ORUN AND AYE – HEAVEN AND EARTH

BOOK ONE

Behind The Dark Veil

Carolyn Holland

Editor: Tia Ross, WordWiser Ink (www.wordwiserink.com)
Proofreader: Brandy Patton, WordWiser Ink
Cover Design: Navi Robins, North Shore Publishing House Inc. (www.nsgraphicstudio.com)
Cover Art: The Art of Salaam Muhammad LLC
Book Interior and Ebook Design: Amit Dey (amitdey2528@gmail.com)

ISBN:978-1-7324693-2-7

Visit my website at: www.carolynhollandbooks.com

DEDICATION

*T*HIS BOOK IS dedicated to the memory of my beloved parents, Robert Leroy Evelyn and Lena Evelyn. Thank you, Mommy and Daddy, for showing me what true love looks and feels like.

ACKNOWLEDGEMENT

THANK THE DIVINE Creator for giving me the talent, the time, and the tools to do this thing that means so much to me. To every member of my family who smiled with loving indulgence every time I dragged them into my imaginary world of Nephilim, angels, demons, and things that go bump in the night, I declare my undying love. Monique, Leon, Jihad, Aliyah, Shamsiddim, Mahasah, Debbie and Saleem: thank you for your patience, thank you for your encouragement, thank you for your love.

Thank you, Sherry Lynn Pitt and Lillie Jean Laws, for taking the time to read my manuscript from cover to cover. Thank you, Bernice Harris and Karen Martin, for reading large segments of each of the books to make sure I stayed "on point" throughout the series. Ladies, I simply adore both of you. I could not have accomplished this without your inspiration, invaluable insights, and candid critique.

My beloved Ancestors have opened so many doors for me, all with the sweetest blessings behind them. I had but to speak the desires of my heart into the universe and they were quick to respond. I needed an artist to create a magnificent cover for this book. The elevated ones sent Salaam Muhammad. I asked for a talented cover designer. Within days I was in touch with Navi Robins. When I expressed the need for someone to design a sleek, professional website for Behind the Dark Veil, LLC, the Ancestors introduced me to the kind and extremely talented Jake Pak. And when I prayed for the best editor in the business, my heavenly family outdid themselves by sending the phenomenal Tia Ross, who took on this unique piece of literature like the consummate professional I knew she would be. Thank you, Tia, for your guidance. Thank you for sharing your resources. Thank you for your many kindnesses. And thank you so very much for the fantastic job you did with my novel!

There are so many other people that I want and *need* to thank. Please forgive me if I forgot anyone; it is not intentional. Many thanks to my *sister by another mother*, Joan Morris-Belcher, for being my biggest fan. I just love you, girl!

Thank you, Charles Lionel Holland, for honoring me with your last name and being a lifelong friend. Thank you, John and Debbie Pereira. Your generous gift actually brought tears to my eyes. Many thanks to my dear friend, Janice Copeland, for listening to countless outlandish scenarios on our daily train commute. After umpteen years of marriage and three grown sons, you still have the ability to blush at my sheer outrageousness. Thank you, Tina Woodson, for your beautiful prayer and that wonderful card you sent me. It made me feel like a published author long before the book was ready. And all I can say about that tall, "cool" glass of water Paul Toombs is "thank you, Pablo" for being such a very good friend and for managing to coax laughter out of me on those rare occasions when I felt like crying. Many thanks to all the wonderful people down at Stone Square Lodge who kept on asking me, "When is the book coming out?" whenever I stopped in for a drink… or two…or three.

Thank you, Ricky Aldarondo, Jean Coriolan, Lisa White, Harry Fisher IV, Daphne and Clifford Gilbert, Shyeka Hopkins, Rickey Fuller, and his North Kackalacky tech friend Mike, who pulled one foot of my dying computer out of the grave. Thank you, Joe Francaviglia, for bringing that half-dead computer back to life.

Whether you read a portion of the manuscript or just gave a bit of encouragement, I thank each and every one of you from the bottom of my heart. All of you are sons and daughters of the Divine

Creator—angels in human flesh. I am so very thankful our paths crossed in this life.

Lastly, I give thanks and honor to the souls of every Black king and queen who held on to his or her faith in a world of darkness so that I might enjoy a glimpse of the light.

GLOSSARY OF TERMS

Anakin	Nephilim working class
Brothers of the Dark Veil	First born of the prefects of the Watcher Angel Shemyaza (Ajuma, Antioch, Boaz, Gilead, Nicodemus, Rephidim, Shiloh, Simeon and Zion, the Nephilim king)
The Dark Veil	A supernatural shield erected by the Brothers of the Dark Veil on all seven continents which allows Nephilim to live among humans without detection
The Fallen	Fallen angels turned demons that serve under Zuet
Gateway	A portal of entry between the heavens, hells, and earth
Ghosting	A mode of Nephilim transportation that involves traveling through space and time as particles of gold dust
Gibborim	Nephilim fighting class
Host	A human whose body is inhabited by one of the Fallen

Houses of the Nephilim	Twelve major Houses of Nephilim royalty: Anane, Arazyal, Armers, Asael, Batraal, Ertael, Samsaveel, Saraknyl, Turel, Yomyael, Zavabe, and Shemyaza, the highest House of the king
King Solomon's Grimoire	A demonically inspired textbook of magic with instructions on how to cast spells, create magical objects and evoke or invoke angels, spirits, and demons
Maroon	Community of escaped slaves in the Atchafalaya Swamp
Mind Meld	Telepathic communication
Mind Swipe	A forceful mental invasion to erase human memories
Nephilim	Half angel/half human descendants of the Watcher angels that landed on Mt. Hermon during the days when the Prophet Enoch walked among men
Rephaim	Member of Nephilim royalty
Vessel	A human who gives birth to a child fathered by one of the Fallen
Zion Shemyaza	King of the Nephilim; oldest and most powerful Nephilim in existence
Zuet	Fallen angel turned demon that rules over all seven levels of hell; arch nemesis to the Nephilim people; known as The Satan

PROLOGUE

~

"FOR WE WRESTLE NOT against flesh and blood, but against principalities, against powers, against the rulers of the darkness of this world, against spiritual wickedness in high places."

— Bible NKJV Ephesians 6

CHAPTER 1

Paris, France
18 January 1724

MARCEL BENOIT'S FALL from grace was swift and painful after being caught in *flagrante delicto* with the wife of one of his wealthy benefactors. He sealed his fate by getting the daughter of that same benefactor with child. Within a fortnight Marcel went from living a comfortable life of relative privilege to that of virtual obscurity and pecuniary loss. Instead of painting portraits of influential members of the ton, the once-renowned artist was reduced to capturing the likenesses of convicted criminals for his new employer, *La Gazette*. He sat in a packed courtroom, surrounded by the dregs of society, with the heat and unpleasant smell of countless unwashed bodies threatening to suffocate him. He wrinkled his nose in disdain.

There was a deafening hue and cry when the defendant, Pierre Wolf, was ushered into the courtroom by the prison screws. Shackled hand and foot and looking neither left nor right, Wolf seemed impervious to the uproarious commotion that erupted upon his entrance.

Marcel immediately went to work, his talented fingers scratching across the parchment, replicating Wolf's high cheekbones and his long patrician nose. Poker straight, platinum blond hair hanging well past Wolf's shoulders appeared on the parchment as if by magic, as Marcel effortlessly captured every subtle nuance of his subject's face in charcoal. He didn't miss one detail as his strokes emulated the whitish-blond brows that soared across Wolf's wide forehead like slashes of an angry painter's brush, then turned his attention toward the cruel pink slit of a mouth that was nearly hidden beneath his bushy moustache and beard. The artist in Marcel was fascinated by Wolf's skin. It was an anaemic white, so pale that he could easily see from across the room rivers of blue-green veins crisscrossing his forehead and the areas at the corners of his eyes. Marcel stopped drawing mid-stroke, holding his breath, when Wolf turned in his direction.

Wolf's eyes were huge—luminous. They were the clearest shade of grey Marcel had ever seen—almost white. Marcel stared trance-like as Wolf's tongue shot out to lick the moustache hairs at the corner of his mouth. Something in that simple gesture made Marcel's flesh crawl. Marcel tore his gaze away with a great deal of effort, sucking in deep pulls of air to compose himself.

"All rise for the Honourable Judge Dominique Renaut," the bailiff proclaimed.

Marcel pulled himself together, picked up paper and charcoal, and waited for the trial to commence.

Dominique Renaut, judge of the high court and close confidante to the king, entered the courtroom to take his place behind the bench with a sour expression on his portly face. He lowered his corpulent figure into the seat of judgment, his long, powdered periwig slightly askew and the weight of his heavy robe causing him to sweat profusely. His jowls quivered with the effort it took for him to wipe the sweat off his face with a pristine white handkerchief provided by his clerk. Renaut lived a double life. He was a dissolute hedonist at night and a renowned jurist, holding the power of life and death in his hands, during the day.

Renaut was miserable. Too much rich food, excessive drink, and far too many pox-riddled, dockside strumpets served to sap

2

Renaut's strength and weaken his resolve. His head was pounding like a bass drum, his mouth as dry as the king's wit. His dimple-knuckled, pudgy hands visibly shook as he reached for a nearby glass of water.

Would that I was anywhere but here, Renaut thought, before he signalled the bailiff to proceed. All conversation in the courtroom ceased.

"Will the defendant please rise."

Wolf rose with great difficulty. His lack of grace was directly attributed to the surfeit of chains surrounding his hands and feet, chains that played their own special music each time he moved his body.

All effects of the previous night's carousing vanished when Renaut turned his attention to the defendant, now fully immersed in his daytime role of dispenser of justice.

"Pierre Antoine Wolf," the judge intoned in a stentorian voice. "You stand before me and your accusers, convicted of the heinous and inhumane crime of murdering your elderly parents, your twenty-two-year-old sister, and her husband of only two weeks."

Wolf had been captured, naked and covered in blood, in the small hamlet of Montbeliard after having hacked his family to pieces with a blunt-edged hatchet. There was evidence that he had cannibalised portions of the bodies.

Someone in the courtroom tried unsuccessfully to stifle a twitter when the charges were read. Wolf's vicious murder of his family had been fodder for the town criers for the past three weeks, and now it was sentencing time. The French were a macabre bunch. They needed—no, demanded—to be apprised of every gory detail.

Renaut had convicted hundreds of men and more than a few women to death. In all his time sitting on the bench, he'd never faced anyone more deserving of a death sentence than the monster standing before him. It gave him great pleasure to sentence Wolf to the gallows—great pleasure indeed. Renaut cleared his throat in preparation for rendering his sentence. He paused dramatically, looking over the assemblage to ensure his words would carry the desired effect.

"This court doth hereby order and adjudge your person be returned to the place from whence you came…" *That would be the infamous Bastille.* "Whereupon you will be fed naught but bread and water until Friday next, at which time you are to be remanded to the place of execution and hanged by the neck until you are dead, dead, dead."

Wolf let out a low growl in response to the judge's proclamation.

Uproarious shouts of approval from all present nearly drowned out the rest of the judge's words.

"After which," Renaut continued, "your remains shall be publicly dissected and anatomised. May God have mercy on your soul."

The prison chaplain muttered a solemn "Amen" as two big burly screws led Wolf back to his death cell. The prison chaplain made a hasty sign of the cross as the prisoner was unceremoniously ushered past him.

An acquaintance sitting next to Marcel said, "'Pon my word, Marcel. Are my blasted ears deceiving me? Or did I just hear that murderous bugger growl?"

"Indeed, you did just hear him growl." Marcel's response was overshadowed by a collective gasp in the courtroom.

Everyone else heard it too. In fact, someone yelled, "String the *lichieres pautonnier* (wicked evildoer) up right now."

"*Brûle en enfer!*" (Burn in hell) someone else shouted.

The suggestion was met with collective declarations of agreement. As far as Marcel was concerned, they couldn't dispatch that nasty bastard fast enough for his liking.

⁂

Place de la Bastile

Wolf's face showed little emotion as he watched the gallows being brought out by a team of high-stepping black horses. It was strategically placed right outside his cell, presumably so that he could contemplate his fate.

Well, fancy that, he thought.

He noticed a large crowd had already gathered around the gallows. There was a decidedly festive air throughout the city. Parisians could think of nothing more entertaining than a good old-fashioned hanging. Broadsides bearing his likeness and advertising his pending execution were being distributed throughout the square, none of which he felt did his natural good looks adequate justice.

Wolf's eyes scrutinised the area surrounding where the gallows stood. He knew from experience that on the morrow, every window overlooking the gallows would be occupied by wealthy citizens willing to pay good coin for the privilege of watching him dangle from the gibbet while they sat in relative comfort in their rented window seats.

Ah. To have such infamy attached to one's name is truly noteworthy and altogether amazing.

As one of his last wishes, Wolf requested a tankard of ale, a meal of artichokes and French beans, and an hour of solitude in the prison chapel. He had also requested that a cross be placed in the execution chamber where he could see it. Soon it would be time to meet with Father Claude Jolliet, the prison chaplain. He thoroughly enjoyed his ale and meal before he was escorted from his cell.

CHAPTER 2

⌒

*I*N THE CENTRE of the chapel was a large enclosure painted black. Inside of the enclosure were seats reserved for prisoners condemned to die. Wolf occupied one of those seats. His hands were chained and his blonde head bowed in silent prayer.

Father Jolliet closed the chapel door behind him. Wolf appeared to be extremely thin and significantly weakened from his imprisonment. Even in his weakened state, with manacles on his wrists and two armed guards stationed outside the chapel door, Wolf was an imposing, frightening figure.

Father Jolliet couldn't help but feel uncomfortable in his presence. He was a vicious killer of the worst kind—a cannibal. Yet, he was also a child of God. Jolliet took a deep breath. He reminded himself that he need only shout or knock on the door and the guards would come to his rescue. The young artist who had been present every day of the trial was also outside the door, with the material of his trade at the ready to capture Wolf's likeness as he walked the final distance to his death. All would be well.

He was surprised when he learned that Wolf wanted a cross in the execution chamber where he could see it. *Maybe there is hope for his wretched soul after all.* As repugnant as his crime may be, it was Father Jolliet's responsibility to minister to Wolf's spiritual needs and prepare him to meet his maker.

"Bonjour, Messier Wolf," he said, closing the door behind him.

Wolf derived an unaccountable sense of peace inside the prison chapel. The reliquary and other religious artefacts served to temporarily erase the ugly sights and sounds just outside the prison walls. He reluctantly raised his head at Father Jolliet's tentative greeting.

"Bonjour, Father Jolliet. Please…come sit." He motioned with his eyes to the seat next to him.

"How fare you, Messier Wolf?"

Father Jolliet's face turned red with embarrassment. He realised the question was an absurd one the moment it passed his lips. How did he expect one would feel on the eve of their death? It appeared Wolf took no offence.

"I suspect that I am doing as well as can be expected under the circumstances, Father. Thank you for asking," he replied politely.

Father Jolliet cleared his throat. It was his job as prison chaplain not only to spend time ministering to the spiritual needs of the condemned, but also to try and extract a confession. Wolf had already confessed. Father Jolliet would persist in his efforts right up to the last moment to obtain as much information as he could as to why Wolf committed his crimes. Father Jolliet hoped that Wolf would not take the reason why he slaughtered his family to his unmarked grave.

"You have readily confessed to committing the most heinous crimes imaginable," the priest began, stating the obvious.

Wolf neglected to remind the good father that he'd had no choice but to confess. After all, he had been caught red-handed, covered in blood, with an empty look in his eyes, a smile on his face, and the bloody murder weapon in his hand.

"Have you no remorse for the things you have done?"

Father Jolliet had no way of knowing that, on the day Wolf killed his family, the demon Travail slipped inside of Wolf's body like it was custom made for him. The fit was just *that* perfect.

Wolf had yet to express any regret for what he'd done. The demon knew what Father Jolliet wanted to hear. It was Travail who answered the good father's question, not Wolf. He turned to look the priest in the eye.

"Father Jolliet, my remorse is deep and profound. I do not understand why I did what I did. It felt like an outside force took control of my body, only to depart once the awful deed was done. I cannot undo the things that I have done. I can only ask for forgiveness and pray the Almighty will grant it."

"It matters not what you have done, Messier Wolf," Father Jolliet said, in a voice filled with the sureness only faith can bring. "The blood of Jesus Christ has wiped even *your* sins clean."

A look of profound relief came over Wolf's face. "That is very comforting to me, Father. It would also give me a great deal of comfort, Father, if you will tell me what will transpire on the morrow."

Father Jolliet had never received a similar request. Most death row inmates wanted to talk about everything *but* their pending death. He would not deny the dying man's simple wish.

"At 7:30 tomorrow morning you will be led from your cell to the Press-Yard where the Sheriff and I will meet you. The hangman and his assistant will be there as well. They will bind your wrists in front of you with cord and similarly bind your body and arms at the elbows."

"You will hear the church bells toll at sunrise or shortly thereafter as the cock crows. You will be led across the yard to the lodge and then out the side door of the prison to climb the steps leading to the gallows platform. The hangman will place the noose around your neck."

Father Jolliet paused to see what effect his words were having on Wolf. The convict appeared to be understandably shaken by Father Jolliet's graphic description of what would occur on the last day of his life. When Father Jolliet paused, he begged him to continue.

"The executioner and officials typically say nothing at the gallows. I doubt that you will be afforded an opportunity to speak. If you are, more likely than not, you will be too frightened to do so.

I will keep up a constant prayer vigil from the moment you arrive in the Press-Yard until you take your last breath. You will not be alone. My voice will be the last voice you hear during the hanging. I will not forsake you. I will read the words of the burial service during the procession to the gallows and continue to pray for you until the drop falls. I give you my word."

"What about my body? The judge has ordered that I be dissected."

Wolf's concern was a valid one. It was not at all unusual for fights to break out beneath the gallows between the dissectionists and members of the condemned's family. There would be no one to fight over Wolf's remains. He'd massacred all of them. The priest decided to spare Wolf that worry with a false assurance.

"I will personally see to the proper disposition of your remains."

What harm could it possibly do? Father Jolliet thought. *After all, the man will be dead tomorrow. There was no need to let him know his body will be chopped up for close examination. Sometimes a lie is better than the truth.* Wolf seemed content. Father Jolliet was more than happy when Wolf dropped the subject.

"Father Jolliet. I have but one more request—that you pray for me tonight and that I be allowed to place my hands on that old rugged cross one more time before I meet my maker."

Wolf walked with Father Jolliet to the front of the chapel like a man on a mission. There was an old wooden cross hanging on the wall. He dropped to his knees before the cross. Father Jolliet held his rosary in one hand and placed his other hand upon Wolf's forehead. He began to pray.

"Almighty and merciful God. You bestow on mankind the gift of everlasting life. Look graciously–"

He got no further. When he reached into the confines of his mind for the next word to the prayer and searched his lungs for his next breath, neither were available to him.

Wolf was no longer kneeling before him. Something that resembled Wolf was now standing toe to toe with the priest, using the manacles on his wrists to strangle the life out of him.

The priest could see the storm clouds swirling in Wolf's inhuman eyes. He could smell his fetid breath. Memories of what Wolf had done to his family inundated his spirit with terror. He was at the mercy of a monster. A madman. A demon.

Jolliet kicked and clawed at Wolf's hands in a desperate attempt to loosen his grip—to get one more breath of air so that he could call for help. Even though his fingernails ripped the flesh on Wolf's hands to the bone, he was no match for Wolf who had the strength of twenty demons.

Wolf continued to squeeze with a wicked smile on his face. The metal rings on the manacles were digging into Jolliet's neck, ripping the skin and crushing the delicate bones in his throat. His body was consumed with an agonising burning sensation from lack of air.

Father, please have mercy on my soul. I am going to die at this monster's hands.

Wolf squeezed long after Jolliet had stopped fighting. His yellow teeth were bared like a well-fed wolf when the priest expelled his bowels. Wolf's tongue shot out to caress the hairs on his moustache as the smell of death and fear surrounded him. He then lowered the dead priest's body to the floor.

Wolf moved silently and with an economy of motion. He didn't flinch as he banged one hand against the wall. There was a loud crack when the bones broke. He stood as still as a defenceless animal to make sure the guards outside hadn't heard anything.

Now that the large bones in his hand were shattered, he was able to easily slip his hand out of the manacle. Next, he donned the dead priest's frock. He pried the old wooden cross from the wall. Pausing before departing the chapel, he looked down on the dead priest.

"Well," he said, "it looks like my voice was the last one *you* heard, Father Jolliet."

Marcel Benoit gave up in his futile attempts to engage the two surly guards in conversation, instead allowing his mind to drift to the singularly unpleasant conversation he had earlier that day with his new father-in-law, the same man whose wife he'd bedded and whose daughter he'd impregnated and eloped with. A nasty situation if ever there was one.

Genevieve's father made it clear that since she had chosen to marry Marcel, she would not get so much as a *le denier mot* from him. His pregnant new bride was officially, irrevocably disowned, and Marcel knew he must now find a means to support her in the manner in which she had grown accustomed. He looked down at the prominent bulge in the front of his pants.

What a fine mess you've gotten me into.

Marcel was jerked from his musings at the sound of the chapel door opening. He reached for his charcoal and the sketch pad lying next to a neat stack of drawings he'd already rendered of Wolf. Finally, he could get the show on the road.

What happened next took place so quickly that it almost seemed to be in slow motion. The chapel door opened, but it wasn't the pious priest who charged through the portal. Marcel's eyes bulged in horror when a thing that looked like Pierre Antoine Wolf, but wasn't, snapped the neck of one guard and then gutted the second with something that looked like a wooden cross.

The murders were executed with an ease that could only be described as inhuman. Wolf paused to pick up the handbills bearing his likeness before turning his attention to Marcel.

Marcel's attempts to escape capture were to no avail. Though he knocked over his chair in his haste to depart down the long solitary hallway leading away from the chapel, Wolf caught up to him as easily as a mongoose catches a fly.

Using Marcel as a human shield with a knife trained at his back, Wolf managed to make his way out of the prison, steal a horse, and ride like the devil himself, with the frightened Frenchman seated on the horse in front of him. When the sound of their pursuers diminished to nothing, Wolf grabbed a handful of Marcel's thick auburn hair and scalped him.

CHAPTER 3

SIX MONTHS LATER, Clidamont Etienne, a Frenchman from the German-speaking region of Alsace-Lorraine, booked passage for himself, his pregnant wife, and four-year-old daughter aboard the ship *Les Deux Freres* (Two Brothers) en route to Louisiana in the New World. At the last moment, he purchased an additional ticket for a young French farmer.

Clidamont was the impoverished third son of a Baron twice removed. He knew he would never inherit his family's modest seat. With the promise of a fresh new start, rich fertile land, and gold virtually available for the taking, he, like many others before him, was lured across the seas from Europe to what had been described to him as a thriving new settlement in the colonies. It was August 20, 1724, the long-awaited departure date. There was a look of intense worry on Clidamont's handsome face. He turned to a nearby seaman.

"How long before we set sail?" he asked.

"Twenty minutes as the wind blows, sir," the crewman replied before climbing up the rig like a monkey in a tree to check the sails.

Clidamont had seen his family comfortably settled in their cabin. He was now standing on deck, anxiously awaiting the arrival of the young farmer he had met a month prior. He and the farmer had hit it off famously. The farmer informed Clidamont that he had lost his family tragically and that he wanted nothing more than to leave France behind him and start a new life.

They made a pact. The agreement was that, in exchange for his passage, the farmer would help Clidamont clear the land he'd acquired in the colonies and build a house for his family. In further exchange for the farmer's help, Clidamont promised to deed over two acres of prime land from his ten-acre tract. The two men had struck a gentlemen's agreement. They shook on it. They had a deal.

The cold wind slid across the churning waters of the troubled sea, whipping at Clidamont's face and rocking the ship. The ship's crew was frantically working in preparation for their departure. The captain would be pulling up anchor soon, and still no farmer. *Did I misjudge the man? The young farmer had seemed so forthright and honest when we met.* Clidamont didn't know anything about farming. Without the young farmer's help, he would surely be lost.

Clidamont's anguish diminished when he smelled his wife Irmgard's soft perfume. Her presence always seemed to soothe him. He pulled her close to inhale her sweet essence.

"You should return below deck, my love. I wouldn't want you to catch a chill," Clidamont gently admonished. Irmgard was three months pregnant with their second child. Clidamont loved his wife and child to distraction. He would do anything for them.

"Oh, poo, darling. I am pregnant, not an invalid," Irmgard said with a sparkle in her bright blue eyes. "You seem worried, my darling. I welcome whatever burdens you wish to share with me," she said sweetly.

Clidamont wrapped his arm around her waist. He certainly didn't intend to share his fears with his wife. She thought the sun and the moon set at his feet. He intended to keep her thinking that way. He would not worry her in her delicate condition.

"All is well, my love. I am just anxious to start our new life together."

They stood side by side in silence. They would watch the shores of France recede together. Whether the farmer showed up or not, Clidamont was determined to find a way to provide for his family. Maybe he would be able to hire help once they arrived in the New World.

BEHIND THE DARK VEIL

Just as Clidamont was about to give up all hope that the farmer would make an appearance, Pierre Antoine Wolf ran up the gangplank. Wolf made it just before the ship set sail. Clidamont let out a sigh of relief.

All will be well now.

✦ ✦

La Louisiana, "The Louisiana Territory"

There was no work today. Today was a day of celebration. The two men hunted down fresh game that morning. They'd partaken of a delicious feast prepared by Irmgard. Now the two men sat in companionable silence in front of a waning fire. Clidamont drank deeply from the bottle of aged cognac he had been saving for a special occasion, then passed the bottle to Pierre who also drank deeply. The cognac warmed their blood. They had much to be thankful for.

Clidamont stood, gazing over acres of land that extended farther than his eye could see. Tears burned behind his eyelids. *This land belongs to me*, he thought. *Irmgard and I will raise our sons and daughters on this land. One day, our children will raise their children here.* Pierre stood beside Clidamont, both lost in their own private thoughts.

Clidamont extended a work-callused hand to Pierre. The two men shook. Clidamont was overwhelmed with emotion. His gratitude for the assistance Pierre had given was so great that a mere handshake would not suffice. With tears of gratitude in his eyes, Clidamont pulled Pierre to him in a firm, manly embrace.

"At long last, we can enjoy the fruits of our hard labour. I owe it all to you, dear friend."

Pierre returned the embrace reluctantly. He was unaccustomed to praise of any kind and found it difficult to respond to Clidamont's display of heartfelt appreciation. Pierre extricated himself from the awkward show of affection.

Clearing his throat, he said, "It was my sincere pleasure to be of assistance, Clidamont. You and your family have been good to me. You deserve every happiness."

He then turned to look in the direction of the land they had worked so hard to cultivate. The strong emotion in Clidamont's eyes let Pierre know that his expression of gratitude was sufficient.

Over the past several months, the two men had become fast friends, staying up late at night long after Irmgard and Frieda, the Etiennes' four-year-old daughter, were fast asleep. On these occasions they would sit before the fire under the waning light of the moon, sharing their dreams for the future in this wild yet promising new land.

Pierre remained a mystery to Clidamont. When questioned about his family or his past he always changed the subject or responded in vague generalities. Clidamont could see that it was painful for him to speak of the past. He had decided long ago that he would respect Pierre's privacy. His past didn't matter. They were in the New World, and Pierre deserved a fresh new start just as much as Clidamont.

The two men stood proudly in front of the home they had built. They had reason to be proud. It hadn't been easy for them. When they first docked in what was supposed to have been the settlement named after the Duc d'Orleans, they were shocked to find there was no settlement at all. Only a village of Cyprus huts inhabited by prisoners, slaves, and bonded servants who had been sent from France to populate the new territory.

To make matters worse, the village was surrounded by swamp and disease. The once-friendly Native American Indians were now hostile due to the settlers' continued acts of duplicity. Despite the daunting odds against them, Clidamont and Pierre eventually managed to clear Clidamont's land.

The first thing they did was to construct a temporary shelter in the region located on the west bank of the Mississippi River called *Cote des Allemands,* the German Coast. The shelter was built in the centre of a copse of mature magnolia trees just upriver of New Orleans on a prime stretch of fertile land in St. John the Baptist Parish.

Next, they cultivated and seeded the acres surrounding the shelter. Come next fall they would have crops to trade. Lastly, they constructed a handsome log cabin which they attached to the original shelter. Clidamont would expand the cabin as his family grew, and, from the looks of Irmgard's burgeoning belly, it would not be long before they had a new addition. They had beaten the odds. They had tamed a small portion of this land and made it their own. It was late. Clidamont and Pierre walked toward the cabin.

"Tomorrow we will begin construction on a similar dwelling down the road for you, Pierre," Clidamont said, as they neared the cabin door. "I am a man of my word. I promised you a portion of my land, and you shall have it."

Clidamont did not add that he would be honoured to call the hard-working, soft-spoken Frenchman his neighbour. He assumed it was understood.

"In the meantime," he added, "you will continue to reside with us for as long as you desire. Come. Let's enjoy the rest of the feast Irmgard prepared for us."

That night they slept under the shelter of the newly built cabin for the first time. The fragrant smell of freshly cut timber perfumed the interior of the Etiennes' new home. After eating their fill of the savoury rabbit stew Irmgard had prepared, the two men enjoyed a pipe by the fire and several more cups of the costly cognac before lying down to sleep. Tomorrow would be a busy day. They planned to cut down the trees to commence construction of Pierre's cabin.

CHAPTER 4

THE SOUND OF steady breathing and light snores filled the cabin. Wolf lay awake on his pallet, mentally counting the space between each of the Etiennes' breaths. Once he determined all were in a sound, dream-free sleep, Wolf silently rose from his sleeping pallet. He was guided by the light of the moon toward a small cache of tools in a corner of the cabin. These tools were intended to construct the Etiennes' furniture.

Wolf grabbed a small hatchet. He hefted the tool in his hand, testing its weight, size, and manoeuverability. Satisfied with his choice, he walked on feet as silent and fleet as the hostile Indians the colonists had come to fear. He positioned himself at the head of Clidamont and Irmgard's pallet. Hatchet in hand, Wolf hovered over the peacefully sleeping couple.

Sensing a nearby threat, Clidamont opened his eyes. It was at that moment when Wolf knelt down with a frenzied look in his eyes and, swift as a hawk, took hold of a handful of Clidamont's long, sleep-tousled hair. With one blow, Wolf ruthlessly brought down the sharp end of the hatchet on the top of Clidamont's head, scalping the unsuspecting man. The second blow landed in the centre of Irmgard's forehead.

The blow was struck with so much force that the hatchet blade was driven clear through Irmgard's head and embedded in the wood beneath it. It took two hands to dig that hatchet out of Irmgard's horror-stricken face. It was messy work, but Wolf took his time and got the job done right. Soon Irmgard's bloody scalp lay in a corner next to that of her husband's.

By now little Frieda was wide awake, having witnessed the carnage. Her eyes were huge with fear. She clutched her blanket to her chest as if it could somehow shield her from the evil in front of her. The little girl cowered in a corner, whimpering like a frightened animal, as Wolf shucked his bloody clothing and approached her with slow intent.

Wolf kept Frieda alive for a week after he'd murdered her parents, torturing and brutalising the four-year-old before he finally grew bored with the innocent child and slit her throat. He saved the scalps he'd taken from Clidamont and Irmgard, blaming the Indians for their deaths. Later he would state the Indians had taken Frieda and that the scalps belonged to Irmgard and his helper, Pierre Wolf.

Pierre Antoine Wolf was no more. Wolf assumed the land, possessions, and identity of Clidamont Etienne. He purchased three slaves. When he worked all three to death, he purchased three more, eventually losing count of how many slaves he'd killed to build a more substantial, much larger structure atop the graves of the Etienne family. His home would later be known as the infamous Magnolia Hill Plantation.

♒ ♒

Magnolia Hill Plantation
River Road, St. John the Baptist Parish
New Orleans, Louisiana
(1748)

Magnolia Hill wasn't just a place. It was a living, breathing, foul-breathed monster that sucked the essence out of anyone who stepped foot on its soil. The plantation itself was a boil on the face of the earth and a blot on humanity. A place where other planters threatened to sell their slaves off to when they wanted to scare the sweet bejesus out of them.

BEHIND THE DARK VEIL

Gone was the humble cabin Etienne and Wolf built so many years ago. The house proper now sat high atop a grassy knoll, surrounded by densely planted magnolia trees, and thus Magnolia Hill came to be. It was a sprawling beauty, built on the west bank of the Mississippi River between New Orleans and Baton Rouge, about a quarter mile south of the fiery gates of hell.

The plantation was a self-contained southern fiefdom. Old man Clidamont was the bloodthirsty mad king. Claude, his son, was the vicious, despotic prince. Clidamont's two muckraking grandchildren, Julien and Henri, fashioned themselves as the dandified duke and the malicious marquis, respectively.

The slaves at Magnolia Hill were expendable commodities. They were used and tossed away like a pair of beat-up old shoes that had lost their shine. The slaves that weren't killed outright were either worked into an early grave, or they had their spirits beaten out of them to the degree they became the walking dead.

Every acre of land on Magnolia Hill was shrouded in a dark cloud of hate and despair. Its rich soil was fertilised in blood and watered with the tears of countless men, women, and children whose mournful spirits wailed for retribution.

⟞⟑ ⟒⟝

A night owl's portentous hoot and the piteous moans of a slave left to die in the "hot box" chased the weary slave woman from the Big House. The light of a full moon presented her face in sharp relief as she ran. She had once been very beautiful, but now her face was marred by two long disfiguring scars resembling permanent tears, one on each cheek.

She hurried on bare feet to the plantation kitchen which was housed in a separate building up-wind of the main house. This was where the plantation cook, Mother Ethel, was watching her three-day-old baby and where she slept on a thin straw pallet on the kitchen floor.

The rag she had carefully packed herself with earlier that day was soaked clear through with blood and clots. Warm blood trickled down her leg with every step. She could smell the stink of it. She could also smell the cloying shroud of Mistress Felicity's blood. It attached itself to her clothing like a clinging vine and followed her like a storm cloud chasing the moon.

The slave woman's name was Abayoni, but her mama and everyone else who knew her called her Sorrow, because that was all she was ever gonna know.

Sorrow was not yet healed from birthing her own baby but a few short days ago, yet she'd been up all day and into the night working like a pack mule to bring Mistress's child into the world. It had been an extremely long and difficult labour which ended badly for both mother and child, just as she prayed it would.

Try as she might, Sorrow couldn't muster a shred of pity for the woman or her dead child. The corpse whose body was growing cold in the Big House right now belonged to the same woman who had watched Sorrow's man get whipped to death and fed to the pigs. She was the same woman who sat on the front porch sipping a mint julep while Sorrow lay in the dirt, screaming in anguish.

Felicity Etienne's death was grounds for celebration. It represented merely one less white person to deal with, and the death of her child represented one less child that would grow up to be a white person she'd have to deal with. Sorrow silently prayed the devil was sticking a pitchfork up both their asses.

While the white folks were clicking glasses and celebrating the pending birth of another somebody to make Sorrow's life miserable, Sorrow had busied herself rushing to the kitchen to melt down the tallow to make a candle. She used the ash from the cooking fire to stain it black. Then she moulded that black candle into the shape of a pregnant Mistress Felicity and Masta Claude.

She heated the blade of the knife in the fire. When it was white-hot, she sliced the candle down the middle, symbolically severing Felicity's connection to her husband and her child. Then Sorrow called upon the Orisha gods and goddesses of war to bring down pain and destruction on the Etiennes. She stabbed the still-hot blade of the knife into the belly of the candle representing Felicity. Praise be to the goddess, Felicity Etienne and her baby were now both dead.

CHAPTER 5

⁓

SORROW WAS A natural born healer. She delivered all of the babies at Magnolia Hill and most of the babies on the neighbouring plantations—slaves and whites alike. Just like her mama and her grandmama before her, Sorrow was a powerful Obeah conjure woman.

She had inherited her renowned healing skills with herbs and such from her mama, the daughter of an African-born princess from Yoruba. After Masta Clidamont worked her mama to death, Sorrow became the official go-to person by default whenever a slave took sick or a baby needed birthing. It is mighty hard to minister to the needs of folks you hate.

When she wasn't healing, Sorrow worked behind the scenes in the Big House or in the kitchen with Mother Ethel. She didn't have to enter the dining area to serve the white folks food anymore. Masta Clidamont said her sliced-up face spoiled his appetite.

The women in Sorrow's line had a long and twisted relationship with the Etiennes. After Masta Clidamont's first wife was weakened from three miscarriages, the white doctor told Clidamont another pregnancy would kill her. Clidamont didn't care. He kept coming to her bed until his seed took.

Sorrow's mama delivered Masta Clidamont's only son Claude. She told Sorrow that Claude's mother had been a poor sweet girl of good reputation sent from France to New Orleans to find a husband. She found one alright. White folks should be careful what they ask for.

Women don't last long on Magnolia Hill. That poor creature died under suspicious circumstances right after she pushed Clidamont's only son out of her wasted body— at least that's what the white folks whispered behind Clidamont's back. Sorrow's mother said she saw Clidamont pick up a pillow and smother the woman to death with her own eyes. After the dirty deed was done, she heard him say, "I'm going to name our son Claude darling, after the priest I murdered in France. Give him my regards when you get to hell, won't you?"

The last shovel of dirt hadn't been thrown over the first wife's coffin before Clidamont took him a second wife whose name escaped Sorrow at the moment. The second mistress didn't live long enough for the slaves to remember her name. One thing for sure, she fit in with the Etiennes like tea in a kettle. The slaves were glad to see her put in the ground after the fever took her.

Then Masta Clidamont's son Claude started courting Lorelei Poche from Poche Plantation between Gonzalez and La Place, and him just barely a man, still wet behind the ears. Things went badly with the newlyweds from the start. There was enough fighting and fornicating going on between them to test the patience of Job himself. Then Henri was born.

One day Mistress Lorelei was sitting up at the Big House making everybody's life miserable. The next thing Sorrow knew she was no longer around and a fresh grave had been dug up on the hill.

Masta Claude married his current wife quicker than a jackrabbit jumps out of his hole during a brush fire. His younger son, Julien, was born of this union. Sorrow delivered Julien. And wouldn't you know it? Neither one of Claude's sons were worth the shit that came out their asses. The apple doesn't fall far from the tree. When the tree is rotten to the core, it can't help but bear rotten fruit.

Claude Xavier Etienne was mean as a snake and filled with the devil himself. He came by his streak of meanness honestly, because his father Clidamont Etienne was a pure unadulterated son of a bitch. The two sons Claude would eventually sire, Henri and Julien, were devil spawn.

Nosiree, women don't last long on Magnolia Hill.

***

A blast of heat from the kitchen cooking fires confirmed Sorrow's belief that she was indeed in hell on earth. When she reached for her baby, the old cook Ethel's rheumy eyes surveyed her sorry condition as a thick drop of blood plopped onto the dirt floor.

"Go on and clean yourself up, gal. Won't hurt me none to look after this little baby a bit longer. Now go on."

Ethel shooed Sorrow along while massaging the baby's little back, making cooing sounds.

Sorrow hastened to do Ethel's bidding. Somehow she managed to express her thanks through lips that had long ago forgotten how to smile. Once she was cleaned up, Sorrow took her baby from Ethel. She immediately put her baby to the tit. The babe suckled hungrily.

"Did the mistress have that baby yet?" Ethel asked while stirring the stew that would be served for the evening dinner. Sorrow bit into one of Ethel's hot buttery biscuits before answering.

"The baby dead," she said without emotion. "And soon, if it ain't happened already, Mistress Felicity gon' be dead too."

"Lord have mercy," Ethel said, dropping her fulsome arthritic figure down heavily on a nearby stool.

Sorrow held her newborn on one hip while she steeped some herbs to make a tea she would drink to heal her insides from the recent birth.

"Masta Claude and his daddy must have ice water flowing through their veins," Sorrow declared. "Masta Claude stood at the foot of the birthing bed like he was betting on a racehorse. When the baby came out dead, Masta Claude screamed at me to git out the birthing chamber, even though Mistress was bleeding like a pig stuck with a pitchfork. He wouldn't even let me pack her to stop the bleeding. She bled out before I turned my back to open the door." Sorrow handed Ethel a cup of the tea. It wouldn't do the old woman any harm.

"Thank you, baby," Ethel said, blowing on the tea to cool it off before taking a sip of the steaming brew. "You know how white folks is, child," she opined with the wisdom that comes from a lifetime in captivity. "Now that Masta Claude got himself an heir and a spare *and* Mistress Felicity's money, he don't have no more use for her. I 'spect he'll just go out and get himself another victim."

Sorrow nodded in agreement. Felicity Valcour Aime came from money. She was the only child of Armond Valcour Aime who was the owner of St. Joseph Plantation in St. James Parish. She brought a huge dowry into the marriage.

Sorrow jumped up when she heard the sound of horses' hooves. She went to peer out of the window. "Ethel. You ain't gon' believe this. Masta Clidamont and his nasty ass son Claude just saddled up. I bet they on their way to town to carouse at that black whorehouse."

Ethel's expression was pinched. "Hmph, I guess they gon' leave the mistress and that dead baby till morning without a second thought. It's a shame before God."

Her huge breasts shook with merriment. "If we leave it up to them, they'll do us a big ole favour and kill off every white woman this side of St. John the Baptist Parish. Then we'll only have to deal with the white menfolk!" The women laughed companionably. Sorrow stared out the window long after the dust settled from the Etiennes' horses.

"Now both of them been through two wives," Sorrow said, then added in a more sombre tone of voice, "I only wish the angel of death had plucked the two of them up along with the mistress."

Sorrow never met a white person she didn't hate, and she never hated one more than she hated Clidamont Etienne. It didn't much matter that he was her daddy.

BEHIND THE DARK VEIL

(Ten years later…)

Old Mother Ethel was long gone, dead and buried and feeding the worms in the old slave cemetery that bordered the woods behind the plantation. Sorrow was now the plantation cook, midwife, and healer. She and her daughter, whom she named "Flossie," could have continued to live in the kitchen, as they had while Mother Ethel was alive. Sorrow didn't want to be that close to the white folks in the Big House. She preferred to live on Slave Row. Besides, folks ran in and out of the kitchen all day and night. Sorrow needed privacy to practise the rituals passed down from her mother.

Flossie was dark, like her daddy. She had to be of good use if Sorrow wanted to keep her only child out of the fields. Folks didn't last long in the fields. The fact of the matter is—folks didn't last long period on Magnolia Hill. Sorrow passed on her vast store of knowledge about healing, herbs and delivering babies to her daughter Flossie so that she would be more valuable to the whites. She also passed on her knowledge about the Ancestors and the Orisha gods and goddesses to her daughter.

It had been more than 10 years since they killed Sorrow's man. Still, the hatred that festered like an open sore was blazing as white-hot as the fires of hell. She was consumed by it. Sorrow found a small sense of satisfaction every single day she sprinkled some of her poisonous herbs in the Etienne's food before serving it. Slow and easy—that's how you do it. She wanted to see them suffer.

CHAPTER 6

⁓

𝒯HE DAY THAT would irrevocably change the fabric of Sorrow's existence began like any other. It was daybreak, and the sun framed the plantation like a beautiful water coloured painting. Clidamont and his son sat side by side astride their massive horses from a vantage point that allowed them to take in the verdant vista that was Magnolia Hill.

They never travelled alone. "Nameless," a minor level malevolent spirit from the third level of hell, hovered over Clidamont Etienne like the stink on a rotting corpse.

"Nothing," yet another demon, clawed the inside of Claude's frayed soul, making him restless and anxious to be about evil.

The pride and avarice oozing from their black-hearted souls fed a basic need for the spirits' existence. They grew stronger with every day their hosts drew breath. Now, the demons were nigh on invincible. Soon—very soon—*they*, and not the hosts, would control their steps, and then, the lowly demons would be in a position to petition the Satan for a promotion. In the meantime, the hosts were doing a fine and dandy job on their own at being deliciously wicked. Nameless sent a telepathic message to the demon inside Claude. It rubbed its hands together in anticipation of some fun.

It whispered in Clidamont's ear. "It's killin' time, boss." Nameless laughed when Clidamont jerked in the saddle. He'd just tickled Clidamont's cock as a little treat for being a really bad boy. Seconds later, Clidamont and his son Claude spurred their sweaty horses like two wild Mohicans on the warpath.

They viciously whipped the sides of the winded beasts as they rode hell-bent for leather through the gates of Magnolia Hill. They'd been out all night, drinking and whoring. Now they were out for blood, and they knew just where to find it. They veered their horses in the direction of the slave quarters.

"They is back, Flossie!" Sorrow hissed. "Go hide yourself in the woods behind the patch of hemlock 'til I give you the signal to come out. Go on now. Hurry!"

The love in Sorrow's eyes softened her scar ravaged face. Flossie hurried to do her mother's bidding. Sorrow had practised this drill with her daughter many times over. It became necessary when she noticed Masta Claude sniffing around her daughter like an old randy hound dog with the devil riding its back.

The pounding of Masta and Young Masta's horses' hooves sounded like a death knell, generating fear in the hearts of every slave in the quarter. This wouldn't be the first time the Etiennes swooped down on the slaves like hungry vultures on wild game, nor would it be the last.

The sound drew nearer and louder as the woods behind Sorrow's cabin swallowed her daughter. It wouldn't be long before the double dose of evil was right there, kicking in or pounding on somebody's cabin door. Sorrow expelled a sigh of relief she hadn't even realised she'd been holding when they rode right past her cabin, kicking up dust and dirt in their wake.

Praise be to God, this time it ain't my door they are darkening, Sorrow thought. *Some other poor wretch will have to service her father and her half-brother's twisted needs this morning.*

The two large stallions reared up on their spindly hind legs. They were whinnying in pain from being ridden too hard and from the rider's crop the Etiennes wielded like madmen.

Clidamont and Claude tethered their horses two doors down, in front of young Sylvie and her little boy Isaac's cabin. It wasn't long before Sylvie's cries for mercy were heard the length and breadth of Slave Row.

Sorrow covered her ears and closed her eyes to drown out the sound of fists connecting with flesh and grunts of pain, but the sounds kept on coming, travelling through the thin walls of her cabin to invade the space in her mind. Sylvie and little Isaac's cries were eating her alive.

I can't take this much longer. Obatala, deliver me from these feelings. They will only lead to my destruction, and the destruction of that one thing you have allowed me to love—my daughter.

Then she heard it. The too familiar gut-wrenching sound of a wounded animal scraped the surface of her soul with its jagged finger-nails with each of Sylvie's piteous wails. After that, there was a silence more frightening than even the screams had been. A terrible sense of foreboding dropped over Slave Row like a damp blanket covered with mould.

Sorrow hastened to the place where she hid her ileke, the multico-loured beads she prayed with. She was an Orisha priestess, an Obeah conjure woman. Tonight, she would stand before the hidden altar in the woods and lead her followers in prayer for the destruction of the whites. Today she would pray to the gods alone. Sorrow closed her eyes.

"Olodumare, I beseech you. Smite Clidamont Etienne. Render him unable to walk, talk, eat or sleep. Then mighty Olodumare, I ask you to smother the life out of him—nice and slow. I want him to struggle for each breath, to suffer. Then make him die hard and burn in the sewers of hell for eternity."

There has to be a special place in hell reserved for that foul demon spawn Claude, she thought. Sorrow asked the Gods to instil him with a sense of fear such as he'd never known. She wanted him to experience the same fear he made every slave on Magnolia Hill feel every single day of their miser-able lives. Nothing short of Claude's death could drown out the sounds of him panting and grunting on top of her and the wet mongrel smell that followed him even after he'd bathed.

"I claim in your mighty name Olodumare and in the names of Elegba, Obatala, Shango, Ogun, Oshun, Oya, and Yemaya—every god in the pantheon, that there will always be discord in the Etienne house-hold, and that Claude Etienne's sons Julien and Henri will always be at odds with one another, and that they will know nothing but suffering all the days of their lives. Stamp out their seed Mighty One so that the Etienne line will be no more."

Tears ran down Sorrow's face and her chest was heaving with emotion. She was so absorbed in her vengeful prayers and clutching the ileke with such fervour, it broke apart in her hands. The sound of the beads hitting the dirt floor snapped her out of the spiritual trance she was in. She opened her eyes to find Clidamont Etienne standing in the open doorway.

Sorrow won't know sorrow no more.

ᴄᴏ ᴏ

Not far from Magnolia Hill, well hidden behind the mystical dark veil that separates the realm of mortals from the realm of spirits, was a band of half-breed angels known as Nephilim.

Nephilim society is built upon a strict caste system consisting of Rephaim, Gibborim, and Anakin. The Rephaim represent the Nephilim upper-class. This class of Nephilim is further divided into twelve Houses. The heads of each of the twelve Rephaim Houses and their respective families represent the crème de la crème of Nephilim society—the aristocracy. Alliances through arranged marriages abounded to strengthen their angelic bloodlines. House, reputation, and wealth were paramount to a good match.

The heads of each House make up the Grand Nephilim Council, a twelve-member tribunal responsible for bringing the concerns of their constituents to the ear of the Nephilim king.

The Gibborim represent the Nephilim middle class and members of the Nephilim military. Every Gibborim must swear fealty to the House of a Rephaim Grand Council Member. Any Nephilim without a House affiliation will be ostracised by Nephilim society and at the mercy of enemies of the Nephilim Nation, i.e. demons and/or humans.

Anakin are part of the Nephilim lower working class. They are born to serve in one of the twelve Houses and are indentured to their respective Houses for life. An Anakin male can work his way up to Gibborim status by serving in the military or apprenticing under a master trades-man. An Anakin female can marry up to Gibborim status after receiving the proper dispensation to do so from the Grand Council Member heading her House. The Nephilim society is patrilineal. Any children born of a union between an Anakin female and a Gibborim male will assume the class designation of the father.

The Rephaim members of the Grand Council answer directly to a group of powerful Nephilim generals known as the Brothers of the Dark Veil. The Brothers of the Dark Veil sit on the Supreme Nephilim Council and are close intimates of the Nephilim king. They command legions of Gibborim warriors and are charged with protecting members of the Nephilim Nation against humans and demons on each of the world's continents. They are an elite corps of Nephilim who are given direct access to the Supreme Grand Guardian, the king, by right of birth.

These Nephilim possess extraordinary preternatural powers far and above those of the average Nephilim. Unlike all other Nephilim, they are powerful preternatural beings who have the ability to raise the Dark Veil, a supernatural wall of protection behind which Nephilim can exist in tandem, yet undetected by humans.

Collectively referred to as Brothers of the Dark Veil, they are Nicodemus of the House of Urakabarameel; Ajuma of the House of Akibeel; Gilead of the House of Tamiel; Simeon of the House of Ramuel; Boaz of the House of Danel; Antioch of the House of Asael; and Rephidim of the House of Azazel. The Brothers of the Dark Veil report directly to Zion Shemyaza of the House of Shemyaza, their mighty matchless king and the most powerful Nephilim in existence.

The Rephaim are direct descendants of those Watcher Angels who served as officers under their leader, a Seraphim named Shemyaza. The descendants of the remaining Watchers were either of the Gibborim military-class or the Anakin serving-class, depending upon their ancestral rank in the angelic hierarchy prior to the antediluvian flood. Because of the sins of the father, every one of them was cursed by The Ancient of Days to have to drink blood to survive and to never enjoy the light of day.

CHAPTER 7

1756 Atchafalaya Swamp

⌒

*T*HE WELL-COMPORTED Anakin servants were invisible to the elegantly dressed Rephaims. The Anakins had no more importance than the chairs their betters sat upon or the table on which they ate. They were born to serve and nothing else. Not one of the Rephaims spared them so much as a glance as they quietly performed their duties.

The dinner was in honour of Ephraim of the House of Armers and his fiancé Nephthys of the House of Samsaveel. This was to be their engagement dinner. The marriage contract had been signed by their parents before they were born. They were meeting each other for the first time tonight.

Ephraim was the adored only son of Silas, a Nephilim bearing the blood of Cherubim Angels. His father and, therefore, he, were direct descendants of Armers, a prefect of the original 200 Watcher Angels who descended from the heavens to land on Ardis, the highest peak of Mount Aron. Ephraim's ancestors inhabited the earth during the time when the ascended Prophet Enoch still walked among men.

Ephraim's mother, Delia, was of equally impressive lineage. She was a descendant of Zavebe, a noble house in its own right, though not quite as lofty as her husband's. Zavebe was also an original Watcher Angel who served in two angelic orders, that of the Watchers and the Virtues. The blood of these two powerful orders flowed through Delia's beautiful body and the bodies of the son and daughter she bore to Silas.

The combination of the two impeccable bloodlines placed Ephraim and his sister in the highest echelon of Nephilim nobility: the Rephaim. The blood of mighty throne angels ran through Nephthys' veins. As such, both families enjoyed a lifestyle that exceeded those of even the wealthiest mortals. Ephraim's father, Silas Armers, held the position of Chairman of the Grand Nephilim Council while Nephthys' father, Bertram Samsaveel, was a revered Council member.

❧ ☙

Ephraim Armers was a prime catch. He was handsome, favoured with the tight ropey muscles of his father and the burnished bronze skin and deep, penetrating black eyes of his mother. As with all of his kind, he was near perfect in face and form. His physical beauty was directly attributed to the surfeit of angelic blood flowing through his veins and what humans would commonly refer to as the "good genes" passed down from his parents.

Young Nephilim females fell at his feet. They swooned when he graced them with so much as a smile. He was already well over six feet tall, not nearly as big and tall as his frame promised he would eventually become once he reached his majority and filled out. Ephraim was considered a teen among his people. Ephraim, his sister, Sara, and his fiancé, Nephthys, were the youngest of the diners; each of them was nearly fifty years old.

He was also rich. The lifespan of the Nephilim eclipsed that of humans by hundreds of years—in some cases, thousands. Over the centuries, members of the Rephaim class amassed obscene amounts of wealth and were able to enjoy all the luxuries money can buy.

The air of obvious wealth, refinement, and privilege were incongruous with the reality that the dinner party was being hosted in the bowel of a huge cave in the middle of the Atchafalaya Swamp.

BEHIND THE DARK VEIL

The Armers didn't have to exist as one of the Atchafalaya Swamp's best-kept secrets. They made their home in the swamp by choice. Silas was a loyal supporter of the Nephilim king. However, he wanted the autonomy to rule his people as he saw fit outside of the king's close scrutiny. He chose to set up his household in the swamps where humans dared not tread.

⁂

The Rephaim aristocrats took their Anakin servants for granted at their own peril. The lead server, Moultrie, who had been with the Armer family for some 700 years or more, was paying very close attention to them—watching every move they made like a snake preparing to pounce. In fact, Moultrie had seen young Ephraim slip out of the compound without his parent's knowledge on more than one occasion. He had followed the young master at a discreet distance.

It is not safe for a Nephilim to be caught out late at night all alone. It is especially unsafe when the Nephilim is young and not yet at peak power. Some of the white humans could catch him or, even worse, a demon could get hold of him.

Moultrie wasn't following Ephraim to protect him. If that had been the case, Moultrie had only to inform Silas and Delia of Ephraim's nocturnal wanderings and extremely reckless behaviour. He had no intention of doing that. He had come to hate every member of the Rephaim class, including those he served this night.

Moultrie's human blood was mixed with the lowest class of celestial being—that of an angel. He resented the caste system that allowed the Rephaims to have so much and the Anakins to have so little due merely to an accident of birth. Because of his inferior blood, he was forced to serve others. Moultrie wasn't the only Anakin who held these sentiments. Unlike the others, he planned to do something about it.

He practised the forbidden art of black majick which had been outlawed by the king. In fact, he was a master practitioner—an archmage wizard of the first order. He intended to turn the world of the aristocrats upside down and strengthen his already prodigious powers tenfold in the process.

He hid a secret smile. He was overjoyed with the knowledge that he had spit in the food they seemed to be enjoying so much. It was a small reward indeed, but gratifying nonetheless. He would continue to follow Ephraim on his late-night forays until his efforts bore fruit.

Who knows what tasty tidbits of information I will garner from my due diligence. I will endeavour to turn whatever I learn to my own advantage. I will bide my time and wait.

～❧ ☙～

Ephraim's parents had spared no expense for the celebration. Each guest lifted the deliciously prepared food to their aristocratic mouths on exquisite Renaissance Baroque flatware designed by Benevento Cellini. They sipped 100-year-old Bordeaux from Baccarat goblets the servants continuously kept filled.

The soft strains of violin music could be heard in the background while the Anakins moved silently from guest to guest serving the third course of an eight-course meal. The latest course consisted of truffles, wild rice, and stuffed quail which each servant artfully plated in the centre of china dinnerware dating back to the Tang Dynasty.

The lavish spread did nothing to lift Ephraim's morose mood. He would have preferred the sound of the fiddle he'd heard the slaves playing at one of the nearby plantations to that of the sedate violin. He would have been well satisfied with much simpler fare.

As the only son of Silas Armers, Ephraim was kept in a cocoon of privileged protection to ensure the continuation of their angelic line. He was told what to do, how to do it, when he could do it, and with whom. Sometimes he felt no freer than the slaves picking cotton and cutting down tobacco under the threat of the overseer's whip on the white man's plantation.

Now he was going to have to marry a woman his parents had chosen for him before he was born. He loved his parents and was, for the most part, a dutiful son, but he honestly didn't know how much more of this he could take.

Ephraim was a restless spirit. He would often slip away in the middle of the night to investigate his surroundings and dream about how different things could be if he wasn't the son of a powerful, well-connected Nephilim aristocrat.

What Ephraim really wanted to do was join the Gibborim Army under the mentorship of one of the Brothers of the Dark Veil and work his way up through the ranks to eventually become an officer. He was a good fighter and well-versed in weaponry. He wanted to use those skills to protect the Nephilim Nation and see the world while he was doing it. Unfortunately, nobody had taken the time to ask Ephraim what he wanted. His life had been plotted out for him from birth to the grave.

He lifted the heavy silver fork to his mouth. The food was rich and well prepared, but he could barely taste it. The idea of marrying someone he didn't know made the food fall like lead to the bottom of his stomach. He lifted his goblet to take another swallow of the wine. He knew he was drinking too much. There was nothing for it.

Everyone seemed to be having a nice time—that is, everyone but him. His father was engaged in a heated debate with Nephthys' father about King Zion's decision to relocate a heavy Gibborim contingency to North America as opposed to Asia. His sister, Sara, and the two matrons were exchanging the merits of imported versus domestic silks while Ephraim drank like a fish and Nephthys sat beside him like a statute.

He was working on his fifth or sixth glass of wine—he couldn't recall which—when he felt his mother's warm gaze fall on him. She'd worked so hard to make a good impression on his future in-laws. His parent's marriage had been an arranged one, and they had come to love one another deeply. His mother wanted the same happiness for him.

Ephraim loved her too much to disappoint her. He had been pointedly ignoring Nephthys since she and her family arrived on the previous evening. It was time he at least attempted to engage her in conversation.

"So, Nephthys, what do you enjoy doing during your spare time?" he asked. She took so long to answer that at first he thought she hadn't heard him.

"I play the pianoforte, and I enjoy needlepoint," she replied in a voice barely above a whisper.

Ephraim waited politely. There had to be more. If Nephthys didn't have her head down like she was afraid to look at him, she was sneaking peeks at him and giggling like a silly twit. He didn't know which annoyed him more. The idea of saddling himself with an empty-headed female who jumped every time he looked in her direction or one who giggled at inopportune times. Neither option presented a promising future for him. In fact, it sounded downright depressing.

Ephraim took a good look at his intended. She was pretty enough. He'd give her that. Her *café au lait* skin was as smooth as moon-kissed porcelain. She had brown eyes as large as a frightened doe's and long brownish red hair that she wore pulled back in a sedate bun. She was of medium height and build with a virginal look about her that made her appear fragile and untouchable. Ephraim felt nothing for her.

He suspected she didn't even know how to tie her own shoes without the assistance of an Anakin. She seemed to be a beautifully formed empty shell without an original or interesting thought in her pretty little head.

Ephraim shot a despairing look in the direction of his sister who was sitting across the dining table from him. He and Sara were very close. She hid her return look of commiseration before bowing her head to hide her unkind feelings about her future sister-in-law. She too had attempted to engage Nephthys in intelligent conversation without success. After a few more attempts, Ephraim concluded that engaging Nephthys in conversation was like pulling good teeth. He finally gave up.

Ephraim politely excused himself when the diners adjourned to the parlour for aperitifs. He desperately needed to feel the kiss of the night air upon his skin—to be alone with his troubled thoughts.

CHAPTER 8

The Maroon Camp

⌒

*J*UBAL SNUCK UP on Abena like a thief in the night, blocking her path as she rounded the bend on her way back from the outhouse.

It was after midnight. The cook fires had long been extinguished, and most of the camp had bedded down for the night. Abena found herself all alone in the woods with a man who had a look of lust in his eyes—a man she loathed. Fear gripped her belly like a vice.

Jubal made no secret that he desired Abena. He undressed her with his eyes whenever he was near, making her feel unclean. With the features she'd inherited from her African-Haitian father and her Dahomean mother, Abena was an exquisite mixture of her parents.

Abena had never had a man, but she knew enough about male and female relations to know that she didn't want Jubal. He was a vicious runaway slave with big pink lips, a nose that was so flat it looked like it had been smashed in with a cast iron pan, and close-set hooded eyes that were always a sickening bloodshot red and yellow. He was ugly, thick, and squat like a bull, with dull ashy skin and chipped yellow teeth. Worse still, he was as ugly inside as he was out. Abena despised the ground he walked on.

Abena lived in an armed camp of runaway slaves known as Maroons. Her father, Francois Andre, was a houngan—a voodoo priest—whose

French Creole master brought him from Haiti to the Louisiana Territory after the Haitian Revolution.

Not long after he arrived in Louisiana, Andre and four other slaves escaped the cruel conditions of plantation life, killing the sadistic plantation overseer to facilitate their escape. During his escape, Andre kidnapped an innocent housemaid named Annamae who would eventually bear his only child, Abena.

Andre led the runaway slaves into the nearby swamps, one of the few places where white men feared to tread. They managed to eke out a humble existence in the heart of the swamp, making periodic raids on nearby plantations to assist runaways and to steal the supplies they needed. It was during one such raid when Andre was shot in the side, barely escaping with his life. They got the bullet out, but a fever set in, permanently sapping Andre of his former vigour and vitality. He became a shell of the man he once was.

Five years later, 150 African slaves overtook the officers and crew members of the slave ship transporting them to Louisiana. They waited until land was in sight and hacked the white men to pieces with machetes, hoisting their heads on pikes for the sea vultures to feast upon. They swam toward shore in the dead of night, but the whites onshore picked many of the slaves off with their rifles before they could emerge from the water. Out of the original 150 insurrectionists, only fifty survived.

A fearless warrior from Ghana, Jubal was the leader of that rebellion and one of the fifty survivors. He and his followers trekked toward the swamp with a hefty bounty on each of their heads. Should they ever be caught, they would be tortured and executed as an example to other slaves.

Abena's father knew he was no longer strong enough to protect his people. Jubal had proven himself to be the stronger man, but many of the Maroons were leery of Jubal's leadership. Abena was little more than a toddler when she was promised in marriage as a means to unify the Maroons. Her father soon became leader in name only while Jubal became leader in fact.

BEHIND THE DARK VEIL

As more runaway slaves made their way to the swamps, they banded together to form a community. As they continued to raid and pillage nearby plantations and free more slaves, the Maroon community grew even more.

⁂

Abena attempted to hide her fear with bravado. "Get out of my way, Jubal."

The shaky timbre of her voice gave her disquiet away. Jubal picked up on her trepidation like a shark smelling blood in the water.

She tried to go around him, but he moved when she moved, boxing her in and blocking out the moon, the stars, and all chances for a clean escape. As fast as lightning flashes across the sky, Jubal backed Abena up against a tree, slobbering on her face and neck with wet open-mouthed kisses. The cruel projections sticking out of the bark dug into her back. His big musky body pressed intimately against her.

She could feel his desire through her thin cotton dress. It was a short fat club, as wide around as the bottom of her father's coffee cup and as white-hot as a branding iron. Jubal was forcing one of his thick thighs between her legs just like he was forcing his tongue into her mouth. She couldn't breathe.

It was bad enough that she would have to sacrifice herself for the good of the community. But she'd be damned if she would allow that ugly motherfucker to take liberties with her one minute—no, not one second—before she had to.

Abena struggled against his unwanted amorous embrace. Finally, in a state of sheer desperation, she bit down on Jubal's tongue and twisted her face away.

"Get off of me! *Mwen rayi ou. Gwet maman ou!*" (I hate you, motherfucker.)

She always reverted to her father's native Creole when she was upset. Abena was *really* upset.

Jubal drew his fist back to strike her but stopped himself before landing a blow that would have probably killed her. He'd wait to tame the little bitch after they were wed. He moved his tongue around in his mouth to assess the damage. It felt like she had bitten off a piece of his tongue. It was killing him. *Shit!*

"You are going to pay for that, bitch!"

Abena didn't care if she hurt him. She wished she'd bitten the fucking thing off. Maybe then he would leave her alone.

"*Alo vouzan, Jubal!*" she spat. (Go to hell, Jubal!) "You don't own me. You have no right to put your filthy hands on me. "*Mwen rayi ou!*" she repeated. (I hate you!) "And I will always hate you."

Jubal knew Abena hated him. He could see it in her beautiful dark eyes every single time she looked at him. She was like a fire in his blood. He wanted to strip her naked and fuck her until that cool look of detachment she seemed to reserve for him alone turned to passion. If he couldn't make her want him, he would make her fear and respect him. Either way, she would be his.

"Stop fighting me," he ordered. "Soon you will be my wife. I will be able to touch you, to kiss you, to do whatever I want to you."

He had her trapped against the tree with his hands on both sides of her head. His stinking breath fanned against her face like hot fetid wind when he moved in to kiss her again.

"Give me a little taste of that honey, baby," he growled. "No one will know."

Jubal clasped her face in his big callused hands and plunged his tongue so deep inside of Abena's mouth that she gagged. Then he grinded his sweaty body into hers, leaving no doubt about his intentions.

This time Abena brought up her knee, connecting with the blood-engorged piece of steel between Jubal's thick thighs. He dropped to his knees, roaring like a lion with an amputated paw. Abena stepped away from him.

"Well, I'm not your wife yet, Jubal, so you had better keep your hands to yourself until then or I will scream the entire compound down. I am sure you wouldn't want your men to know you had to force a woman to lay down with you."

BEHIND THE DARK VEIL

The swamps swallowed Abena as she took off running, leaving Jubal holding himself and cursing up a blue storm.

❧ ❧

Abena ran. Branches cut her calves and arms. Rocks and vines injured her feet as she ran through the thick foliage. She ran with her mouth wide open in a silent scream with tears streaming down her face. She didn't stop running until the sounds of Jubal's pursuit diminished to nothing.

She finally stopped, pressing her back against a broad tree to conceal herself. All she could hear were the night sounds of the swamp and her own laboured breathing. Her chest heaved and her throat burned from the exertion. Her body was covered with sweat borne of fear and the uncomfortable steamy night. She had escaped Jubal's unwanted advances—this time—but each time he caught her alone he grew bolder.

"I won't do it!" she said aloud to no one.

She was trying to convince herself that the inevitable wasn't going to happen. She raised her eyes to the starlit night and hissed. "I tell you I will not marry that ugly baboon-looking motherfucker." Abena swiped her hand over her mouth and spat on the ground to remove the taste of Jubal's slimy kisses. He made her flesh crawl.

What am I going to do? she thought. *I cannot tell my father about Jubal's assault. He would challenge Jubal for touching me, and he would die. My father is no match against Jubal. Few among the Maroons are.*

She had to do something. The thought of Jubal's hands and mouth on her made her sick. His smell was on her skin, her clothing. It had invaded her soul. Abena bent over to throw up. She emptied her insides, and yet the taste of Jubal's slimy tongue still lingered inside her mouth like a sickness. His smell assaulted her sensibilities.

She'd been restless of spirit since her flowering, yearning for something she didn't quite understand. Whatever it was she was looking for would not be found in Jubal's arms. She ran through the swamp to a nearby creek, determined to bathe the stink of Jubal off her.

CHAPTER 9

⌒

ON THE NIGHT Ephraim first saw Abena, the ever-capricious fates danced upon the tips of the brightest stars, aligning themselves just so. Then they blotted out the light, leaving lesser beings bereft and cold from their fickle abandonment.

He had left the safety of the Nephilim encampment to wander the swamp, to think. His mind was troubled. He'd just had dinner with the woman he was supposed to marry, and he found her wanting. There was no doubt in his mind that he would do his duty, but that didn't make things any easier for him. He wandered through the swamp, eventually finding himself at the mouth of a creek. That was when he saw her.

The light of the moon reflected off the water in which she was bathing, creating shimmering crystals around her dark skin, giving her an otherworldly appearance. Ephraim was utterly and completely spellbound. He stepped upon a nearby root and it cracked. The sound startled her. She quickly grabbed the dress she had carelessly abandoned at the edge of the pool and ran.

From that night forward, she haunted Ephraim's dreams. He had to see her again. He returned to the creek every night for more than a week with the hope he might see her one more time, even though he knew that one more time would never be enough.

Just when he despaired he would ever see her again, she returned. He didn't think it was possible, but she was even more beautiful than when he first saw her.

It was an insufferably humid night. The moisture in the air was so heavy it weighed down the leaves of the trees and coalesced into a thick murky fog which floated a foot from the ground.

Abena was naked as the day she was born, standing waist deep in the cool creek water when she felt his presence. She knew he had been watching her on that first night when she escaped Jubal's unwanted attention. His eyes caressed her like a lover's questing hands. She loved every single minute of it.

Her lips parted in a secret smile as she cupped her hands in the clear water, scooping a handful of the liquid gift from God over her shoulders. She arched her back, giving him a clear view of her shapely silhouette. The water beaded as it ran down the length of her smooth, moist back, soothing her feverish flesh from the night's heat. It did nothing to cool the heat of passion that was pulsing between her shapely thighs.

For weeks Abena had been aware of the tall, dark youth who had taken to hiding himself amongst the thickets bordering the creek, watching her with longing in his mysterious eyes.

Abena knew it was dangerous to court the attention of a stranger, but something in his eyes called out to her. Though he lived among the people her father warned her to stay away from, somehow she knew he would never hurt her.

She felt the heat of her secret admirer's eyes upon her. His gaze was as potent as a tight grip between her thighs. She wanted him. She threw her head back in abandon, feeling freer than she'd ever felt before.

∽ ∼

The woman of Ephraim's dreams had finally returned to what he would later call the sacred creek, granting him the guilty pleasure of watching her wash her beautiful body. He eagerly watched her, knowing she was very much aware of his presence.

BEHIND THE DARK VEIL

She looked like one of the exquisite African queens his father frequently told stories about. The only difference being that the beauty standing before him was real and not a memory recalled from days gone by.

Ephraim actually gulped at her suggestive pose. He would have given anything at that moment to be one of those droplets of water covering her body, especially the drops that trailed down her back to pool in the cleft between her tight round buttocks. He broke out in a sweat that had nothing to do with the hot, humid night and everything to do with the erotic display taking place before him. He licked his lips, hungry to taste her.

When Ephraim thought he would lose his mind with wanting her, she looked over her slender shoulder at him and flashed a smile brighter than the sun he'd never been allowed to see. In that moment, Ephraim was lost. In an instant, his family, his fiancé, and his obligations were forgotten. His heart belonged to the lovely human and no one else.

Abena sucked in a breath when his dark eyes locked with hers. Her eyes grew round with astonishment when she realised what he was doing. *Oh, my god. He's taking off his clothes!*

Now it was Abena's turn to gulp. Ephraim felt her look of astonishment transform into a hunger that matched his own. His body reacted like a springboard, flaring to life wherever her dark eyes landed. He smiled mischievously, showing a dimple in his left cheek, as he undid the buttons of his shirt one by one. Then he knelt to kick off his boots.

He was a potently masculine male, long and lean, with the face of a Black Adonis, and tightly corded muscles from an active lifestyle. Her hands positively itched with the desire to touch him.

The look on the beautiful human's face expressed how much she wanted him far better than words ever could. Ephraim knew exactly what he was doing. His deep, sexy laugh tickled her insides, making her breath hitch and her heart pound when he caught his fingers in the waistband of his trousers and slowly lowered them in a sensual striptease before his audience of one. Then he stepped into the creek in all his naked glory. Abena's knees nearly buckled.

O bon Dye, men li ap vi n pran mwen. (Oh, my god. He's coming to get me.)

She loved the way he moved, like a lithe jungle animal on the prowl. She thoroughly enjoyed every movement he made as she watched him through the light of the moon shining through the trees.

His hands shook with emotion as he cupped her delicate heart-shaped face, kissing both cheeks, the cleft in her chin, her forehead, and finally her soft, full lips. For a moment the former strangers became one and were totally lost in each other and their surroundings.

She was disturbingly beautiful—captivating with rich dark skin that shone like polished ebony. About a foot of thick bushy hair framed her delicate heart-shaped face. Her eyes were as dark as onyx, expressive with long lashes that curled at the tips.

His eyes travelled down her body. The water in the creek was not deep, only coming up to her womanly thighs. Her breasts were full and high. Her waist was impossibly small. Her hips were lush and ample. She was created for lovemaking. Her eyes beckoned him.

He took his time with her. His tongue lathed the inside of her mouth, savouring every single bit of her sweetness like it was the finest wine. She let him know how well his skillful kisses affected her. She moaned into his mouth, completely giving herself over to him with untutored reckless abandon. There was no artifice between them—neither were there any inhibitions. She was too innocent to know how to play those kinds of games. Their being together was as natural as breathing, almost as if God designed them specifically for one another. Ephraim felt like he had been drugged when the kiss ended.

"What are you called, beautiful one?" Ephraim asked, his voice filled with passion. The deep velvet tone made Abena melt in his arms.

"My name is Abena," she responded in a husky voice that made him as hard as steel.

He repeated her name with wonder. "Ah-bee-nah."

Then he took her hand and led her out of the creek. Ephraim retrieved his shirt. He spread the light cambric garment upon the ground to cushion Abena's body from any twigs or stones hidden within the grass. Then he gently laid her down on a grassy patch of earth. Ephraim rose, his arms extended while he balanced himself on the heels of his hands.

"My name is Ephraim, sweet Abena. You will know the name of the male who will claim you this night."

CHAPTER 10

BENA SPREAD HER thighs wide beneath Ephraim. He was thick and long. The weight of his manhood caused it to sway between them. They both watched in wonder as his cock disappeared inside Abena's body.

Abena cried out. It hurt, like a red-hot blade splitting her asunder, but the pain was quickly replaced with a sensation she didn't have the words to describe. He withdrew his member with slow purpose. Ephraim hissed when a second later he seated himself from tip to balls inside her hot body. When he withdrew again, he was slick and wet from Abena's excitement and the blood of her lost innocence.

Ephraim's large body eclipsed Abena's womanly frame. Wild swamp birds with majestic wings soared above them and the night animals that made their home amongst the swamp's dense vegetation bore witness to their passionate lovemaking.

Ephraim grunted. She felt like heaven inside. Like a wet, hot glove rhythmically clamping around his cock to milk it dry. Abena's breath hitched in concert with the sounds of the swamp. The feeling got so good Ephraim could no longer control himself. His firm buttocks rose and fell in a steady relentless rhythm, plundering the grasping wet womanhood between Abena's widespread thighs, filling her with steel plated meat just short of madness. She took all he gave her and greedily sought even more.

Abena's fingernails scored crescent moons in the ropey muscles in Ephraim's broad back. She arched beneath him, her beautiful face contorted by the sensation overload while Ephraim gave her the ride of her life. Abena never knew being with a man could feel so damn good.

"Yes, baby. *Ah NAY!* Yesss!" She screamed to the heavens and beyond, switching between her mother's native tongue Twi and English. "*Ah NAY!* Split me open with your long hard cock. *Ah NAY!*" Her voice echoed through the night sky, bouncing off the moon and the stars before returning to earth in a shower of love-infused sweat that made both of their young bodies glisten.

Ephraim felt his release building as their sweat-slick bodies pounded against one another. Like molten lava, his semen soared to the tip of his thick manhood, building and churning as he tightened his buttock muscles to drive even deeper inside Abena's yielding body, striving to become one with her.

He was about to erupt. Abena's slick inner walls began to convulse and clutch at his manhood, threatening to milk him of everything—his seed, his mind, his very soul.

The veins in Ephraim's neck bulged as he threw his head back and opened his mouth wide to accommodate a pair of long, sharp fangs. He growled deep in his throat like a jungle animal and then plunged his fangs into Abena's neck at the same time his steaming hot semen splashed against her pulsing feminine walls, flooding her insides and temporarily cooling the fires which burned deep within her.

Ephraim then began to suck—deep, slow and steady—savoring every swallow of her sweet blood. He was exceedingly gentle as he fed from her, making sure not to take enough to weaken her or compromise her health. He was strong, and he recognised her fragility. He would never do anything to hurt her.

Abena felt the beginning of yet another orgasm. It felt like Ephraim's mouth was everywhere, sucking clear down to her centre. She came, and came, and couldn't stop coming until both of them had their fill.

Now that the blazing hot fire of passion was temporarily abated, the enormity of the situation they found themselves in came crashing down on the lovers like a century-old wall.

Their being together was wrong on so many levels, but Ephraim didn't care. He couldn't get enough of her lips, her smell, or the feel of her smooth dark skin. Her voice was like sweet music to his ears. Now that he'd had her, he knew that the sound of her sultry voice would stay in his head, haunting him and making it impossible for him to think straight. He had no idea he could feel like this.

Ephraim was aware that the Maroons warned their children to stay away from his kind, but the Nephilim were no better. Even though they were part human, their prejudices and disdain for humans ran deep.

Ephraim tenderly licked the side of Abena's neck to close the puncture wounds. He closed his eyes, savouring the taste of her blood on his tongue. To Ephraim, Abena's blood tasted like nectar from The Ancient of Days, sustenance fit for angels. He knew of nothing that could possibly be sweeter.

Using the lush forest grass as their bedding, he cradled her in his arms, inhaling the fragrance of her soft hair. She smelled like hot buttered honey and the fresh pine needles on the huge tree covering the entrance to his family abode. Indeed, with her in his arms, he felt as though he had come home.

But for now, all they had was this moment. They must treasure the precious little time they had together, as though it was their last. Before long, it would be morning and she would have to hasten back to her village and he would have to return to the large cavern that housed an underground city where he dwelled with his family. Neither of them was ready to part. Ephraim squeezed her tightly against his body and kissed her on the temple. He could feel the rapid beat of her heart against his lips.

"This is insane," he said. "I just met you and already I know that no matter how much time we spend together, it will never be enough."

He could not see her face clearly from the position they were in, but he felt her smile. She kissed his chest in that place directly above his heart where he was most vulnerable, where only she resided.

Abena's feelings for Ephraim were also strong. "I will think about you all the time, Ephraim, wondering what you are doing when we are apart and who you are with. When I go to sleep, I know that I will dream about you. You will be the first person I think about in the morning when I wake and my last thought before giving myself over to sleep at night."

When Abena looked at him the way she was looking at him right now, it made all the risks they were taking worth it. "Would you think I was crazy if I told you that I love you, Abena, even though I am engaged to wed someone else? I do not want to hurt her any more than I want to hurt and disappoint my parents," he said with a troubled look in his eyes.

I did not set out to fall in love with a human. It just happened, he thought to himself.

Abena raised her hand to caress his cheek. Ephraim kissed the centre of her palm. "I understand exactly how you feel, Ephraim. I, too, am promised to another. His name is Jubal. I feel nothing for him. Before I met you, I was resigned to do my duty for our people. But now that I have met you—loved you—I know that I cannot marry him under any circumstances."

Ephraim loved to hear Abena speak. Her speech pattern was not like that of most slaves. "You do not speak like a slave, Abena. How did you come by such refined speech?" he asked.

"I do not speak like a slave, Ephraim, because I am not a slave. I am a Maroon, the daughter of escaped slaves. I am free. Before my father brought my mother here, she had been the personal maid of the plantation owner's wife. She mimicked the mannerisms and speech pattern of her owners and passed them onto me. I also know how to read and write," she added proudly.

Ephraim entwined his fingers with Abena's. "I don't know what the future holds for us, sweet Abena, but I do know this. As long as we are together we can overcome anything."

The young lovers caressed and whispered tender words of love to one another under the canopy of the lush swamp trees. All the while, Moultrie hovered a foot above the ground in a semi-transparent form, concealed behind a copse of dense foliage.

BEHIND THE DARK VEIL

He could barely contain his excitement. He'd followed Ephraim as was his custom and had the privilege to witness his steamy exchange with the lowlife, stinking human. A huge smile split Moultrie's face. He knew someone who would pay dearly to get their hands on a young Nephilim aristocrat. He ghosted out of the swamp to set his diabolical plan into motion.

CHAPTER 11

⌒

PERCHED UPON A sturdy limb in a tree high above Ephraim and Abena sat a two foot tall creature with the face of a miniature goblin and the outer flesh of a skinless fire-breathing dragon. His palms, fingertips, and toes were covered with enlarged pores that secreted a sticky substance which enabled him to easily cling to or climb up any surface like a monkey.

His back was permanently curved forward and his head hung below his shoulder line as he dispassionately eavesdropped on the lovers. His name was Feo, and he was one of several imps patrolling the swamps. The heavily leafed tree which had at first appeared to be a perfect location for Ephraim's and Abena's late-night tryst hid nothing from the eyes and ears of the mischievous little imp.

Feo's triangular face was all smooth bone with no skin to hide the stark dips and grooves of his skull. Since imps don't eat, drink, or speak, instead drawing sustenance from the aura of others, there was nothing but shiny smooth bone where a mouth should have been.

The skin atop Feo's head was a bright lime green, graduating in degrees on his arms, legs, and abdomen to a green as dark as the most verdant grasses of the swamps. The tips of his fingers and toes were inky black. He had a lethal barb-tipped tail, twice as long as he was high. It undulated like a contented cobra, poised to strike if necessary.

He cocked his funny-looking little head to the side, growing still as stone, as Ephraim and Abena continued to speak in whispered voices below. Feo watched the innocent lovers with widespread deep-red eyes, his eyelids blinking side to side like a lizard while he took everything in, making sure not to miss a single nuance or gesture. He dared not leave out any of the pertinent details when he gave his report to his master.

With Ephraim's preternatural hearing, he had the ability to detect the approach of animal or man from as far away as a mile. With the aid of the wind he could sometimes hear from an even greater distance. His keen sense of hearing, coupled with his preternatural sense of smell, made it virtually impossible for anyone to sneak up on the couple as they shared words of love with one another.

But it would have been difficult for Ephraim to detect the presence of the imp, even if he were not so engrossed in Abena. Feo's natural odour was masked by an arch mage wizard's spell, and his scaly lizard skin naturally blended in with the night, occasionally shimmering in iridescent shades of green.

Feo shifted his bony arms like a monkey and swung quietly to a lower limb. He needed to get closer. He grabbed on to the limb with hands that consisted of only four fingers, each of which were tipped by a long, curved claw as were his toes. He easily gained purchase of the limb and briefly hung there upside down. Feo had heard and seen enough. The information the wizard had given him was accurate.

Had Ephraim been paying attention, he would have easily mistaken Feo for a bird when he spread his leathery wings to glide out of the tree and into the open sky. Imps are not capable of flying long distances, but he certainly could fly far enough to deliver the news he'd just discovered to his master.

Wind burned Feo's face and leaves from the tops of trees sliced into his leathery wings as he made his way anxiously out of the swamps to his master's domain. He sought to deliver his message with all haste. Who knows? His master might even reward him with a nice warm bath in newborn baby blood. His razor-sharp tail spun in excitement at the prospect of such a reward.

His destination was Magnolia Hill Plantation, the largest of five stately plantations lining River Road. The master of the manse was

BEHIND THE DARK VEIL

Clidamont Etienne, a profligate paederast with a gambling habit and a penchant for sadistic cruelty. He was also diseased with the pox and syphilis, a blink of an eye away from total madness, and ripe for demonic possession.

All was quiet as Feo cut through the night air, landing like a bird of prey upon the open windowsill of Clidamont's bedroom suite. Feo patiently perched on the narrow sill with his head awkwardly cast to the side. Eventually, the sleeping man began to stir.

Clidamont's sleep was troubled. His diseased body shook and quivered under Feo's watchful eye as though in the throes of a bad dream. Sensing he was not alone, Clidamont's eyes sprang wide open like a sleepwalker on the other side of a trap door.

The eyes of the sleeping man were not Clidamont's watery greyish-red veined orbs rendered thus from sickness and too much drink. The eyes Feo looked into were the blood-red demon eyes of his master Tyranny, one of The Satan's wicked sons.

Tyranny squinted to see through the cloudy lenses of Clidamont's insipid eyes like they were a dusty telescope. He wore the weak mean-spirited man's skin like an ill-fitted suit, to be worn until the threads frayed apart and discarded.

Tyranny was an insidious demon on a mission. Once he took up residence in a human's bodily temple, they may as well stick a rifle in their mouth and pull the trigger. That would be a more merciful death than the one Tyranny would mete out once he was done with the body.

Tyranny forced Clidamont to sit up in bed like a puppet. Vapour sifted out of the man's eyes, ears, nose, and mouth like smoke from a dying fire, filling the bedroom suite with a hazy essence until it finally coalesced and materialised into the ghostly shape of a translucent man. His voice was deep and gravelly, packed with a promise of bad tidings and evil acts.

"You had better have good news for me, cretin," the demon stated, prompting Feo to immediately adopt an obsequious manner. He bowed his head between every swing of his tail like a broken metronome. In a form of code used only by imps, Feo delivered his urgent message with the tip of his barbed tail. The message was short and to the point because he knew Tyranny had little or no patience with dissembling.

"Oh, yes, sire. I have very good news for you, very good news indeed. Less than a mile from here, a male Nephilim is rutting upon the body of a human female for all he's worth. I can take you to him, Master. If we move quickly, we can apprehend him."

Tyranny's breath hitched in excitement. This was good news indeed. Centuries of enmity existed between the fallen angels, now known as demons, and the half-angel, half-human hybrids known as Nephilim.

At long last, one of the Nephilim had been foolish enough to venture outside of the protection of one of their secure compounds. Tyranny had long suspected there were Nephilim holed up in the Louisiana swamps. He just didn't know exactly where. Hopefully, tonight would change all that and more.

His determination and persistence were finally paying off. Feo, one of the imps he had cleverly stationed in strategic areas throughout the swamp, had just reported a splendid bit of news. An arch mage wizard among the Nephilim has betrayed his own kind. *I will see that the traitor is amply rewarded,* he silently promised.

Feo's initial report was followed by even better news. "Sire. The foolish lad dallying with the human is none other than the son of Silas, head of the House of Armers."

Tyranny crowed with delight. *Upon my word. This is too rich. What a coup!* But it would not do for him to count his chickens before they hatched. He would see this unguarded Nephilim with his own eyes.

He sent a mental message out to two of his brothers. Like unpaid taxes and bad luck, his brothers Travail and Hindrance were soon standing by his side. His brother Incarnadine was trapped on the third level of hell, and his brother Salacious had taken up residence inside of Claude Etienne.

Without a word passing between them, Travail and Hindrance became as mist and slipped into the now peacefully sleeping body of Clidamont Etienne as quickly and easily as a hot knife slides through warm butter.

BEHIND THE DARK VEIL

"Come, Feo," Tyranny commanded. "My brothers will hold down the fort here. Lead me to this son of Silas. This is an auspicious night indeed."

Tyranny's excitement was contagious. Feo didn't want to waste a minute getting back to their quarry.

"But what of the female, Sire?"

Tyranny looked at Feo like he was crazy. "What of her? The human female has served her purpose. We will give her over to a horde of demons and dispose of her as offal. But not the male. Oh, no. I have big plans for the male, Feo."

Tyranny began to chant in Dimoori Sheol, the universal language of the underworld. He became as mist, surrounding Feo's body as the anxious imp took to the air, flying high above the grounds of Magnolia Hill as all quietly slept. Soon they were in the middle of the swamps, not far from where the inquisitive little imp had first spied Ephraim and Abena.

The earth shook beneath Tyranny's feet as they touched down on the spongy swamp earth. Tyranny was now in his natural form, befouling the air in and around the swamp. All business now, Feo watched in fascination as Tyranny spread his arms wide in a stance of pending victory.

"Now lead me to my quarry, imp," Tyranny commanded, following the imp deeper into the swamp.

Together, Tyranny and Feo drew closer to the spot where Feo spied the unsuspecting lovers' secluded love nest, leaving in their wake a path of unparalleled death and destruction. The grass upon which they trod withered and died. The leaves on the trees shrivelled and, like ashes in the wind, fell from their branches to be crushed beneath Tyranny's massive amphibian feet. The animals of the forest scurried for cover, intuitively sensing something evil in their midst. The air stilled in deference to their approach, allowing the swamp to fill unchallenged with the sulphurous stench.

By the time Ephraim's ultra-sensitive nose detected danger, it was too late. A shadow of darkness descended upon the young couple. In the space of a moment, the lives of all those who loved them would be irrevocably altered.

CHAPTER 12

⌒

*T*HERE WERE FIVE thousand Gibborim soldiers on the wrong side of the Dark Veil, each assigned to cover a portion of the thousands of acres that comprised the Atchafalaya Swamp wilderness. They were all loyal to General Ajuma of the House of Akibeel and to their king. Their assignment was to scour the largest swampland in America.

They were on a search-and-rescue mission. The night before, Ephraim, the only son of Silas of the House of Armers, had gone missing. When the youth's sister was questioned, it was discovered that Ephraim was infatuated with one of the Maroon females who resided not too far from the Nephilim compound. In fact, he had been visiting a creek each night where he had first seen the human bathing with hope of seeing her again, even though relationships between Nephilim and humans were strictly forbidden by the Nephilim king.

A few hours ago, Ajuma had come upon the desecrated body of the leader of the Maroons. The remains of what appeared to have been a search party were found not too far away in the centre of a small clearing about a quarter mile south of the Nephilim compound. The bodies had been drained dry and torn apart so savagely they barely resembled anything human. Ajuma assumed the humans had been out looking for the missing female when they met their gruesome end.

The only son of a prominent member of the Nephilim aristocracy was missing and a group of humans wiped out, but for what? Ajuma and his army were there to get answers to those questions.

Ajuma did not condone mixing between humans and Nephilim, but for years the Maroon people had respected the existence of the Nephilim Nation. Because of this, the Nephilim left them to live in peace.

Ajuma knelt to more closely examine the area near the creek. His bright green eyes took in every detail. From the look of things, their search-and-rescue mission may turn into one of search and recovery. The killings clearly bore demonic footprints.

Demons are the sworn enemy of Nephilim and humans alike. However, the Brothers of the Dark Veil, the King's appointed protectors of the Nephilim Nation, were only concerned with the impact the presence of demons would have on their people. The humans would have to use voodoo or witchcraft to fend for themselves.

It stood to reason, however, that if their enemies had somehow gotten to the Maroons, it would not be long before they stumbled upon the Nephilim's well-hidden underground compound. Ajuma and his comrades were determined that would not happen.

Ajuma sniffed the air around him like a jungle animal. His nostrils flared as his keen sense of smell took over. He suspected he was not alone. Like a burst of cannon fire, his olfactory senses were immediately bombarded.

No. I am definitely not alone.

His preternatural form travelled over the marsh grasses at a superhuman speed, becoming one with the haunting and mysterious beauty of the Atchafalaya Swamp. A set of steps to the left and to the right of him mirrored each of his footfalls.

Let the games begin.

The owners of the steps surreptitiously kept pace with him in a futile effort to conceal their presence. Two things gave his uninvited guests away. First, the little hairs at the nape of his neck were standing up like century-old poplar trees. Second, a familiar stench travelled through the bayou on the wings of the wind.

The throat-clogging stench rode on the back of each gust of wind, causing the towering moss-laden bald cypress trees to sway to a mournful tune and the swamp animals to flee in the face of the evil polluting their domain. The undeniable smell of sulphur and shit that always presaged the arrival or presence of a demon hung thick in the moist Louisiana air.

Giving the demons the impression he was unaware he was being tailed, Ajuma continued on through the dense fecund underbrush, his lithe, muscular body becoming one with the dark and sometimes frightening beauty shrouding the swamp in the darkest hours of the night.

He moved with swift deliberation, as silent as a nocturnal predator. He sought to lead his enemies as far from the area as possible, deep within the heart of the swamp that had for centuries hidden a large colony of Nephilim whom he would willingly give his life to protect. Ajuma maintained a blinding pace as he quickly sent out a telepathic message to his second-in-command.

"You might want to hasten to my side if you are interested in questioning some recalcitrant demons before I dispatch them back to hell, Face."

Face was the nickname the Brothers of the Dark Veil had given to Facio of the House of Batraal.

"No doubt I can handle them on my own, but as a gesture of goodwill and brotherly love I thought I'd let you and a couple of the green soldiers have a piece of the action. Why don't you pull a couple of the new guys off sentry detail and bring them along with you."

Face responded to Ajuma's message telepathically. *"I wouldn't miss an opportunity to kick some demon arse for anything in the world. Be right there, General. Try not to kill them before we get there!"*

Evidently tired of playing their little game of cloak and dagger, two demons materialised in front of Ajuma, effectively blocking his path. One of the demons seeking to engage him was short and squat like a two-legged Brahma bull. His fists were the size of Christmas hams and his arms were so thick he was forced to hold them away from his body.

This demon had the look of a mythical Cyclops, with one large eye in the centre of his forehead and a mouth filled with razor-sharp teeth dripping thick, viscous saliva. His weapon of choice was a spiked cudgel that seemed to fit his huge fist perfectly. Ajuma had no doubt the demon knew how to use it.

The second demon held a huge rip-hook sickle in his hands. The light of the moon shone off the curved metal blade as the demon shifted the wooden handle from hand to hand. He had blood-red reptilian eyes, the large leather wings of a giant bat, and the physique of a well-built man. His eight-foot-tall body was covered from head to toe in thick metallic scales.

Fuck. It won't be easy to take this one down, Ajuma thought, preparing himself for a good fight.

But what got Ajuma's attention was the size of the scaly skinned demon's member. He nearly choked on his laughter. The demon's cock stood out in an obscene display. It was at least the width of the bottom of a six inch cup, if not thicker, and its surface was covered with putrid, runny sores. What appeared to be at least two feet of diseased cock protruded between the scales at the demon's groyne, oozing a thick pus-like substance from the wide slit at the tip that winked at Ajuma like a pox-riddled strumpet in a low-class whorehouse.

Ajuma grimaced as the stench of the infected member reached his nose and tunnelled down his throat. If he didn't need both hands for the upcoming fight, he would have covered his nose to block the godawful stench.

Both demons had an evil gleam in their eyes as they cautiously closed in on Ajuma.

Check that, he thought. *The stocky one had an evil gleam in his one eye.*

The big-dicked demon strutted back and forth like a peacock, his huge cock bouncing up and down like a wooden seesaw as he waited for an opportunity to strike. Meanwhile, the two-legged Cyclops attempted to inch his way behind Ajuma, seeking to attack from his blind side.

Ajuma became still in spirit, waiting for the demons to make their move. He felt hot breath on the back of his neck just seconds before Cyclops attempted to strike him from behind, but Ajuma was ready for him.

BEHIND THE DARK VEIL

In the blink of an eye he drew a fifty-two inch, double-edged, tempered, carbon steel sabre from the scabbard at his hip, meeting his enemies' deadly weapons with cold, hard steel. Ajuma swung his weapon like a madman, viciously fighting off his attackers.

With his first swing he cleanly sliced off big dick's penis at the base. The demon's roar of pain was so loud it probably resounded to the lowest level of hell. The maimed demon's mouth yawned open, piercing the night air with an inhuman scream as black demon blood sprayed like a fountain, splashing on Ajuma's face like black rain.

The demon clutched his groyne where his monstrosity of a cock used to be in a vain attempt to stem the blood that spurted through his gnarled fingers. His careless action left him wide open, affording Ajuma an opportunity to arc his deadly sword and lob off the demon's hideous head. It fell from the demon's neck to land beside his severed cock.

Cyclops didn't spare a glance for his fallen comrade. Before Ajuma had an opportunity to bask in the glory of his victory, pain radiated through every inch of his body. The one-eyed demon's cudgel connected with his shoulder, shattering the bone and giving Ajuma a new understanding of the word 'pain.' Now it was Ajuma's turn to roar. *That shit hurt!*

Despite Ajuma's arm hanging uselessly at his side, he fearlessly advanced upon the Cyclops with murder in his green eyes. "You ugly motherfucker!" he bellowed.

Cyclops took an involuntary step back as the trees in the swamp vibrated in the face of Ajuma's inhuman rage. It didn't take the demon long to regain his courage and advance again.

Ajuma raised his sword as the Cyclops came toward him. The demon's face bore a vicious smile. He was confident Ajuma would fall in the face of his injury, but the demon would have to get in real close and personal to use his cudgel against Ajuma's much longer weapon.

Ajuma waited until he could feel the heat of the demon's foul breath. With lightning speed, he reached out with his one good arm and pulled the demon's eyeball right out of its socket. It came away with a wet, squishy sound. Veins and bloody strings of muscles and flesh hung from it. For the sheer pleasure of it, since the demon could no longer see, Ajuma squeezed the oversized eyeball until it burst apart in his raised fist like an overripe melon left too long in the sun.

While the demon was on his knees howling in pain, Ajuma raised his sword and decapitated him. He kicked the severed head with his booted foot toward the other demon's head. One side of the head burst open, leaving blood and brain matter atop Ajuma's foot.

"That's what you get for hitting me with that unholy weapon, you one-eyed bastard." Ajuma spat and locked his intense green-eyed gaze on the stinking remains of one of the demons. The demon started to smoulder, then burst into flames. He dispatched the other demon in a similar fashion.

So much for questioning the motherfuckers! Where the hell are Face and my men, he wondered. *I told them I could handle this on my own, but I didn't think they would take me at my word. Gotdammit, what if I'd really needed them? I'd have been shit out of luck! I'll have their hides for leaving me slightly wounded and in this fucked up predicament.*

He was just about to send out a nasty mental message to his men when a tall, translucent demon with long, flowing blond hair and blue eyes as cold as chipped ice appeared out of nowhere. The demon walked boldly toward Ajuma with a cruel smile on his perfect face. He brandished a wicked-looking cutlass with a jagged-edged black blade. Smoke came out of his nostril and mouth with each breath he took.

Aw, bugger me!

The demon that was quickly closing the gap between himself and Ajuma was none other than Tyranny, one of five sons of a fallen angel turned demon called Zuet. Zuet held the title of The Satan. He ruled over all seven levels of the hells. Parlour tricks wouldn't work on this demon because he had an endless repertoire of his own to work with. Tyranny was purported to be a mean motherfucker and hard as hell to kill.

Ajuma sent out yet another telepathic message. *"Ah, Face? Nico? Is any fucking body there? It would be mighty nice if anyone within the sound of my voice could get their black asses here as soon as possible. Satan just sent up one of his pups and it's about to get ugly. Any assistance would be appreciated!"*

Tyranny licked full, red lips that were still stained with Ephraim's and Abena's blood. His chest heaved in anticipation of the fight to come.

"Sending out a message to your little half-breed toy soldiers, huh?" His laugh was dark and sinister, reminding Ajuma of slow, painful death and the rot of the grave. "You'll be waiting a long time for them to get here, whoreson. They are a bit tied up at the moment with a half legion of my nastiest demons," he boasted.

Before Ajuma could truly assimilate the ramifications of Tyranny's taunting words, Tyranny transformed into a monstrous fire-breathing creature and leapt through the air. Ajuma instinctively went airborne. Demon and Nephilim met head on. They shook the swamp floor, slamming into one another like Titans, their swords playing an unholy tune as steel clashed against steel.

Tyranny did not slow down when Ajuma's superior swordsmanship cleaved his weapon in half. Instead he fought on, snarling, clawing, and biting in vicious hand-to-hand combat. Tyranny's hands became lethal claws which he swiped down the side of Ajuma's body, ripping the flesh wide open from just beneath his armpit all the way to his hip. The pain was blinding.

Tyranny's claws felt like they had been dipped in acid. Ajuma shouted in agony. Whatever poison laced Tyranny's claws was weakening Ajuma at an alarming rate. Still, he fought on like a beast, ripping Tyranny's flesh with his sharp teeth and slamming his superior weight down on the demon, anxious to weaken or incapacitate him.

Ajuma knew he was fighting a losing battle when Tyranny called in reinforcements, but Ajuma was a shape shifter. Realising the odds were heavily stacked against him and wanting to live to fight another day, he shifted into a 1,000-pound spotted Smilodon cat. He beat a hasty retreat with blood gushing from the open wound in his side and the sound of Tyranny's sinister laughter echoing through the swamp.

CHAPTER 13

Magnolia Hill Plantation

～

LOSSIE WASN'T QUITE sure what her actual age was. Her best guess was that she was about 16 or 17, much older than her mother was when she had her. She recalled her mother once telling her that she was born during the fall of 1742. The same year a terrible hurricane nearly destroyed the newly rebuilt city of New Orleans.

During the storm, the building which housed the temporary chapel on St. Anne Street was levelled. Her mother said she pushed Flossie out of her body at the same time the sturdy, thick chapel walls came crashing down like the walls of Jericho in the white folks' bible. Her mother said she took one look at her newborn baby's face and she knew that Flossie would one day become a powerful Orisha priestess, more powerful than her own mama. Flossie liked the idea of coming into this world on the wings of a storm. If only a similar storm would lift her up and fly her away from Magnolia Hill.

Flossie's mother, Sorrow, had been the Big House cook and the go-to person whenever a slave took sick. She had been renowned for her healing skill with herbs. She passed those skills on to her daughter.

Sorrow was also a midwife. She delivered all of the babies at Magnolia Hill and most of the babies on the neighbouring plantations, slaves and whites alike. Flossie's mama had also been a powerful conjure woman, for all the good it did her.

The Etiennes didn't allow dark-skinned slaves inside the Big House. Flossie was delicately built like her mama and not strong enough to work out in the field. Her skin tone was just light enough to allow her mother to slip her inside the Big House undetected, where she once worked as a maid. That is how Flossie came to catch the eye of her granddaddy's son and her mother's half-brother, Claude Etienne.

Flossie's mama delivered both of Masta Claude's boys. Her mama told her that when Masta Claude's second wife tried to deliver their third child after what turned out to be a long and difficult labour, he told her to get out of the birthing chamber, even though his wife was haemorrhaging. Not long thereafter, Flossie's mother was unceremoniously thrown out of the birthing chamber by Masta Claude, and Mistress quietly bled to death.

Flossie's mama said Claude and his daddy had ice water flowing through their veins because they left the bloody body of Mistress and the dead baby on her stained death bed until near sunset of the next day while they rode into town to carouse at a local whorehouse.

The slaves whispered that Masta Claude didn't have any more use for Mistress after she had dutifully provided him with the obligatory two sons.

Flossie never knew who her father was. All she knew was that he was a pure-blooded Black African from Yoruba named Afolabi. Flossie's mama said Masta Clidamont didn't cotton to heathen names, so he renamed her father Jim. Afolabi put Flossie inside her mama's belly just before Masta Clidamont staked him to the ground at high noon and whipped him to death. Then he fed her daddy's body to the hogs.

By the time Flossie's father was thrown in the ground, he had been stripped of everything he had once been—even his name. Flossie's mama said she was proud of her man because he had remained defiant to the very end, spitting in the eye of his enslavement. Whoever her father was, the whites couldn't break him, so they did the next best thing. They killed him.

BEHIND THE DARK VEIL

After Clidamont killed her father, his son Claude used Flossie's mama's body until he just about used her up. Didn't matter to him she was his own sister. As far as he was concerned, spilling his seed inside a slave, sister or not, was just like tupping a barnyard sheep or a dog. You did it, but you just didn't admit to it.

Flossie's mama was willing to endure just about anything to keep Clidamont and his nasty son from putting their hands on Flossie. Every night her mama drank a bitter herbal tea to make sure Claude's seed didn't catch.

Old man Clidamont liked his women small and childlike, with little breasts and narrow hips. Quietly as it was kept, what he liked more than anything were little children. The bodies of countless slave children rotted in an unmarked shallow grave in a large patch of ground near the stables. It didn't bother old man Clidamont one bit if he ripped open the insides of a little slave boy or girl; he didn't consider them to be human. Flossie didn't know which one was worse, the father or the son.

Flossie would never forget the day Claude dragged her mama kicking and screaming from their cabin. Everything happened so fast. Flossie had just come back from hiding in the woods to see her mama hitched to the back of Masta Claude's big black stallion and dragged around the plantation until the skin fell off her. One day Flossie had a mama, and then she had no one—no one but the gods—and a heart filled with fear.

To this day, Flossie didn't know what her mama had done to get herself killed like that. Truth be told, you didn't have to do much to get the skin stripped off your back or get sold away from family and friends at Magnolia Hill.

The Etiennes ruled Magnolia Hill with a bull whip, an iron fist, and vicious intent. They were teaching their good-for-nothing wastrel boys to follow in their footsteps. If only Mistress had taken that last one with her when she departed this life, the lives of half the slaves in St. John the Baptist Parish would be exceedingly better.

Flossie would never see her mama again, at least not on this side of creation. She was thankful that her mama taught her all she knew about herbs, midwifing, conjuring, and the Orisha gods and goddesses before her spirit flew away. Flossie appealed to the gods and goddesses to shield her mother in a wall of protection wherever she might be.

Flossie's mama wasn't gone one full day before Masta Claude started sniffin' around her like a randy dog. Flossie did her best to stay out of his way. Knowing it was just a matter of time before he struck, Flossie had the foresight to slip a little chaste tree berry, better known as Monk's Pepper, in the bourbon whiskey he favoured. Claude was a drunk, so he ingested a healthy portion of the herb each night.

Try as she might to avoid him, one afternoon Claude managed to corner her alone in the hallway outside his son Julien's chambers. They grappled as he pulled her into one of the unoccupied bed chambers, pushed her against the wall, and pulled her skirts up around her waist. She pleaded with him to stop, but he was like a man possessed. Her pleas only seemed to anger him. When he told her, "Gal, I'll slit your black throat and feed you to the hogs if you don't stay still," Flossie knew that he meant it. Masta Claude had the fattest hogs in St. John the Baptist Parish. As bad as things were, she was not yet ready to die.

The gods were with her. Over time her powerful concoction of Monk's Pepper had built up in Claude's bloodstream and was racing through his system even as he was unbuckling the thick belt holding up his trousers.

Try as he might, he couldn't get his manhood up. Flossie had dosed him with enough chaste tree berry that his manhood wouldn't get up even if it was propped up on a board with twine wrapped around it. Her deep fear of the next encounter with Masta Claude prompted Flossie to brave the perils of the swamp to get to her hidden altar.

The flimsy door to Flossie's cabin creaked as she tried to quietly pull it shut behind her. She held her breath for a moment, making sure her late-night surreptitious departure was not observed by anyone in the slave quarters.

She scanned the row of ramshackle cabins, taking in her surroundings with eyes as big as an owl's and as sharp as an eagle's. Word of unusual behaviour on Slave Row had a way of spreading like poison ivy in the woods. All she needed was for one person to see her doing something she had no business doing, and she would be done for.

The white of her coarse, simple linen skirt and top made for a sharp contrast to her smooth milk chocolate complexion and the inky blackness of the night. The baleful sound of a lonely owl cut through the darkness, reminding her that she was never alone. She sent up a silent prayer that Olodumare's creatures would watch over her on this night as they had on all the other nights she had managed to slip away from the slave quarters to pay homage to the gods.

Flossie clutched a heavy black sack close to her chest as she beat a hasty retreat down the length of Slave Row. The sound of crickets played background music to the soft fall of her bare feet. She was spurred on by the cries of the spirits who only come out at night and the restless souls of those who had died at the hands of the whites on the hill. Having no desire to join them, she ran for all she was worth, widening the distance between the plantation and the woods.

Clidamont Etienne was Flossie's granddaddy, but that wouldn't save her if she got caught away from the cabin while practising Obeah. He'd skin her alive and make every slave on the plantation watch. She didn't have a minute to lose. Before long, the merciless sun would cover the moon and daylight would wake the sleeping giant that was Magnolia Hill.

CHAPTER 14

⁓

UNDER COVER OF darkness and led by the bright light of the full moon, Flossie ran barefoot through the wooded area outside the boundary line of the plantation. She was an Orisha priestess. Her altar and a small patch of dangerous herbs she'd planted nearby were hidden behind a veil of weeping willow trees where the swamp met the northwest boundary of Magnolia Hill's property. If the altar or the herbs were ever found, Flossie's life wouldn't be worth a hay penny.

Few had the courage to venture past the buffer of trees that separated Magnolia Hill from the mysterious secrets of the dark fog shrouded swamp. Even fewer would do so in the dead of night. Whites and slaves alike were afraid of the fierce fighting Maroons who were rumoured to have a large camp deep in the heart of the swamps.

Since the residents of New Orleans were superstitious by nature, they were even more fearful of the spirits that some said came alive at night in search of souls to feed on.

The Maroons were escaped slaves who would slit the throats of anyone who dared to threaten their hard-won freedom. If Flossie chanced upon a Maroon during one of her nocturnal visits to the mouth of the swamp, she would willingly go with him or her. That is, if they didn't kill her on the spot. Better to take her chances with a runaway slave than to remain at the mercy of the Etiennes. She was not afraid of the Maroons. Nor was she afraid of any spirits that walked the night.

The dead can't hurt you, but the living damn sure can.

In Flossie's world the whites were her enemies. Of spirits she was not fearful, but she was afraid of that blond-haired grey-eyed devil Claude Etienne and his sire. They took her mother from her. They killed her father before she'd even been born, and they'd taken a large part of what was left of Flossie's self-respect, working her from sun up to sun down with just enough food to keep her from starving to death.

She'd eaten well when she worked in the Big House, but things were different now that she was in the fields. If it weren't for the little patch of garden she maintained behind her cabin and what she could steal from the scraps thrown out from the Big House, she would have starved to death.

Flossie was not willing to give up anything else to the Etiennes—not if she could help it—and especially not the precious jewel between her thighs. Neither would she pretend to hand over her passion to her enemies as her mother had been forced to do. Tonight she would give a blood offering to Yemaya for protection against the Etiennes, both junior and senior. She would place her fate in the hands of the gods.

As she ran through the woods with her light cotton skirts billowing behind her, she laughed to herself, remembering the spectacle Masta Claude made of himself panting like a bitch in heat with his face as red as the beef steak tomatoes in the garden behind her cabin.

Claude had tried everything in his power to shove his pale limp member inside Flossie's unwilling body, to no avail. In a fit of anger and frustration, when his man root wouldn't get hard, Claude Etienne beat Flossie until she passed out. He revived her with smelling salts, and then he beat her some more.

He wasn't done with her after the beating. Just for spite, Claude sent Flossie to work out in the fields, knowing full well that the backbreaking work would be a slow, cruel death. Mayhap she should count herself fortunate he didn't kill her outright though it may have been kinder to do so. The Etiennes didn't know what kindness was.

BEHIND THE DARK VEIL

As she broke through the small clearing where she'd erected her altar to the Orisha gods, she raised her hand to her cheek. Her face and body still bore bruises from the vicious beating she had taken, but at least for now the jewel between her thighs was still intact. She could only pray it would remain so.

That was hers to give—not Claude's, Clidamont's, nor anyone else's to take. There were enough little slaves running around Magnolia Hill with brown skin and Claude and Clidamont Etienne's evil features stamped on their faces. Tonight she would give thanks to the gods for sparing her that fate and ask for their continued protection.

Breathing heavily from her exertion, Flossie finally reached the safety of the clearing. First giving thanks to her venerable ancestors, both known and unknown, and then paying proper obeisance to the spirits of the dead who were constantly with her, Flossie prepared herself for the protection ceremony.

Her thick, bushy hair was wrapped tightly in a light blue scarf. She donned an ileke, a blue and white beaded collar. She knew the colour of her clothing would be pleasing to her patron. She immediately felt the energy as Yemaya's ileke began to infuse her with rays of protection, working to keep her safe from harm. If Flossie were to be exposed to anything negative, her ileke would absorb the negative energy and break away from her slender neck.

Flossie pulled a live chicken out of the sack she carried. The chicken's sensibilities had been dulled with a paralysing herb. She worked efficiently with deft hands, preparing her sacrifice. As dictated by the ritual, the chicken was pure white. Yemaya preferred to feed upon the blood of white chickens. To garner her patron's favour, that is what Flossie would offer her. Flossie expertly snapped the chicken's neck, pulling the chicken's head away from its body with an ease garnered from years of practise.

Off in the distance, she could hear the muted beat of a drum signalling another lonely soul who had braved the night to commune with the gods. Flossie's message would travel upon the waves of the mysterious African drummer and land in the open palm of her patron. She freed her mind, allowing the drum beat to take control of her body as she began to sway and chant.

❧ ☙

Ajuma's bloody sides heaved with exertion. His injuries had prevented him from ghosting, a gift all mature Nephilim were born with. He had been travelling in animal form for miles. He believed he had lost Tyranny and his horde of demons, but he would have to double back to erase his tracks to make sure.

Nephilim healed at an accelerated rate. If he could just find a secluded place and ingest some life-sustaining blood, he'd be good as new in no time. That wasn't likely to happen since Tyranny and his motley crew had run off all form of animal life within ten square miles with their demonic stench. Animals tended to flee in the face of evil.

Just when Ajuma thought the chances of his getting any blood were slim, he heard a sound. He grew still. He travelled the distance toward the sound with the stealth of the animal he had become.

A short while later he came upon a small clearing where a lone woman stood before an altar. She had a chalice in one hand and a dead chicken in the other, which she appeared to be offering to the gods. Ajuma listened quietly as the woman beseeched her gods to protect her from the master's lustful eyes, to curse him with impotence, and bring down all manner of misfortunate upon him and his family.

He didn't know if her gods would answer her prayer for protection, but he knew for a fact that his god, Attiq Yomin, had certainly answered his prayer. He needed blood to regain his strength and this woman would supply it. Nothing and no one would prevent him from taking the healing blood he needed from this woman—nothing. He charged through the clearing toward his unsuspecting victim.

❧ ❧

Flossie heard a frightening low growl, followed by the sound of an animal charging through the woods. It had the ponderous footfall of a large swamp predator, snarling and breathing heavily like a coyote or maybe even a massive wolf.

Hot blood was still gushing from the opening of the chicken's neck when a thick copse of trees and shrubbery seemed to open like velvet curtains. A huge green-eyed, brown and tan spotted Smilodon, the world's largest sabre-toothed cat, broke through the clearing, shaking the earth beneath his feet with all 450 pounds of his massive body.

Flossie had never seen anything like it. Its powerful jaw encased serrated teeth that were at least seven inches long. Flossie dropped the bloody chicken as a voice inside her head warned her to run.

When she turned to flee, an exact replica of the frightening beast she had just turned away from blocked her escape. Everywhere she turned, she found herself confronted by the growling cat as he played his cruel game, taunting her like a cat teases a mouse before the kill.

Flossie saw her death in its eyes. As if it could read her mind, the cat transformed into a man right in front of her. He was big and brawny with muscles atop of muscles. His muscles were bigger than any buck who worked the Magnolia Hill fields. His skin shimmered as if it had been dipped in gold. His hair was coal black, only making his vivid eyes appear all the more green. Astonished, Flossie couldn't turn away if she wanted to.

He was naked and proud as he stalked her. A self-satisfied grin spread across his handsome face, revealing a hint of fangs. He took his time walking toward his paralysed prey. Flossie stood frozen in fear as her ileke fell away from her throat. She clutched her neck and shaped her mind to die.

The last thing Ajuma expected to encounter in his wild run through the swamps was a human female—especially one such as this. She was a tiny human, cocoa brown with a pinch of cream and exquisitely formed.

Because of their justifiable fear of the unknown, few humans lived in the swamps. Most humans were more afraid of the preternatural creatures rumoured to walk the swamps at night than they were of predatory animals, poisonous snakes, quicksand, and the like.

The shadows of the night were created to conceal beings like himself, Nephilim, angels, devils, demons, and things that go bump in the night—not humans. Yet here she was, a petite girl/woman, garbed in a simple homespun garment with a set of beads tightly clinched in her small fist as though they were a talisman to ward off evil. Talisman or no, at the moment, she was shaking like the leaves on the trees in a wind storm.

Ajuma moved closer, sniffing the air around the frightened little human like a feral dog. The sweet smell of her blood mingled with the fear-laced sweat coming through her pores, making his mouth water with wanting her. The sound of her racing heartbeat drummed inside Ajuma's head. *Lub* as one valve opened to allow blood to flow through and *dub* as the second value snapped shut. The *lub-dub* rhythm picked up speed as her trepidation increased, vibrating inside Ajuma's head with a consistent drum-like cadence.

Her scarf had come loose, revealing a thick bushy head of hair as soft as cotton and as fragrant as a spring blossom. Her eyes were twin saucers, slightly slanted at the ends and clearly expressing a near heart-stopping degree of fear. It was no wonder she was afraid. Not many humans could lay claim to witnessing an animal transform into a man in front of their eyes. Ajuma would have to wipe her memory clean of the events of this night. Right now, he just wanted to look at her.

BEHIND THE DARK VEIL

Flossie was still unable to move as Ajuma took her to the ground, gently placing his hands on each side of her face. *Someone has hurt her*, he thought. He could not help but notice the bruises on her face. Ajuma had an uncontrollable urge to kill whomever had hurt her. He examined every angle of her face, finally staring into her eyes, mesmerising her and melting away any resistance and all of her fear.

"Do not fear me, human. I wish you no harm."

He brought her hand to his side. That was when Flossie realised he was wounded. His side was split open clear to the hip. That was also when she realised that a naked man was lying on top of her. She tensed.

Ajuma felt his nature rise even as he drowned in the depths of her eyes. Her dilated pupils were dark, but so bright they appeared to have lanterns lit behind them. Ajuma had to catch himself before he fell victim to their alluring beauty. He licked his lips in anticipation of a feast as his canines descended. He had the fleeting thought that The Ancient of Days always answers prayers, just before he plunged his sharp fangs into the helpless human's neck.

Nephilim are extremely carnal beings with strong, almost insatiable sexual appetites. The act of feeding is an extremely intimate and pleasurable one, frequently presaged or culminating in sex. Flossie felt his hardness against her leg and she was neither afraid nor repulsed.

He held her face firmly, but gently, as he fed. The human's blood was delicious. It burst upon his tongue like shooting stars, nearly blinding him with its rich, heady flavour.

The moan that came from deep in Ajuma's throat vibrated through Flossie's entire body. She felt a million fingers playing between her thighs with every pull of his sensuous lips on her vein. Soon, she too began to moan.

Never in her life had she seen a more magnificent, more beautifully made man. Flossie knew he couldn't possibly be human. The saints preserve her, she didn't care. When he lifted her skirts and nudged her legs apart with his knee, Flossie gladly let him in.

CHAPTER 15

Bavaria, Germany

⌐◦⌐

"*T*ELL ME, CAPTAIN Facio. Why am I speaking with you and not General Akibeel?"

King Zion Shemyaza sat in his office before a roaring fire while the notably nervous Gibborim captain stood front and centre. The fire did little to warm Facio. It was brutally cold out, but nowhere near as cold as the look in Zion's angry golden gaze.

Zion found it difficult to hide his ire. He had specifically requested an update on the situation in the Atchafalaya Swamp from Ajuma, only to get another no-show. Ajuma Akibeel was closer than a brother to Zion. Friend or no friend, Zion could not countenance even the slightest disrespect from any of his subjects. He tried to relax his fierce expression a bit. It didn't pay to shoot the messenger. He would deal with Ajuma himself.

Facio didn't know how to answer the king's question without somehow disrespecting or compromising his position with General Akibeel, his superior. King Zion's cold stare drilled Facio to the wall, ramping up his sense of apprehension. Facio swiped his large hand across his forehead to remove the sudden cold sweat that appeared. King Zion was waiting for an answer to his question. Facio cleared his throat and chose his words carefully.

"General Akibeel has assigned me the task of relocating The People of the Blood from the swamp, Sarrum, but Councilman Silas refuses to allow me to arrange for the evacuation of the rest of his family until young Lord Ephraim or his remains have been found. He has dug his heels in and will not be moved even though the swamp is now swarming with demons and no longer safe. The other families have decided to follow his lead."

When the king didn't interrupt, he continued. "There is more. General Akibeel said the disappearance of Ephraim has Tyranny's signature stamp written all over it. He was engaged by Tyranny and a couple of low-level demons while on his initial search."

The air in the room stilled. Zion and Tyranny had butted heads on more than one occasion over the centuries. Zion intended that the next time they met would be the last. One of them would die, and he didn't plan for it to be him.

Zion stood to lean against a huge ornate wooden desk and expelled a long, soft whistle, obviously impressed.

"Are you sure, Face? The demons don't know where the Nephilim compound is located. If they did, we would have had wholesale slaughter and not just Ephraim missing. Tyranny is a pretty big gun to be unleashed upon a band of escaped slaves. I would think his presence would be better served by spreading the bubonic plague or burning down monasteries with innocent monks inside. Don't you agree?"

Face was quick to dispel Zion's assessment. "I wish it were not so, Sarrum, but I was there. The area where Ephraim was last seen bears Tyranny's unmistakable footprint. He made it a point to leave his special brand of stench behind."

Zion frowned. He couldn't hide his concern. "The Ancient of Days save Ephraim's poor soul if he is in the foul clutches of *that* evil pile of dung for even a second."

Zion shivered when he thought of what might have happened to the youth. He wouldn't wish the likes of Tyranny on his worst enemy—not even on a human.

Zion moved to sit behind his desk. He brought his fingers before his face in a steeple, deep in thought. "I wonder what good old Zuet has up his wicked demon sleeve this time. I am sure his use of Tyranny in Louisiana has a deeper purpose than one can discern from the surface."

Facio remained silent while the king contemplated the possible ramifications of adding Tyranny to the already muddied mix they would be forced to deal with in Louisiana.

"Do you know Tyranny's history?" Zion asked.

King Zion was the first son of the Watcher Angel Shemyaza. He was the oldest Nephilim in existence. As such, his eyes had seen and recorded thousands of years of historey.

"No, Sarrum, I cannot say that I do," Face said with a look of interest on his face. Without realising it, he leaned closer to the king. He was waiting in anticipation of the knowledge Zion would impart when, seemingly out of nowhere, a lovely female Anakin appeared.

Zion motioned the servant to pour each of them a glass of whiskey. He returned to the sitting area before the fire and bade Facio to be seated, then crossed a long leg in a negligently refined manner. He took a sip of his drink and a moment to gather his thoughts. Facio patiently waited for the king to begin.

"As you are well aware, Face, a demon is naught but a fallen angel. Tyranny is the oldest of Zuet's five sons. The others are called Travail, Hindrance, Salacious, and the youngest and by far most perfidious of them all is known as Incarnadine." Zion's voice was deep and well-modulated, almost mesmerising as he spoke.

"Before the fall, Tyranny was the angel who meted out the Lord's punishments. The Ancient of Days could not have chosen an angel who was better suited for the job. Even when he called heaven his home, Tyranny was evil, hostile, and adverse, always bent upon destruction. His nature as a false accuser and purveyor of injustice was instrumental in his being demonised and summarily tossed out of the heavens."

Facio took another sip of his drink, enraptured by the storey that was unfolding. He felt honoured the king would spare this special time with him. He would treasure it always.

Zion continued. "Tyranny is a cunning adversary and must be dealt with, with extreme caution."

Zion appeared to be speaking to no one in particular as he stared into the bright flames in the fireplace. "I have first-hand experience of the perfidy Tyranny is capable of."

Facio knew this statement to be fact. As a Gibborim destined to serve in the Nephilim army, he learned at a young age about how King Zion and the Brothers of the Dark Veil were taken prisoner by Zuet. They were held for 200 years in the lowest level of the hells, where they were tortured for not disclosing the secret location of the Nephilim to their enemies. Had they not been so fearless, Zuet would have wiped every Nephilim off the face of the earth. Zion took Facio back in time.

"Tyranny's angelic name is Mastema. It is derived from the Hebrew noun that means hostility. He is a high-ranking Satan in the realm of hell, a title conferred upon him by his father for countless barbarous acts. Humans view Satan as an evil entity when, in fact, Satan is a title conferred upon demons by Zuet."

"The battles between my esteemed father and Tyranny were the stuff of legends. They first locked wings during the war in heaven. It was my father who ripped off the wings Tyranny had once been so proud of, causing him to plummet to the earth along with the other defectors." Zion's chest swelled with pride when he spoke about his father.

"My father encountered Tyranny yet again during the pre-diluvian days when he was charged with leading the Watcher Angels while on earth. As he recounted to me, his experience with the demon was extremely unpleasant—so much so that he was not inclined to go into specifics or to dwell upon what had actually occurred between them in light of my tender age. Suffice it to say, my father and Tyranny bore permanent physical scars from their second battle."

"The last time my father had the misfortune to butt heads with Tyranny was during the days preceding the flood. Ever the trickster, Tyranny used his legion of demons to lead the sons of Noah to commit sin and idolatry. As you know, these were crimes our own fathers were wrongfully punished for instigating." A look of disgust marred Zion's striking features. "Our descendants may have been guilty of lying with the daughters of man, but they did not lead them to do evil. That guilt should have been placed at the demons' door."

"Many years would pass before Tyranny showed his ugly face again. This time he would be forced to face the son and not the father." He lowered his voice to just above a whisper. "By this time, my father and his men were all long dead." Facio didn't miss the look of pain that washed over Zion's face.

There was something the king shared with each of the Brothers of the Dark Veil that no other Nephilim would ever be privy to. As much as Facio held each of the generals in high esteem, he believed some things were best left in the shadow of secrecy.

Zion continued. "I served as a thwart to Tyranny's plans during the days of Abraham. You see, it was Tyranny who urged The Ancient of Days to test Abraham with the sacrifice of his son Isaac, and it was I who intervened. Tyranny meant for the boy to die."

Facio remained silent. Much of what Zion spoke of Facio already knew through his Gibborim historey lessons, but it was rare when the king revealed any portion of his past. He was an extremely private male. Facio would hold on to his words like precious stones, not knowing if or when he would ever open up again. Facio was so wrapped up in the king's words that he didn't realise his glass was nearly empty. The servant silently refreshed their drinks.

"And then there was the Moses debacle. I will never forget the demon's involvement with Moses and the Africans who would eventually be known as Jews. Tyranny and his brother Travail planted the seed of hubris within Moses' spirit which resulted in his complicity in the theft of the original man's heritage."

Zion looked Facio directly in the eye. "Know this. There was no Jewish baby floating down a river in a basket to be found and raised by a barren white-skinned Egyptian woman."

Facio was only 467 years old, so he hadn't yet been born during that time.

"There was no such thing as a white-skinned Egyptian. Ancient Egypt was comprised of African tribes: Akan, Fula, Wolof, and Mande, to name but a few. Fair-skinned Jews and Egyptians didn't come into existence until centuries later. In fact, they are direct descendants of Cain."

For the first time, Facio was compelled to interrupt. "With all due respect, Sarrum, how can that be?"

"When Cain was cast out of the Garden of Eden to wander in the Land of Nod, he did not leave alone. Several of his siblings chose to leave with him, but he stood out from everyone else because he bore a distinctive mark. The colouring of the original man who was made in Attiq Yomin's image was stripped from his skin. The purpose of the mark was to ensure that no one he encountered took his life. His punishment was to live and to suffer as the first albino in the midst of blackness. He procreated with his sisters. Fair-skinned children were born of these unions. He eventually founded and populated a city called Canaan. Prior to his punishment, Cain was as black as you and I. So, you see, Moses was a Black African as were all the Egyptians. Thus, the great deception began."

Zion was warming to his subject. "In fact, Moses was a member of the Egyptian priesthood and next in line to become pharaoh. Instead of claiming his place as pharaoh, he was overlooked by one of his relatives. The new pharaoh then exiled Moses and had his name removed from all Egyptian records as if he never existed."

Zion could not confess to having inside knowledge as to why Moses was not allowed to succeed as the next pharaoh. He suspected a perceived flaw in his character might have been the reason.

"Be that as it may, Moses did have a following among serving-class Africans. He willingly accepted the pharaoh's edict that he be exiled, but he met with opposition when he sought to take his followers with him. It was Tyranny and Travail who churned up the emotions of the pharaoh and the Egyptians in opposition to Moses' people departing Egypt. They hardened the Egyptians' hearts against Moses and his followers. Tyranny succeeded in imbuing the new pharaoh's magicians with the magic to compete with Moses at every turn, blinding the pharaoh to the substance of Moses' words. Eventually, they were allowed to leave."

"Moses didn't go empty-handed. Prior to his departure on foot with six thousand men, women, and children, Moses stole secret religious documents which were sealed away in the Egyptian archives. The theft of the ancient Egyptian stories would serve as justification to enslave people of colour for centuries to come. Tyranny had his hand in that bit of dirty business too. These documents consisted of Egyptian historey and ancient stories that would later become the outline for the Book of Genesis."

"The men, women, and children who made the exodus with Moses would one day relocate to Canaan and become the Jews and Hebrews whose historey would distort and, in many instances, replace that of the original man in the bible."

"Have you never asked yourself why so many biblical stories in the Old Testament and the Book of Proverbs bear such close similarity to the ancient Egyptian text called *Instruction of Amenemipet Son of Kanakht* which was authored prior to the bible?"

Facio's face took on a sheepish expression. "To be honest with you, Sarrum, I have not yet had an opportunity to read the famous tome."

An almost indiscernible smile touched Zion's lips. "Ah, I see. Every good soldier should make it a point to read about ancient warriors, Face. The bible is replete with many such brilliant tacticians."

Suitably chastened, Facio responded, "I assure you that I intend to rectify this oversight at my earliest convenience, Sarrum."

Zion nodded in acknowledgment. When Zion stood, Facio knew that their talk had come to an end. He was being dismissed.

"I think that is enough of a historey lesson for one day, Captain Facio."

Facio knelt in obeisance before his king and ghosted back to Louisiana.

CHAPTER 16

IMMEDIATELY AFTER FACIO'S departure, Zion sent out a telepathic message to three Brothers of the Dark Veil. Nicodemus and Antioch were the first to ghost to his castle in response to his mental command. He could clearly hear his manservant Jon speaking to them in the foyer. Shortly thereafter, there was a soft knock at his office door announcing their arrival.

"Sarrum, Generals Urakabarameel and Asael are here to see you. Do I have your leave to usher them in?" Jon asked. Zion nodded at the trusted manservant.

"By all means, please do so, Jon. And please send General Ramuel in as soon as he arrives."

Less than a minute later, Antioch, Nicodemus, and Zion were comfortably seated before a blazing fire with drinks in their hands and cheroots clamped between their bright white teeth. Each was fashionably attired in long waistcoats with pleated panels at the seams, lace-trimmed shirts, breeches with silk stockings, and leather shoes fastened with buckles.

They eschewed the prevailing fashion trend of powdering their hair or wearing large high parted wigs, choosing instead to wear their naturally long hair clubbed at the nape of their necks with black ribbon. Their mode of dress and manner were quite unusual given the times when people of African descent served instead of ruled. They were all big, strong, powerful-looking males, each handsome in his own right.

Zion was engaged in lighthearted banter with Antioch and Nicodemus when a servant ushered Simeon of the House of Ramuel into his office. Simeon barely had time to hand his tricorne over to the servant hovering nearby before he was captured in a tight bear hug by Nicodemus. There were smile lines around Nicodemus' eyes when he stood back to get a good look at Simeon. All the Brothers of the Dark Veil were extremely close. He had not seen the brother in far too long.

"If you are not a sight for sore eyes, I don't know what is!" Nicodemus exclaimed. "I cannot believe it. Zion, Tee, and I were just discussing you and, like a genie let out of the gotdamned bottle, you appear!"

"More like a bad penny turning up, I'd say!" Zion interjected laughingly. The study filled with deep, masculine laughter.

Each male was a member of the Brothers of the Dark Veil organisation. Nicodemus was in charge of protecting the continent of South America. Antioch protected Asia. Simeon protected Antarctica. The absent brothers, Ajuma, Gilead, Boaz, and Rephidim, covered North America, Australia, Africa, and Europe, respectively. They all answered to Zion.

Each Brother of the Dark Veil had a legion of Gibborim at his disposal to ensure the continued prosperity and wellbeing of Nephilim residing on each continent. Rarely were all of the king's generals able to meet in the same place at the same time. It was not safe to do so. That is why Zion only summoned the three.

Shouldering Nicodemus out of the way, Antioch moved in to extend a proper greeting to Simeon. They too exchanged a heartfelt embrace. "How fare you, my brother? It has been far too long since you have graced us with your presence."

It was apparent all three males held a great deal of affection for one another, but King Zion, Nicodemus, and the absentee Ajuma were especially close. That is why Ajuma's defection was all the more troubling to Zion.

Antioch's statement could not have been more true. It had been a stretch since they'd seen each other. The Satans were very busy walking to and fro upon the earth, and each brother had been kept equally busy combating them and their minions' evil works throughout the globe.

Zion's gaze touched on each of the males with sincere warmth. "Tee is right. It has been far too long since I have laid these world-weary and jaded eyes upon each of you." Then he turned to Simeon. "Rest assured, Sim, our previous discussion about you was of a positive nature."

"I would certainly hope so, brother," Simeon replied, with a crooked smile on his lips.

A male Anakin servant silently appeared at Simeon's side. He spoke in the cultured dignified manner of all Anakins.

"May I offer you some liquid libation, General Ramuel, and maybe a bite to eat?"

Simeon nodded his assent and graciously thanked the servant. Soon Simeon had a drink in hand.

They sat in companionable silence, listening to the crack and pop of the logs burning in the fireplace. The king waited for the door to close behind the servant before he spoke again. As nice as their little reunion was, Zion realised there was no getting around the purpose he called the meeting.

"As I just stated, it is always good to see you, my brothers, but I called each of you here for a reason. I just had a lengthy discussion with Ajuma's second-in-command. Captain Facio informed me that things have gone from bad to worse in Louisiana."

Antioch, Simeon, and Nicodemus collectively leaned forward, giving Zion their full and undivided attention.

"Speak to me, my brother," Antioch said with a sense of urgency in his voice. "What news did Face bring?"

"He said Silas is being bullheaded. He refuses to allow the Gibborim to evacuate his family until either his son is rescued or his remains are found. His intractability is spreading like a fungus. Now, several of the other families are taking the same stance."

A muscle in Nicodemus' face pulsed in anger. The fact that a hand- ful of councilmen refused to accept the protection afforded behind the Dark Veil was a sore subject with the usually congenial general.

"I predicted that something like this would happen a long time ago. Now that Silas has lost his precious son, he expects us to work miracles to get him back. I say let him stay in the swamps if he wants to, and let the demons have him!" Nicodemus belted down his glass of whiskey and quickly reached for the bottle to pour another one.

"Would that it was that easy, Nico. Facio said the swamp is swarming with demons and is no longer safe. If it were just Silas, I would say let the devil take him, but there are his wife, his daughter, and at least 500 innocent Anakins to consider. I will not leave them to die because of Silas' foolishness," the king responded.

"And there is something else you should be aware of. Ajuma was engaged by Tyranny and a couple of low-level demons while he was on his initial search for Ephraim. That can mean only one thing. Since Tyranny cannot walk on earth in his natural form for any length of time, he must be using a human's body as his host. He can hop from human to human. It will be almost impossible to smoke him out."

The ever-pragmatic Simeon responded in the fashion he always did. "Alright, Zion. What do you propose we do?"

"Two things. First, we need to get every single Neph out of that fucking swamp as quickly as possible. Second, we need to track down Ephraim or retrieve what's left of him, if possible."

"I can see us accomplishing the first endeavour, Zion, but how do you propose we accomplish the second?" Antioch asked, a look of concern on his face.

Zion clearly had a plan in mind. "Isn't Ephraim the young Neph who was wounded some time ago during a hunt?" he asked, directing his attention to Antioch.

Antioch quickly responded. "Yes, Zion, I believe you are right. He was and, if my memory serves me correctly, he showed a keen interest in one day becoming a member of the military."

Simeon provided further confirmation. "Yes. Now that you mention it, I recall the situation quite clearly. The young man was both brave and impetuous. He was seriously injured after joining a hunting party he shouldn't have been on in the first place. He sustained a grievous wound which was healed through the blood intervention of Brother Ajuma."

Nicodemus had a pretty good idea where the king's chain of thought was leading. Once two Nephilim share blood, they are bound for life. The sharing enables them to sense each other. If they are within a reasonable distance of each other, one Nephilim can track the other through the blood.

The king stood to address the three generals. "Well then, this is what we will do. Antioch and Simeon, I want each of you to choose 1,000 of your most trusted soldiers to accompany you back to the swamps. Place your seconds-in-command over your territories during your absence."

"You will evacuate the Nephilim to safety. I believe there is a community of free blacks located in Texas. They should be able to easily blend in at this location. Offer Silas and his people the choice of relocating there or to one of the safe havens behind the Dark Veil in Africa or South America. Anyone who gives you any trouble will have to answer to me. I will contact Boaz, Gilead, and Rephidim to assist you in the move."

"I charge each of you with the task of exterminating the swamps of the demon infestation. Flood the godforsaken swamp with Gibborim and flush out and kill every single demon. Do it with extreme malice."

Zion then turned to Nico. "Nico, you will travel to that slave plantation and find Brother Ajuma. Go with the speed of light, my brother. It is time to call the prodigal son back home."

There was not much Zion wasn't privy to. He was well aware of Ajuma's dalliance with a human slave. The mere thought of the illicit relationship left a bad taste in Zion's mouth. What Zion didn't know was that Ajuma recently confided to Nico that he had already fathered a son on the human and that his seed had caught yet again. Soon he would be the father of two human children with Rephaim blood.

Nico would do what he was ordered to do without question. First, he needed to air his reservations. "Zion, each time we have called upon Ajuma of late, he has come, but reluctantly. More often than not he sends Brother Face in his stead, as he did today."

Zion knew where this was going. Nico was trying to say he didn't know if he could prevail upon Ajuma to heed Zion's command.

"I don't want to hear it, Nico! Bring Ajuma back into the fold. I mean it. I don't care how it is accomplished. Just get it done."

This softly spoken pronouncement was not made by a friend or comrade in arms, though he was both to all four males. It was made by Zion, King of the Nephilim. It was his final word on the subject and he would brook no dissention.

Simeon and Antioch stood next to the king in silent agreement. The decision to bring Ajuma back appeared to be unanimous.

The king looked into each of the male's eyes when he spoke. "Ajuma has had more than two years to play with his human pet. We have need of his special skills here and now. We cannot afford the luxury of waiting until the human is either killed by her white master or dies of old age."

"Nor can we afford to wait until he comes to his senses," Simeon chimed in. Simeon was preaching to the choir as he continued to press his point. "If we wait until he has had his fill of her, the situation in Louisiana will escalate from a search-and-rescue mission for Ephraim to a recovery-and-burial detail for members of the Nephilim Nation. The affection I feel for Ajuma is deep, but he has been derelict in his duties for far too long. It is time he returns to lead his soldiers."

"Then it is settled," Zion said. "We will use Ajuma's blood connection as a tracking device to ascertain the location of the remains of Silas' son." Zion stood, indicating the meeting was over.

Nicodemus bid his king farewell with a strong hand grasp. "I will report back to you with any new developments."

"That will not be necessary, Nico," the king promptly replied. "Tyranny and I have unfinished business. I intend to travel to Louisiana. On second thought, I will accompany you during the evacuation as well."

Zion Shemyaza was not just a king. He was a warrior. As such, he intended to fight side by side with his generals and their subordinates. He sent out a mental command for his manservant to attend him. Within seconds, Jon ghosted into the office.

"Jon, send word to Mavis and Samuel to prepare *Grato Quies* for our arrival within the week."

Jon bowed his head in acknowledgment of the king's orders and backed out of the room.

"It shall be done, Sarrum." There was much he needed to do to prepare for Louisiana.

CHAPTER 17

Atchafalaya Swamp, Louisiana

~

ZION SUPPED AT Silas' table on two previous occasions, during which time he was treated according to his status. Royalty. The Armers' residence bore no resemblance to the place he last visited. Everything was in utter and complete chaos. It seemed no one knew exactly what to do. The Anakin servants, usually extremely capable, were at a loss without the direction of the lead manservant, Moultrie, who had gone missing at the exact same time as Ephraim. The servants didn't know whether they should prepare the household for departure or prepare for the next meal.

Ephraim's mother Delia had taken to her bed; she was so overcome with grief. It had been over two years since her son was taken. She suffered as if it were yesterday. Tears and wailing could be heard coming from the back of the house. The Anakin servants tiptoed around the house, afraid to disturb Silas or Delia.

Zion did get an opportunity to converse with Ephraim's sister, Sara. She nursed an unhealthy burden of guilt in her bosom. Her father blamed her for the state of affairs, placing no blame upon his son, whose impetuous actions were responsible for the tragic situation.

The younger sister could not help but think that had she not kept her brother's secret, maybe he would be safe with his family right now and preparing to leave this place of evil demons bent upon their destruction.

Ephraim's fiancé, Nephthys, sat off to herself in a corner of the well-appointed receiving room. The swollen-eyed, tear-faced young female was obviously in shock and more than a little hurt and embarrassed. The marriage contract between the families had clearly been breached.

In spite of her good family name and their impressive assets, her value on the marriage market would be significantly diminished after this. To be passed over in favour of a human was the ultimate humiliation. The prospect of her entering into another such advantageous marriage contract as the one she had with Ephraim was slim. Zion could not help but pity the girl. It was a bad situation all the way around.

Silas strode into the salon like a man on a mission after letting Zion cool his heels for far more time than was proper. His face clearly reflected his attitude. He was so bent upon getting his son back that he had temporarily forgotten he was dealing with his king.

Zion sat in a relaxed pose, long legs crossed, on a velvet settee. He immediately took control of the situation. "Sit, Silas."

Like a puppet on a string, Silas froze mid-stride.

"I said sit."

Silas immediately sat on a sofa directly across from Zion. "Listen to me and listen clearly. I must concern myself with the welfare of *all* families of the Blood, not just yours. The situation we are in is, to say the least, untenable. However, I cannot allow the good of one to outweigh the good of many. I ordered my officers to relocate you and the other families, and my orders in all things will be obeyed."

Silas blinked his red-ringed eyes like a frog too long out of water.

"We will make every effort to locate the whereabouts of your son, but you and your family will have your servants pack your belongings quickly and prepare to leave."

Silas' lips trembled and blood tears streamed down his face. "But what about my son, Sarrum? What about my son?"

Zion's face bore no hint of mercy or emotion. He rose from his seat, moving closer to where Silas sat.

"I will say this one more time. We will make every effort to find your son, Silas, but I cannot and will not delude you. Chances are he is either beyond our reach or dead. You must prepare yourself for the worst."

Zion's words were intentionally harsh, striking Silas like a million poison darts piercing his skin. Silas appeared to shrink before Zion's eyes, but he could not be spared. He needed to accept the reality of the situation and give a care for the remainder of his family and household members. Zion knew he thought him a cold-hearted bastard. His opinion dimmed in light of the necessity to get the families to safety as quickly as possible.

"You are the head of a proud angelic family. You have a wife and a daughter whom The Ancient of Days has placed in your care. You also have a household of servants who look to you for direction and many constituents scattered throughout this swamp. Would you condemn them to death because of your weakness?"

Silas answered the king's question in a low voice. "No, Sarrum. I would not. Forgive me for my momentary weakness. I will direct the servants to close down the house and prepare the household for departure."

"Good male, Silas. Good male."

Zion sent a mental message to Facio to have all three families prepare for departure.

⁊⁊ ᠺᠵ

Grato Quies, Baton Rouge

Grato Quies (quiet resting place) was one of many lavish estates King Zion owned throughout the world, and it was one of his favourites. It was to this home he returned time after time when he needed to think and regenerate spiritually.

Each room in the sprawling estate was designed and constructed on a massive scale by the master architect of King Solomon's Temple, Hiram Abiff. It was purported that Abiff was a reincarnation of the man bearing the same name, a man who had been raised from the dead by King Solomon himself. Abiff had done a splendid job with Zion's office/war room. What would have otherwise been considered a draughty, cavernous space was lent a great deal of warmth and charm with a high curved oak-beamed ceiling and three large brass chandeliers.

Zion's office/war room was filled with tasteful Renaissance furnishings, artefacts, and paintings. The floor was covered with bright colourful Persian rugs. One wall was filled ceiling to floor with first edition leather-bound books. Voltaire's *Candida*, Swift's *Gulliver's Travels*, Walpole's *The Castle of Otranto*, and Defoe's *Robinson Crusoe* and *Moll Flanders* were but a few of the hundreds of first edition works of literature lining the shelves.

Zion was an avid reader and, time permitting, would occasionally allow himself to be swept away in the sheer beauty of the written word. He once commented that lyrically written literary works were like a gentle caress to his soul.

King Zion had the Midas touch. He was richer than Croesus and could afford to surround himself with the best of everything. The elegant surroundings were in direct contrast to the preternatural power that positively oozed from the pores of each of his generals. Have no doubt: the Nephilim boasted hundreds upon thousands of soldiers, but the males who would soon be sitting in the king's office were the heartbeat of his army.

The beautiful hand-crafted desk Zion sat behind was made to suit his six foot, six inch frame comfortably. It served as a focal feature in the tastefully decorated office which resembled a royal receiving room more than an office/war strategy room.

The one-of-a-kind solid wood desk he sat behind as well as the petite camel-back sofas and chairs covered in rich brocades, velvets, and damask, and the intricately carved tables had all been commissioned from the famous cabinetmaker Thomas Chippendale.

BEHIND THE DARK VEIL

Lion's paws were carved into the feet of each piece of furniture. The model used for the paws was a full-grown lion that was at that moment reclining not far from his master's desk. His long, pink tongue lolled out and he lazily licked his huge sharp-clawed paws. It was this environment where King Zion chose to meet Ajuma.

"I will not give her up, Zion," Ajuma stated emphatically.

Although this pronouncement was made with all due respect, it was also made with implacable determination. Moss green eyes met piercing amber ones as Ajuma stood before his king.

"Then, by all means, keep her. When have I ever interfered in the personal lives of any of my generals?" Zion replied. "All I demand of you is that you serve me and those you are charged to protect. The only reason you are standing before me right now is because your association with this human is at odds with your job, Ajuma."

Ajuma lowered his eyes in shame. He knew Zion was right. There was no denying it to himself or anyone else. He'd been acting like he'd lost his mind ever since that night he came upon Flossie in the swamp. If he had indeed lost his mind, he had better find it if he wanted to continue to lead his army. He had to get control of his emotions.

The two males were in the sitting area of the king's private office. Soon the remaining members of the Brothers of the Dark Veil would arrive for a strategy meeting. The king had summoned Ajuma for a pre-meet. He wanted to talk to him privately about the human he was involved with and the adverse effect this association was having on his command.

Ajuma ran his large hand through ink black shoulder-length hair, so thick he could barely get his fingers through it. Without prompting, he confided in the male who was not only his king but his friend. His voice was little more than a whisper even though they were alone with no one else to hear his words.

"She's a priestess, Zion, an *Iyalawo* (mother of mysteries), no less. Sometimes I feel like she has cast some kind of spell on me, even though I know there is naught but goodness in her spirit and that a demon would flee in the face of her faith. There have been many women in my life, some far more beautiful than she, but I swear before The Ancient of Days Zion that I have *never* felt this way before. Never. What I feel for this woman is so sweet that it pains me."

Zion took a moment to digest Ajuma's words. "I do not profess to understand the tender emotions you feel for this woman, Ajuma, but I do respect them. I will turn a blind eye to this relationship with the proviso that you never engage in pillow talk with this human. Ancient of Days knows that I cannot tell you not to feed off her. I have tasted the blood of humans. It is sweet."

"Having said that, it also goes without saying that you are *never* to disclose any Nephilim locations, be they behind the Dark Veil or otherwise. Last, and most importantly, you are to wear a French letter whenever you are intimate with your human. Are we agreed?"

Ajuma felt guilty as hell when he nodded his agreement. He wanted to come clean, but he could hear others approaching.

A knock at the door interrupted Zion's train of thought. It was the butler, Samuels, informing the king that his generals had arrived. Ajuma automatically stood, assuming his private audience with the king was over.

"It appears our brothers are anxious to start the meeting, Zion."

"It appears you are right, Ajuma. Let them wait."

Zion then informed Samuels to tell the generals he would be with them in a minute. "As I was saying, I don't understand what you are feeling, yet I do know that your feelings are as genuine as you are. Your Flossie is fortunate to have your love, brother, and I am fortunate to call you both comrade and friend. I am sure you will find a way to balance your time with Flossie and your duties. Don't let me down again."

Ajuma's eyes welled up. That was the first time Zion referred to Flossie by name. It was an emotional moment. Both men stood to embrace. Ajuma quickly masked the hint of fear that flashed in his eyes.

"Thank you, Zion. Thank you."

This was a side of Zion few were allowed to see. It didn't last long. He moved to sit behind his desk before instructing Samuels to usher his generals in.

CHAPTER 18

*I*T HAD BEEN two years and eight months since young Ephraim, son of Silas of the House of Armers, had disappeared. His disappearance had created nearly three years of agonising uncertainty for the members of the House of Armers and a general atmosphere of fear among Zion's subjects as a whole.

Since Ephraim's disappearance, the Brothers of the Dark Veil had been making nightly forays into the Atchafalaya Swamp. They'd searched every single inch of the Atchafalaya Swamp, turned every stone, and walked the bottoms of every dark cave and grotto in search of Ephraim's remains—all without any meaningful success. The plan to sniff out Ephraim through Ajuma's blood connection had also failed. They were at a dead end.

To make matters worse, the swamp was now teeming with demons and was no longer a safe haven for the Nephilim. For every demon they killed, ten more popped up in its place. If they didn't find a way to stamp out the strain of demons in the swamp, there would be spill over into the human population where the demons would find useful hosts.

The Brothers of the Dark Veil were meeting with their king to formulate a strategy as to how they would get Ephraim's body back, ascertain who orchestrated his abduction, and make them pay for it. There was a moment of awkwardness when the other generals saw Ajuma, but it was fleeting. They were all part human, and, therefore fallible. They readily accepted Ajuma back with no recrimination.

Since Ephraim's disappearance, Zion's generals and the Gibborim Army they commanded had engaged in countless battles with low and mid-level demons. Most were murdered outright while others were captured, interrogated, and ultimately dispatched with extreme prejudice. No information about Ephraim was garnered during any of the interrogations.

It appeared young Ephraim had vanished without a trace and was, for all intents and purposes, presumed dead. Their mission had changed from that of a search and rescue to a search and recovery. At the very least, King Zion owed Ephraim's parents the closure they could only receive from the return of their beloved son's remains so that he could be buried with the honour and respect due his father's rank.

Zion could not take the chance that anyone else among his subjects would meet a similar fate. He personally saw to it that all three houses located in the swamp—the House of Armers, Batraal, and Zavebe— were immediately relocated. This was no mean feat because all this had to be accomplished without alerting their departures to the demons swarming throughout the swamp like biblical locusts.

Zion sat deep in thought with his fingers in a steeple, partially concealing the lower portion of his handsome face. His steeple-fingered pose was a familiar one to each of his honour guard. The expression they had come to recognise over the centuries was indicative of focused concentration. The long, elegant fingers of hands that had delivered death to countless demons were now relaxed. To the untrained eye they appeared more suited to a piano keyboard than for killing.

Now that it was full night, the curtains covering the wall-to-wall bank of ceiling to floor windows behind the king's desk were thrown open, allowing the sounds of the night to serve as background music to the serious exchange between the king and his generals.

Zion was the picture of elegance and refinement. His lean, muscular body blended in with the dark stain of the wood of his desk, drawing attention to the crisp white sleeves of his tailored shirt and the expert cut of his waistcoat. Other than the fact that he was black, he was the perfect picture of a refined southern gentleman.

Behind the king's well-tailored garb and impeccable manners beat the heart of a vicious killer. Few demons had the good fortune of meeting Zion of the House of Shemyaza in battle and surviving the meeting. Those who were forced to face him, as a rule, only met him once.

The Dark Veil Honor Guard had come directly to their king after battling demons in the swamp and surrounding area. They were frightening to behold, each filled with hate and bloodlust. They had yet to come down from that distinctly identifiable high all fighting Nephilim feel after battle. The fragrant scent of furniture polish and lemon oil battled with the smell of demon blood and death reeking from their hair, clothes, and bodies.

Brother Boaz and his army had only recently returned to the states. They had been in Europe for the past year, battling demons responsible for the period known as "the year without a summer." Boaz had been battling severe climate abnormalities, famines, volcanic eruptions, and the demons who caused them while the rest of the generals were fighting demons in the swamp. Zion listened intently as his trusted men brought Brother Boaz up to speed on the recent developments.

Boaz turned his deep penetrating eyes upon Ajuma who sat closest to him. "How much time elapsed between the time when Silas sounded the alarm that Ephraim was missing and the boy's trail was picked up?"

Although they had covered every detail of that fateful night more times than Ajuma could count, his response was immediate. Boaz was an expert strategist. Maybe he would be able to shed a different light on the occurrences of that night since he had not been present.

"Silas sounded the alarm just before sunrise. His daughter came to him when Ephraim did not return to the compound at his usual time. There was nothing we could do until evening. As soon as the sun went down, I ordered my men to split up into three camps to cover as much ground as possible. Two platoons patrolled the northern and southern sections of the swamp while yet another platoon split up to guard the eastern section and the entrance of the compound. I covered the western area of the swamp alone. We searched the swamp with a fine-toothed comb."

"We were not on patrol long before I sent out a mental call for assistance to the nearest platoon. I later discovered my soldiers had every intention of responding to my call for help, but they were engaged by a horde of low-level demons before they could do so. Each of our groups was being attacked simultaneously. Other than an insignificant blood trail leading from a bower of trees in the southwest area of the swamp, we found no trace of the young male."

Boaz pondered the information before he spoke. "Obviously, the attacks were a well-orchestrated diversion on two fronts. One, to keep your soldiers from coming to your aid when you were ambushed; and two, to divert you from the abduction site long enough for the trail to grow cold so that the abductors could sweep the site clean."

Ajuma nodded in agreement. He had already come to the same conclusion.

Nico cleared his throat to get Boaz's attention. "Of course, there is the slim possibility Ephraim was killed in the swamp and his body was thrown into one of the many pools of quicksand throughout the area or even dumped in one of the alligator-infested bogs. That would explain our not finding a body or picking up a blood trace."

Reserving further opinion, Boaz nodded in acceptance of Nico's theory and then turned his intelligent gaze upon Gilead. "What think you, Gilead?"

Gilead had the nose of a bloodhound. He was the one who picked up the boy's blood trail at the creek when no one else could. He sighed before running a large callused hand down the length of his face.

"Nico's theory would be credible if it weren't for the fact that the blood trail led away from the lakes and marshes and not toward any of them. Ephraim was a big strong lad, almost in his prime, Bo. His father trained him well. I find it strange there was no sign of a struggle. He had to have been taken off guard. No way would he have allowed himself to be taken without a fight."

This was an angle they hadn't considered earlier. The king found it interesting.

"Did that discerning nose of yours pick up anything else of interest during your investigation, Gil?"

"Actually, there was. I picked up an underlying smell of sex in the air. It was partially masked by demon stench but still detectable. The smell was distinctly human. Since the only humans in the vicinity are the Maroons, I surmised young Ephraim was dallying with one of the Maroon females. His sister, Sara, eventually corroborated our suspicions."

Something new occurred to Simeon who was pouring himself a drink from the king's well-stocked bar. "Gil, you said you tracked a blood trail that seemed to end in the middle of nowhere, right?"

"Yes, that's right."

Simeon stared into the depths of the amber liquor he held in his hand for a moment before he spoke. "Well, did you pick up a trail, blood or otherwise, of the human female Ephraim was with?"

Gilead was thoughtful. "As a matter of fact, Sim, I did not. There was no body, no blood trail, nothing. If it had not been for the strong mixture of the scent of Nephilim seed and the fluid that coats the human female's vaginal walls when stimulated, I would have thought Ephraim had been alone."

Zion didn't attempt to mask his frustration. Nephilim young were constantly warned to stay away from humans and the demons that walked among them, to no avail. Humans have always been the bane of the Nephilim's existence and the cause for the first war in heaven. Thousands of years later, humans still hold a macabre fascination to angelic beings and Nephilim alike.

"Young Ephraim was promised to a female of good family," Zion said, shaking his head. "I personally sanctioned the match between Ephraim and Nephthys. It would have been a powerful alliance between two loyal angelic houses. I can't understand why Ephraim would throw a bright future away, and his life, to dally with a lowly human slave. I cannot understand what *any* member of the Nephilim Nation would want with a human." The king remembered Ajuma's present situation and added, "Present company excepted." It was no secret Ajuma was smitten by his human. *Hell, he had as much as admitted it earlier.*

It was not Zion's intention to censor Ajuma in front of the other brothers over something he apparently had no control over. We don't choose who we love. Oftentimes it is the love that chooses us and we can do naught but fall victim to it. Zion was thankful to The Ancient of Days that he was not susceptible to that brand of weakness nor would he ever be. One day he would be forced to wed to continue his noble bloodline. He would respect her, but he wouldn't love her because he had no love in him to give.

He had more to say, but as he realised he was preaching to the choir he decided to keep the remainder of his thoughts to himself on that subject.

Instead, he said, "More likely than not, the stench of his attacker was masked by a wizard's spell. That is the only explanation I can think of that can explain Ephraim not smelling the approach of a demon."

Demons have a distinctive stench, familiar to all Nephilim. Since their powers on earth are restricted, demons frequently work hand and hand with humans, playing on their innate greed and avarice by promising them the world while taking advantage of their inherent weakness. They can then enter their bodies, infiltrate their homes, and corrupt their spirits.

"If a spell masked the demon's approach, Ephraim would not have smelled anything until the demon was actually upon him. By then it would have been too late."

Boaz quickly came to the same conclusion as his king. Something big was going on and they needed to find out what it was and quickly. He had a frown on his handsome face when he spoke. "That would lead me to believe that the demons did not come upon Ephraim by happenstance. They must have been lying in wait like snakes under a pile of filth, planning for one of us to fall into their insidious trap. The poor kid didn't have a snowball's chance in hell to escape whatever his fate was."

There was a moment of silence while each man was engrossed in his own personal thoughts. The frustration in Ajuma's voice was apparent when he broke the silence. "I find it more than coincidental that Tyranny was on the scene. He's a coward by nature. He generally sends others to do his dirty work. I was grievously wounded during our fight and in desperate need to feed. He could well have taken advantage of my temporary weakness. Instead, he allowed me to beat a hasty retreat, not even trying to pursue."

Given Zion's previous statement Ajuma neglected to add that he received the healing blood he required from Flossie. To disclose that information would necessitate revealing his growing feelings for the female to the rest of his brothers, which he was loath to do at this time. It was bad enough that Nico and Zion already knew.

"There has to be a connection," he said.

Ajuma couldn't look his king nor his brothers in the eye. He was guilty of two lies by omission. Nico was the only one he'd confided in that he had not only fathered a child with Flossie, but that yet another was on the way.

Zion focused his penetrating gaze upon Antioch. "Tee, when was the last time you communicated with your informant in Beer Shahat?"

Beer Shahat is the third of seven levels of hell. Unlike their demon counterparts, the Brothers of the Dark Veil had unlimited access to the earth, all seven levels of hell, and portions of the lower levels of heaven.

It paid to have connections in the lower realm, and Antioch had more than a few. Entering Beer Shahat had its risks, but the brothers had done so on more than one occasion while on fact-finding missions. Besides Nico, Antioch was one of the more fun-loving, adventurous brothers. He laughed in the face of danger.

The brothers' attention were now focused upon Antioch.

"His name is Devius. I haven't spoken with him in nearly six months. His liaison is a warlock out of Nawlins. I can touch base with the warlock and have him channel Devius if you like."

Gilead couldn't keep himself from asking the million-dollar question. "Can this Devius be trusted, Tee?"

Antioch's broad shoulders shook with laughter. "Now, why on earth would you, of all people, ask me a stupid question like that? He's a damn demon, Gil. What do you think? He'd sell his own mother for the right amount of coin. I'll just have to make sure that he is adequately compensated for whatever information I can get out of him."

Zion stood. He walked over to lean casually on the front of his desk, facing his men. His pet lion growled low in his throat, moving from his comfortable position beside the desk to draw closer to his master.

"It's settled then," Zion stated with resolve. "Tee will meet with the warlock to arrange a meeting with this demon informant of his."

Antioch pretended to be affronted. "He's not my demon, Zion! I just happened upon him several years ago when I was seeing that pretty little succubus on Beer Shahat. I paid him good coin to keep his mouth shut, and we have enjoyed a *quid pro quo* relationship ever since."

"Even with that, I wouldn't trust him as far as I can throw him." Rephidim had been quiet till that point. "You'll sleep with anything," he whispered under his breath.

"Suck my big fat dick, Reph," Tee retorted loud enough for all to hear. The two were constantly at one another's throats.

The king was not amused. "It matters not whether he is your demon or the devil's own handmaiden, Tee! I want you to make contact as soon as you can. I have a feeling he's going to want more than a little coin before he gives you any information. I realize it may take some time before you can set up your meeting. I don't want you to go alone when you meet this demon.

"Once the meeting is set up, I want each of you to assemble ten of your best men for a foray on Beer Shahat to follow up on whatever intelligence Tee gets from the demon. As I expressed earlier, my gut tells me something big is afoot and that it will affect us and my subjects adversely if we don't get a handle on it.

"Ephraim's disappearance was not by chance. I don't know the genesis of the assault, but I do know there is more to what happened than meets the eye. It is imperative we get as much intelligence as possible before we make our move."

Simeon was the quietest of the brothers. He was a soft-spoken, scholarly brother who rarely spoke, choosing to listen and learn. When he did speak, his brothers always listened.

"Where there is smoke, there is fire. Wherever Tyranny shows up, you had best believe one of his nasty siblings is not far behind. Cowards that they are, they sent in lower-level demons to engage Ajuma's men while they did their dirty work undetected."

Nicodemus voiced his agreement. "You are probably right, Simeon. Tyranny wasn't in the swamps for kicks and fucking giggles. He must have had something to do with the young male's disappearance. Trust me, if he was in the swamps, one or all of his nasty siblings were not far behind."

CHAPTER 19

⌒

*T*HERE WAS A beehive of activity in the kitchen at Grato
Quies. One Anakin servant girl chopped and cleaned vegetables grown in the estate's well-tended gardens. Another
kept watch over the many steaming pots on the wood-burning stove
as well as the huge wrought iron cooking pot filled with savoury
stew simmering in the fireplace. Yet another kneaded dough for
the many loaves of bread and biscuits that would soon go into the
wood-burning oven. Eight medium-sized stuffed pheasants were
roasting in the wood-burning oven and the air was redolent with
the succulent smell of the juicy meat of a large side of beef, its
skin popping and crackling as it slow-cooked on a spit over an open
fire just outside the back of the kitchen. Mavis, of the House of
Shemyaza, presided over all.

General Nico had a fondness for Mavis' lemon pound cake. Since
Nico happened to be one of her favourite Brothers of the Dark Veil,
she didn't trust any of the other kitchen staff to prepare the cake.
Mavis would bake the cake herself while supervising every dish they
would prepare, seeing that all was properly served. The pound cake
wasn't the only dessert Mavis would make. There would be peach cob-
bler, and they would use some of the sweet apples growing in the
orchard on the western side of the estate to bake rich flaky-crusted
apple pies. The Brothers of the Dark Veil and the Gibborim soldiers

who served under them risked their lives to keep them safe. The least Mavis could do was see them well-fed.

While Mavis' staff frantically prepared their dishes, Mavis' husband, Samuel, the head butler, and his staff of Anakin servants were busy preparing suites in the huge mansion for occupancy by the king's generals. The suites needed to be ready before sunrise so that the generals could take their rest. The Gibborim soldiers would sleep in the barracks on the other side of the plantation. The men had just returned to their king, bloody and battle weary. Mavis knew they were going to be wanting food and drink, and lots of it.

"Make yourself useful, girl," Mavis ordered her daughter, Dreama. Mavis was in a dither, causing her to display uncharacteristic exasperation in her tone of voice. Her daughter was well-named. Dreama was a dreamer, mooning around the kitchen window, humming a happy little tune and generally getting in everyone's way as if she didn't have a care in the world. Speaking to no one in particular, Mavis stated, "I declare girl, sometimes I don't know what I am going to do with you!"

Mavis was in charge of the kitchen staff in King Zion's Baton Rouge residence, which the king preferred to call an estate rather than a plantation. Ordinarily, Mavis would allow her only daughter to do pretty much as she liked. Not today. Suddenly she had a full garrison of soldiers and a houseful of mouths to feed. Her daydreaming daughter was going to have to do more than stare out the kitchen window while counting the twinkling stars. She was going to have to roll up her dainty little sleeves and help out.

There was more than mere star-gazing going on behind Dreama's doe-shaped, wistful eyes. She had deliberately stationed herself within close proximity of the open kitchen window, hoping against hope she would catch at least a glimpse of a young Gibborim soldier named Jihad, the love of her life.

Jihad served as a private first-class under General Akibeel. Dreama had been beside herself with excitement when she learned the generals

122

and their troops were scheduled to arrive at sundown. It had been weeks since she'd seen Jihad. She ached to be held in his strong arms again and to feel the touch of his sweet lips.

"Take this tray into the king's private office. And come right back, mind you. I want no dawdling from you, young lady. There is plenty of work needing to be done, what with the officers in residence and all. Hurry up with you now. Scoot," Mavis said, sounding more like one of the Gibborim drill sergeants than Dreama's gentle mother.

Dreama waited for her mother to turn her back before she rolled her eyes at her. Her expression was again respectful when Mavis carefully placed the cumbersome tray on a rolling cart with the necessary china and flatware and pointed her daughter in the direction of the kitchen door.

The Cardeihac hand-patterned French serving tray was a heavy, ornate sterling silver affair with a matching domed top. It was laden to near overflow with piping hot, savoury hors d'oeuvres that would serve to tide the officers over until the main meal was served later in the evening.

Dreama still had Jihad on her mind as she made her way to the king's private office. He'd asked her to marry him the last time they were together, and she'd said yes. He'd asked her to keep their engagement a secret until he was in a better position to support her. He didn't want her parents to have any reservations about their being together.

She was well aware that the life of a female wed to a military male would not be an easy one. A soldier's life was fraught with danger. Each day you kissed your husband goodbye to send him off to battle could well be his last. But you can't help who you fall in love with either. Dreama loved Jihad with all her heart. Her prayers had kept him safe thus far and she believed The Ancient of Days would continue to protect her love from harm.

Dreama wheeled the cart up to the closed door of the king's office, her heart pounding like a drum. If General Akibeel was on the other side of that door, that meant, more likely than not, Jihad would be amongst the men in the barracks. Dreama was unable to reach out to Jihad telepathically as most Nephilim couples do. Although they had been intimate with one another, they had yet to share blood. They wanted to save that ultimate intimacy for their wedding night. To do so would open up Dreama's womb. She could get pregnant.

Dreama was born on the Baton Rouge estate, yet she could count on one hand the times she'd had occasion to enter the king's private domain. Accordingly, she was unaccountably nervous.

Dreama could hear the rumble of deep male voices on the other side of the door. Her mother had trained her well. She was a member of the Anakin serving class. She knew her place and she knew proper protocol when entering the presence of her betters. So, she took a deep breath, wiped her sweaty hands against her lightweight cotton skirt, and raised her hand to knock on the door.

King Zion's deep voice drifted to her side of the door like mulled wine. "You may enter."

All conversation stopped while Dreama struggled to push the ungainly serving cart into the smoke-filled room. The sudden quiet in the office amplified every squeak of the cart as she pushed it atop the plush blue, red, and gold Aubusson rug.

Each member of the elite unit known as the Brothers of the Dark Veil wore equally serious expressions on their faces. They were seven lethal demon-killing machines whose very presence would suck the oxygen out of a normal-sized room.

Everyone at *Grato Quies* had heard of the disappearance of Ephraim, son of Silas of the House of Armers. Everyone was afraid, including Dreama. More than once her parents warned her to stay within the safe confines of the king's estate.

Each of the big, powerful males sitting in the king's office had anger in their hearts and a thirst for revenge. Their ire was justified.

BEHIND THE DARK VEIL

The boundaries of their secret world had been breached by an age-old enemy, and one of their young had virtually been taken from right under their noses. Dreama shook in the face of their combined power. Her eyes landed upon Nicodemus and she froze.

Her thoughts had been consumed with the possibility of seeing Jihad again. She had totally forgotten that it was Nicodemus of the House of Urakabarameel who had walked in on her and Jihad while they were making love in the barn. The incident had taken place during his last furlough. It had been their first time together as male and female. Dreama was mortified. She wanted to melt through the floor boards and drift away. She averted her head. *Maybe he won't recognise me!*

Nicodemus Urakabarameel was a legendary ladies' man. His warm gaze landed upon Dreama's face. He smiled like he was seeing an old, dear friend after a long separation. He immediately sought to make the pretty little Anakin girl comfortable when he recognised her as the daughter of Mavis and Samuel. Her parents had been in the service of his king for many years. He was extremely fond of them and especially fond of her mother's lemon cake.

Nico's smile soon turned into a devilish grin. *This is the same girl I walked in on in the middle of a heated tryst in Zion's barn.*

He hadn't made the connection at the time because her lover had been scrambling to cover her lovely body from his gaze. Nico could tell from the look in her eyes and the sudden hot flush creeping up her neck that she realised he did, in fact, recall the incident.

Nico recognised her lover as Jihad of the House of Akibeel, one of Ajuma's soldiers. Nico, Ajuma, and their Gibborim frequently partnered on missions. Jihad was a good soldier and Nico was a romantic at heart. Although he was a confirmed bachelor and an admitted philanderer who did not personally believe in the institution of marriage, he didn't intend to do or say anything to betray their little secret. He beckoned her forth.

"Please don't be afraid, little one. As a rule, we don't eat pretty little maidens."

This comment initiated a spate of ribald laughter from everyone in the room, except Dreama who didn't quite understand what the hell was so damned funny.

Dreama could only stare, dumbfounded. The cat had stolen her tongue and hidden it from her. She was awed by the brothers and the king in particular. Up close, King Zion was otherworldly handsome. She couldn't help but stare.

Nico's voice covered the awkward silence. "I don't know about my brothers, but—" he said turning to the king, "with the king's leave, of course—I, for one, would like to see what you have under the lid of that serving tray that smells so good."

Dreama thought she would faint when King Zion's stern expression changed to a reasonable facsimile of a smile in response to Nico's suggestion.

"By all means, Brother Nicodemus," he said facetiously. "Don't let *me* stop you or any of your gluttonous brothers from satisfying your hunger."

The Nephilim were hedonistic by nature. Their preternatural appetites demanded blood to exist. Yet, the human blood running through their veins appreciated most of the same pleasures humans enjoyed, such as delicious food, good drink, and the comfort a man can only find in the arms of a comely female.

Dreama finally relaxed a bit. Her lovely smile captivated every male in the room, save the king whose expression seldom changed. Dreama quickly proceeded to serve first the king and then each of the Dark Veil Honor Guard one by one. She sighed with relief once everyone was served, demurely asked if anything else would be required of her, and departed the king's office with a bow and a curtsey.

CHAPTER 20

⟋⟍

*U*PON EXITING THE King's study, Dreama nearly barreled into Jihad's friend Kai, who had been dispatched by one of the lieutenants to deliver a message to General Akibeel. Dreama was beside herself with happiness. After giving Kai a big hug, she excitedly pulled him aside. "Oh, thank The Ancient of Days for you, Kai!"

Kai couldn't help but laugh. Dreama was as beautiful as ever. She was talking so fast he could barely understand a word she was saying.

"Calm down, Dreama. You over-excite yourself," he said, trying not to laugh.

Dreama placed her hand upon her chest in dramatic fashion and took a deep breath to slow down her heartbeat. "Kai, you must deliver a message for me. Tell Jihad I will meet him in the greenhouse at midnight."

Jihad, Kai, and Emanuel were closer than brothers. They were therefore Dreama's friends too, but she had to admit that she was most fond of Kai. He was always so good-natured and kind.

"I promise to deliver your message as soon as I return to the barracks, Dreama."

Dreama planted a quick sloppy kiss on Kai's cheek. "Thanks, Kai. I owe you one. I better go before Mama has my hide."

She pushed her serving cart back to the kitchen with a secretive little smile upon her lips and a pep in her step she had not had earlier.

Dreama sucked her teeth when her mother instructed her to check to see that the fire on the spit was completely out. It seemed Dreama's chores would never end. Her mother had managed to keep her busy from sundown to near midnight. The moment she finished one chore, her mother promptly assigned another. Mavis' demands had been merciless.

"Mama, is there anything else you need for me to do?" Dreama held her breath for her mother's response.

"No. Take your lazy little behind upstairs and relax. It's going to be a busy day tomorrow." Mavis lightened the sting of her words with a kiss.

Dreama feigned fatigue and headed up to her bedroom where she quickly washed up and changed clothes. The house was relatively quiet. The front door and kitchen door were out of the question. That left the cellar door.

Dreama's parents' bedroom was on the third floor in the back of the house. Their bedroom window was above the cellar door which tended to squeak when you pulled it shut. Dreama held her breath, closing the door in increments so as not to alert her ever-vigilant mother.

She stepped away from the door, turned, and immediately slammed both hands over her mouth to keep from screaming. Egypt, a stray cat her mother left milk and food for outside the kitchen door, streaked past her like a furry phantom. Her heart landed in her mouth. Surely her mother could hear her heartbeat from the window above her. She didn't move a muscle as she waited to hear that familiar censorious voice.

She finally exhaled when no sound came. She made a mental note to catch that damn cat and throw it in a pot of scalding hot water as she snuck away from the house to make it to her midnight rendezvous.

Dreama's feet flew like the wind across the landscaped grounds of *Grato Quies*. Her heart was racing like the vibrations inside a steel drum as she sent up a silent prayer she would not meet anyone along the way. After all, how could she possibly explain being unescorted in a seldom travelled area of the plantation after midnight with a garrison of young soldiers in residence? She was so anxious to meet her baby, but she did not want to ruin her reputation in the process.

She sighed with relief when she successfully made it to the western portion of the grounds without encountering anyone. She didn't have much farther to go. She picked up her pace during the last leg of her journey.

Dreama deliberately chose the greenhouse to meet Jihad. It was close enough to the barracks for him to get there quickly, and it was far enough for them to be together without raising any undue suspicions. The only drawback was that she would have to pass Widow Solonge's cottage to get there.

Widow Solonge's cottage was located on the fringe of *Grato Quies*, a good distance from the main house and ancillary buildings. Nephilim are superstitious by nature. Unlike their human counterparts, they know with a certainty that things really did go bump in the night.

Over the years, the widow's house had become the equivalent of the Nephilim haunted house. Children and adults cut the old woman who resided there a wide berth. It was because others felt the same as she did and seldom travelled this area alone unless they absolutely had to that Dreama chose the greenhouse to meet Jihad.

Dreama always felt uncomfortable in this section of the plantation. No matter how hot the night, there was always a chill in the air surrounding the cottage. It was the kind of chill that went clear to the bone, similar to the feeling of standing in the middle of an old graveyard. She sent up a silent prayer that she would have the good fortune to put the sight of old lady Solonge's scary cottage behind her as quickly as possible.

Unfortunately, the fates were working against her. Just when Dreama thought she had cleared the cottage, she heard the gravelly wet voice of the elderly female call out to her.

"Come here, girl. I may only have one eye, but I can see better than most who have two. There's nothing wrong with my hearing. Thought you could creep by me unnoticed, huh?"

Dreama kept walking as though she didn't hear, but Solonge would have none of it.

"You best mind your manners, girl, and come here," she demanded, her voice cracking like a whip.

The old female's voice gave Dreama an unpleasant sensation, like dragging jagged broken fingernails across crushed stone. Dreama raised her eyes to the sky in an exaggerated manner. *Attiq Yomin, you know I don't have time for this.* She had less than fifteen minutes to get to the greenhouse to meet Jihad.

As much as she wanted to ignore the old female, Dreama had no choice but to comply with her request. She reluctantly turned around and headed back toward the cottage. She wanted no part of Solonge Shemyaza, but Dreama had been raised never to disrespect her elders, even if they resembled a character in one of the scary stories her mother used to read to her as a child.

The wizened old widow stood on the other side of the closed fence. She started in on Dreama as soon as she approached the fence.

"I know where you're going, gal. Had a taste of that good Nephilim lovin' and got yourself an itch. Going to meet one of them young soldiers that came in with the generals this eve, aren't ya?"

Dreama's face flushed an unattractive shade of red. *I got an itch alright. And as soon as I get away from your ass, I plan on scratching it.* The old woman's words and her tone of voice somehow made Dreama feel unclean, like she was a woman of loose morals or, worse, a whore. Dreama loved Jihad. There was nothing sinful or wrong about what they did together.

Before Dreama could allow her anger to take root, Solonge hobbled closer to the gate, allowing the light of the moon to shine clearly upon what was left of her face. Dreama's anger drained from her body like water through a strainer when she got a clear look at Solonge's ravaged face.

For the second time that day Dreama was rendered speechless. She found it hard to reconcile the old woman's words with her hideous appearance. She'd frequently heard of Widow Solonge's horrible disfigurement, but she had never been close enough to *really* see her. Up close, Solonge's face was truly frightening to behold.

She resembled a crow, dressed all in black from head to toe. There was a huge lumpy growth on the upper right side of her back causing one shoulder to be noticeably higher than the other. Wisps of fine white hair escaped from beneath a black headscarf tied African style. A portion of her neck was buried within the growth extending up to her shoulder, permanently casting her head to one side.

She held her fragile body aloft with the help of a sturdy black cane that had a silver gargoyle carved into its head. Her twisted wrinkled fingers looked like they had been broken more than once. Although she could not have been more than five feet tall, she appeared to be even smaller. One bony hip jutted forward in an awkward position and one twisted little bird-like leg was considerably longer than the other.

It appeared to Dreama that the demons had broken her apart like a child's puzzle and put her back together bent, twisted, and crooked. Dreama hoped Solonge's twisted body was not as painful for the old lady as it was for her to look at it.

As hideous as the old female's body was, it was her face that repulsed Dreama more than anything else. It appeared someone had peeled the top layer of skin off her face and neck in thin uneven strips, not unlike the manner Dreama's mother would peel zest from a lemon to make the filling for her lemon meringue pies.

Apparently, the socket where her right eye should have been was empty because the lid was sewn shut and the skin surrounding the area was smooth and shiny like tanned leather. There was a gaping hole in one side of her face, exposing teeth, gums, bone, and discoloured muscle matter up to her ear, forcing her to speak out of the side of her mouth.

Dreama involuntarily stepped back, nearly stumbling over the root of a huge tree extending under the fence in her efforts to put distance between herself and the ugly little female.

Solonge's deep-throated laugh was squishy and wet from the spittle collecting in her mutilated mouth. Her voice resembled the sound

Dreama's boots made when she walked through a pile of sodden leaves after a heavy rain.

"What? Scared some of this ugliness might rub off on ya, gal? Seems it don't matter what ya look like outside if the inside is empty. Are you empty inside?"

The old woman didn't expect an answer nor did she give Dreama time to reply. "Have no fear, vain little girl. You'll still be as pretty when you walk away from me this night as you ever were, for all the good it will do you."

Dreama took another step back as Solonge moved even closer. She could smell the woman's sour breath.

"I can see past what you see when you look in the mirror. I can see what's inside," Solonge informed her in a disturbing tone. "I'm gonna give ya a warning, girl. You have a thick caul of grief surrounding you. I can see it as clearly as if I had two good eyes instead of one. It's the dark grey of angry storm clouds. Mind me when I tell you it portends heartbreak and misery for you and anyone who draws near. If you care anything about the boy you're sneaking off to see tonight, you'll steer clear; else, the grief you carry will seep into every opening of his body— his eyes, his ears, his mouth, his nose, and his throat. I tell you, no good will come of whatever you're planning this night. Turn your little brazen behind around. Leave that boy ya plannin' to meet be, girl. Turn around and go back to your parents," she warned.

"I tell you, once the grief you carry gets inside of him, your young man will go straight to hell in a handbasket and he'll suck you down with him free of charge. Heed my words."

CHAPTER 21

~

*D*REAMA FELT HERSELF starting to get angry again. Her little chest puffed up in indignation. *The audacity! How dare that ugly old prune try to tell me what to do? She's a mean old lady with a misshapen body and a horrible face. All she wants to do is make others miserable, just like she is. She should go back inside her stinky little cottage and stay there.*

Dreama turned to walk away, but at the last moment changed her mind. She took a deep breath to release her anger. She knew in her heart she should be kind to the old woman, especially after all she had been through. Dreama's mother was good friends with two of the four servants who cared for Solonge.

Attiq Yomin knew Solonge had reason to be bitter. She had once been a breathtaking beauty. You wouldn't know it by the look of her now. She looked like a monster from the worst nightmare, her visage so appalling that she frightened little children and adults alike.

Her husband, Tremaine of the House of Shemyaza, was a Gibborim who worked as a spy for the Brothers of the Dark Veil. He was a truly valiant warrior, always taking on the most dangerous missions and constantly placing himself in perilous situations to advance the safety and continued wellbeing of the Nephilim Nation. He managed to escape the fifth level of hell by the skin of his teeth just before his role as a spy was discovered. A high-placed demon, who was demoted for not filtering out the mole, kidnapped his wife Solonge and their two children in retaliation.

Only The Ancient of Days, King Zion, the demons, and Solonge knew all that took place while she was held captive. She would take most of the things she endured to her grave. The demons forced her to listen on helplessly as her children begged for mercy, screaming for their mother to help them. Solonge could do nothing to save her innocent babes. She watched on in horror as they skinned her children alive. Ugly little imps and newts pranced around with her dead children's bloody skin draped around their shoulders like capes.

Then Solonge's torment began. For seven days and six nights, Solonge was raped and tortured, only to be dumped in front of King Zion's Baton Rouge residence just before nightfall on the seventh day, barely clinging to life. She was horribly disfigured. They'd tortured her and starved her of the blood all Nephilim require to sustain life and heal so her wounds became permanent.

When Tremaine learned of his precious children's fate and saw what was left of his once beautiful wife, he fell to his knees beside her torn body, keening like a wounded animal. He blamed himself for his family's fate. The physicians who worked on Solonge that night did not expect her to live, so dreadful were her injuries. She survived, but she would never be the same. The next morning, Tremaine walked outside and let the sun take him.

It was whispered that Solonge was a black witch and that she'd been inducted in the art of black magic while the demons held her prisoner in hell. Some even said she ate her own children, sacrificing the innocent little babes to the devil in exchange for her own life. Dreama didn't know if the rumours were true, but she did know for a certainty that the old female was stark raving mad and as nutty as a holiday fruit cake.

Even though Tremaine took his own life, he was given a funeral with full honours befitting a high-ranking officer in the Gibborim Army. King Zion always took care of his own, and he could do no less than to provide for Tremaine's widow since, suicide or not, her husband died in his service.

BEHIND THE DARK VEIL

The king gave Solonge the use of one of the five guesthouses on his property where she would live out the remainder of her life until such time as Attiq Yomin called her home. She was provided with four servants—one to cook, one to clean, one to meet any medical needs, and the other to keep the grounds around her little cottage tidy.

The female was as crazy as a loon. Until the king ordered a fence be built around her cottage, which her maid servant dutifully locked each night, the old woman would take to walking the grounds of the plantation, prophesying a future filled with murder and mayhem, blood and gore, demons, and death. Dreama suspected the purpose of the fence was more to keep Solonge in than to keep others out. When she wasn't proclaiming the demise of the occupants of the plantation, she would frequently be heard singing a mournful tune that could be heard through the open window of her cottage.

Other than the four servants King Zion had assigned to provide Solonge's care, no one ever knocked on the old woman's door. Most of the residents of *Grato Quies* were afraid of her. Those who were not afraid of the old woman thought her house was haunted.

But just because something bad happened to her and her husband and children didn't mean it was going to happen to Dreama and Jihad. Emanuel, one of Jihad's friends, had been happily married to his wife for nearly three years. Dreama saw no reason at all why she and Jihad would not enjoy a long and happy married life as well. She would give him many beautiful daughters and strong, handsome sons. She shook off the old woman's dark tidings of things to come and made to take her leave.

All elders were addressed as "Mother" or "Father" among the Nephilim. Dreama automatically afforded Solonge the same respect.

"With all due respect, Mother Solonge, I appreciate your concern, but I assure you there is no foundation for it. Now, if you will please excuse me, I will take my leave."

"Well, ain't you the little miss hoity toity! Mark my words, girl. The next time I see you, your pretty little eyes will be filled with tears. Go, do what you must, and may Attiq Yomin be with you."

Dreama stalked off in a huff, refusing to listen to another word that came out of that mean-spirited old lady's mouth. She had a date with her man and she did not intend to miss it.

***

Kai delivered Dreama's message to Jihad as soon as he got back to the barracks. Jihad was so anxious to see Dreama that he arrived at the greenhouse thirty minutes early. He sat upon a wooden worker's bench, rolling a smoke while waiting for her to arrive.

He took a deep satisfying pull of his smoke. The tip of the lit tobacco interrupted the darkness with one bright orange dot of light. He let the smoke out in a slow exhale. Now the aromatic smoke was competing with the fragrance of the lovely greenhouse blooms, evening the score.

Jihad was low born. His father, Raguel, was a member of the lowest order of angels and his mother, Ernestine, long dead now, had been a human. Both of Dreama's parents and her parents' parents' were Anakin through and through. Relationships between Nephilim and humans were frowned upon. It was considered a further dilution of their angelic blood. He feared his parentage would be an impediment in Dreama's parents' eyes.

Jihad had seen the opportunity to rise in the angelic ranks and he seized it, moving up from the Anakin serving class to the Gibborim fighting class. Just because you are born on the bottom doesn't mean you have to stay there.

Just two short years ago, after a gruelling ten-year training stint, Jihad entered into service under the Brothers of the Dark Veil as a private. Since then he had already moved up two more ranks. He was a male with a plan. He would become a career serviceman, a vocation that was both honourable and vital to the future wellbeing of the Nephilim Nation.

He intended to distinguish himself in the line of duty and claw his way up the Nephilim military ladder by hard work and sheer dint of will. He had incentive to succeed. Jihad was madly in love, and his female had faith in him. But even having done all that, he was still unsure what reception he would get from Dreama's father when he finally drummed up the courage to ask for her hand in marriage.

Jihad knew without a doubt that he wanted to make Dreama his wife. He needed Dreama as much as he needed his next breath. They were two parts of a whole, but before he could even think about approaching Dreama's parents on the subject of marriage, he had to find a way to support his lady love. Dreama's life was a comfortable one. Her family had been in service to King Zion of the House of Shemyaza for centuries.

He would speak to Dreama's father about marriage after he attained the rank of sergeant, which would place him in a higher pay grade and enable him to comfortably support a wife and the children Dreama planned to bear him. Until then, they would have to keep their relationship a secret. He stood to prepare for Dreama's arrival.

"Jihad?"

Jihad heard Dreama whisper his name from the entrance of the greenhouse. "I'm back here, baby. Just follow the trail of rose petals."

He'd pulled the petals off the white roses and strewn them on the greenhouse floor for her to follow. He placed the two candle stubs he found in one of the gardener's cabinets near the path. The light from the candle stubs flickered like the light of a dying camp fire. Dreama flew into his open arms. They melted into each other. Every part of them touched—their lips, their hips, their souls. Dreama moaned while Jihad made love to her mouth with his tongue. His kisses were deep, intimate, searing. They said far more than words could say. Dreama was breathing heavily when she broke away from the kiss to look into Jihad's dark sensuous eyes.

"This is what I defied my parents for, Jihad. It is all for you, baby. I'd do *anything* for you. I love you so much."

Jihad pulled her even closer to him, groaning like a starving man who had been offered a feast. "I love you too, baby. I would do anything for you. You are *everything* to me, Dreama."

He tipped her chin up with the tip of his finger, forcing her to look even deeper into his eyes. His dark brown eyes were soulful. They were rich and as soft as warm cognac.

"*Everything*, Dreama. I love you more than my life."

The next kiss was searing hot. Jihad had a hint of a moustache—just enough to tickle her face when they kissed. His lips were full and surprisingly soft for such a powerful male. Dreama's tongue explored every inch of his mouth. He wore his dark wavy hair cut close to his head. Her short fingernails gently scored his scalp as they kissed. She moaned in need when Jihad took a step back to unbutton his shirt, allowing the shirt to fall from his body. A thin sheen of sweat coated his smooth, deep almond-coloured flesh, accenting his manly chest and the cluster of muscles on his stomach. Dreama licked her lips. It was Louisiana-hot out, the kind of heat that seeps into your pores, reminding you of steamy nights and hot passion.

His body was sleek and toned everywhere with muscles from a life of hard military training. Dreama's eyes feasted on him. He was perfect. She would never tire of looking at his handsome face, his rock-hard body. He was absolutely delicious, and he was all hers.

The sounds of the night made special music while Dreama and Jihad pointedly ignored the tiny, annoying bugs that teased their faces.

Now it was Dreama's turn to titillate. She kicked off her shoes. They landed somewhere near the orchids. Her cotton skirt and top soon joined them. Jihad's nostrils flared in excitement. She stood before the male she loved in her simple cotton chemise. He ate her up with his eyes. He stroked himself while Dreama pulled the chemise over her head and shook her hair loose of its hair tie. Dreama would have had to be blind to miss the tent in the crotch of his pants. Suddenly, the temperature in the greenhouse went up a thousand degrees.

Their heavy breathing drowned out every other night sound when Jihad reached for her. Dreama stepped away, cupping her breasts in her hands enticingly. He growled deep in his throat. Dreama responded by flicking her hard nipples between her thumb and forefingers.

Jihad pounced, lying her squirming body down on the bough of rose petals he'd prepared for her. He blanketed her with his muscular body, lying partially on his side so that he could see every inch of her.

The ceiling of the hothouse was all glass, allowing the starry night to shine through. It was a night made for love and passion. The sky was clear with enough stars to light up the entire world. They felt surrounded by the oversweet fragrance of greenhouse flowers. Even in the dark, they were nearly blinded by the riotous rainbow of colour of the various blooms.

The lavender jacaranda, the fuchsia cypress vine, and the bright red peregrine competed with exotic flora from all over the world in shades of orange, yellow, and every hue of pink, peach, and green imaginable. It was the soft white rose that they lay upon that most drew Jihad. It reminded him of Dreama—simple, elegant, and so very beautiful.

He squeezed one of her breasts with his callused hand before bending his head to taste it. The pleasure was exquisite. Dreama shut her eyes to savour the intense sensation. She felt each hungry pull of his mouth all the way to her pulsing core.

"Oh, Ancient of Days, that feels so good, baby," she panted, offering her other breast to him for similar treatment. Jihad was happy to oblige. He sucked it hard, wetting her breast with his hot saliva. Jihad thought she tasted like heaven.

"You taste so damn good, baby."

His kisses travelled a path from her sensitive breasts to her throat and back to her kiss-swollen lips. His other hand slid down her stomach to that place between her thighs that had been disturbing his sleep since the first day he'd met her.

He slid first one and then two of his long, thick fingers inside, stretching her for his invasion. Dreama's thighs fell open, giving him all the access he needed. He didn't waste any time taking it. He slid his fingers in and out, nice and slow. She was wet and ready for him. The tips of his fingers glided against every nerve ending inside her slick opening. The scent of her female arousal overshadowed the scent of the strongest greenhouse flower. She whimpered when he pulled his fingers out to suck on them.

"Mmmm, you taste good, baby—everywhere."

She was out of her mind, pumping her slender hips in desperation, her eyes and her body entreating Jihad to put out the fire he had ignited. Jihad clutched a handful of rose petals. He rubbed the petals against her undulating belly before cupping a handful of the fragrant petals between her widespread thighs.

"Oh, Ancient of Days, yes, yes, yes!" she screamed, raising her hips off the ground as Jihad rubbed the handful of petals against the sensitive bundle of nerves between her lips.

"That feel good to you, baby? Answer me!" he barked, when she took too long to answer.

"Yes, yes! I can't take any more!"

His deep, sexy laugh tickled her insides. "Well, if this feels good, I got something that is going to feel even better."

He came up on his knees, lifted her thighs over his shoulders, and took everything Dreama had to offer. He pounded into her wet, tight sheath until his liquid heat tunnelled from him to her. Before he even realised what he was doing, he bit her. All Dreama could do was hold on to the nape of his neck as her world spun out of control. Later that night, Jihad held Dreama in his arms while he shared his plans for the future.

"Now that I have tasted your blood, sweetness, it is even more important than ever that we wed. The next time an opportunity for a special mission comes along, I intend to take it," he promised.

CHAPTER 22

Magnolia Hill Plantation

~

DEMONS HAD A stronghold on just about everyone on Magnolia Hill, both whites and slaves alike. Flossie didn't know them by name, but she could see them in the dark shadows that hovered like a cloud of smoke over the white overseer wielding the whip while astride his big, black horse. She saw them in the disdainful looks she received from the same house slaves with whom she had once worked side by side. She could hear them cackling in the face of her misery and whispering profane words in her ear.

Today was going to be different from every one before it. She just knew it. The gods had told her so. Even though she'd armoured herself in prayer, the cloud of demons in the air was so thick they changed the colour of the sky. Their evil chatter was deafening.

It was the beginning of the fall season and hot as the fires of hell. The slaves had been working eighteen- to twenty-hour days, performing an endless cycle of planting, hoeing, weeding, harvesting, and grinding. It was time for endless, backbreaking chopping. Everything but the cane they chopped hour after long hour was burnt, blistered, and dried up. Flossie felt her spirit withering under the relentless rays of the harsh Louisiana sun.

It didn't matter that she was nearly eight months pregnant. Mr. Mike, the white overseer, was riding her especially hard, hollering and threatening to take the whip to her if she didn't speed it up. Flossie kept on swinging that machete like her life depended on it, pretending the cane was Masta Clidamont, Claude, and the stinking overseer. She kept swinging that machete because she had no choice.

The raggedy, sweat-stained straw hat Flossie wore did little to spare her from the torture of the blazing hot sun. Sweat trickled down her back, pooling in that place Ajuma loved to kiss, where the small of her back and her round buttocks met. The sweat left a dark stain across the back of her faded white calico shirt.

Jessy, a big-boned yella gal with funny-coloured grey eyes just like Masta's, tried her best to help Flossie keep up. They had something in common. Both had once been house slaves, and both had been booted out of the Big House to work in the fields. Try as she might, even Big Jessy couldn't cut cane for two.

The sugar cane was cut by gangs of slave labourers. Each gang was supervised by a driver who was usually a fellow slave specifically selected by the white overseer to ensure the slaves worked in tandem cutting, stacking, and loading the cane stalks onto nearby mule-drawn carts. The loads of cut cane would then be taken to the cane mill for processing. The sugar cane had to be juiced within twenty-four hours of harvest or it would spoil.

The slaves worked in silence. There was no humming or singing of Negro spirituals as they worked. They were too hot, too tired, and too beat down in spirit to talk, much less sing. The slaves performed their backbreaking task in a similar rhythm, so it was noticeable when Flossie began to lag farther and farther behind.

Flossie would have given anything to stretch her straining back a bit or have a cool drink of water from the creek. She dared not stop working, not even for a second. Even now she felt Koby's eyes on her.

Koby was the driver who supervised the gang Flossie worked on. He hated Flossie as only one black can hate another. It didn't matter that white folks hated them. Black folks on Magnolia Hill hated each other enough to surpass any hate the whites had for them.

BEHIND THE DARK VEIL

Flossie knew Koby would be more than happy to alert Mr. Mike if she slowed down again. Then he'd get a chance to whip the skin off her. Koby cornered her one night while coming back from the fields. It happened right after she'd had her son Jake. He told her he wanted her. That he didn't care if Masta put a hundred suckers in her belly. He would still want her. Everyone assumed Jake was the Masta's seed. Ajuma was a light-skinned black with green eyes and curly black hair. Her son Jake looked just like his father spit him out.

Not only did Flossie spurn Koby's advances, but now she was pregnant again. Flossie hadn't turned away from Koby because he was a field hand. She didn't want anything to do with him because he was flat-out mean. She'd seen him in action. He'd been known to beat a fellow slave more viciously than Mr. Mike, and he smiled while he was doing it. It seemed Koby's hatred for Flossie grew every day, right along with her swollen belly.

"Pssst," Minnie hissed when Koby finally rode ahead of them on his big black roan. Flossie looked around, frowning in confusion. None of the field slaves *ever* spoke to her unless they wanted something.

"Yeah, I'm talking to you, gal!" Minnie didn't even try to hide her dislike. It was clear in her facial expression and in her tone. "You best speed it up, gal, or baby or not, Koby gon' be up in that ass."

Minnie shook her head to silence Flossie when she opened her mouth to thank her for the unnecessary warning. Flossie knew better than anyone what Koby was capable of. If Flossie thought for a minute that Minnie's warning was generated from any concern she might have for her wellbeing, Minnie didn't waste any time disabusing her of that foolish notion.

"You keep fallin' behind and you gon' get us all whupped—or worse."

Well, there you go, Flossie thought. *I should have known Minnie didn't give a rat's ass about what happens to me.*

Minnie did have a valid point though. The Etiennes drove their slaves like mules to the market. You either kept up or you'd be beaten down and stepped over like the hot steaming dung the mules left in the sugar cane field. Flossie pulled on her last reserve of energy and picked up her pace.

It had been two years since Flossie had been unceremoniously tossed from the Big House by Claude Etienne, and still the field hands hated her. *What in the blazes do I have to do for them to accept me,* she wondered. *Die?*

The Willie Lynch theory was applied at Magnolia Hill with precision, separating the slaves in accordance with skin colour, hair texture, and facial features. The field slaves hated the house slaves. The dark slaves hated the lighter ones. The hate just kept on rolling in one big, growing circle.

"Don't mind that old black heifer, Flossie. She just mad 'cause her man left her for that gal who work in the dairy. She can't take it out on her, so you the next best thing."

Flossie laughed ruefully. "It's kind of funny, Jessy. They always manage to forget their dislike of me when they need me to help bring their babies into the world or prepare a medicinal or potion for them to get rid of them." Flossie shook her head in disgust.

Even though she'd delivered all four of Minnie's children, Flossie knew that if she was to pass out right then and there, Minnie wouldn't move to spit on the best part of her. The only thing that kept the field slaves from doing Flossie some harm was their fear of retaliation. After all, slaves were a highly superstitious lot, and Flossie *was* a powerful conjure woman.

Jessy's scary-looking grey eyes were filled with concern. "How you doin', Flossie?"

"How you think I'm doing?" Flossie snapped, running her shirt sleeve over her sweaty forehead. The pain in her lower back was getting worse by the minute. The herbs she had steeped earlier to ease her discomfort while she worked the field were not working. The baby was sitting low in her belly. If she didn't know any better she would have thought it was positioning itself to leave the safety of her womb.

"I swear, Jessy, if I didn't love this baby's daddy so damn much, I would have prepared one of my special concoctions to spare this child the life of a slave. Better to send his or her little soul to be with the gods before it's born than to watch the baby suffer like this."

Jessy was barren and quick to chastise Flossie. "You hush now. It ain't right for you to say thangs like that about a little unborn baby."

They both knew Flossie wouldn't be the first slave woman to contemplate killing the seed growing in their body. She wouldn't be the last either. Hell, most of the time Flossie was the one who prepared the herbs to deliver the women in the quarter of their unwanted burdens.

"The fact of the matter is, Jessy, that I do love my baby's daddy—more than life itself."

For the next few moments all that could be heard was the rhythmic sound of their machetes slicing through the cane. Flossie's mind drifted to Ajuma. The father of my children is a beautiful black angel, she thought. *The gods sent him to me bleeding and wounded from a battle with demons during the darkest hour of the night.* She would bear and love his children gladly.

Jessy never let an opportunity pass to question Flossie about the identity of her children's father. Today would be no different. "Tell me this, Flossie, is he one of them yalla bucks from over Raveneau Plantation?"

Flossie pretended not to hear the question and kept on cutting. Friend or no friend, it wasn't anybody's business who fathered her babies. No one but her children would know that their father had deep golden-brown skin and eyes as green as the moss that crept up the side of the plantation guest house. He was a god amongst angels and men, so gloriously handsome that at times it hurt Flossie's eyes to look upon him. His name is Ajuma.

Finally, the sun was starting to wane. The slaves would be given a few minutes to eat and drink some water before they went back out into the field. Apparently Koby had spoken with the overseer about Flossie because now Mr. Mike had his watery blue eyes glued on Flossie like a hungry badger on a fat hare, waiting for the moment he would strike. Since the last thing Flossie needed was to feel the bite of Mr. Mike's whip across her already aching back, she stepped away from the line at the well and went to sit down under a nearby tree, hoping against hope that his attention would be drawn somewhere else.

She watched him with dread in her eyes as he and Koby walked toward the wagon where the cane her gang had cut was loaded. Now they were both focusing their attention on her. She wanted to run, but where would she go?

It felt like a million fire ants were marching across the surface of her skin with each step Mr. Mike and Koby took toward her. Her body was ungainly when she stumbled to her feet.

"You come up short." Mr. Mike shot a mouthful of tobacco juice out of his mouth after he made his pronouncement. He raised his voice so all could hear. "All you nigras gather 'round so I can show you what happens to sluggards." He nodded a signal in Koby's direction.

Koby had to drag Flossie away from that tree. The heels of her feet left runnels in the dirt as he pulled her kicking and screaming. The last thing she wanted to do was to appear cowardly before a bunch of folks she knew hated her, but she'd be double goddamned if she was going to take an ass whupping with a smile on her face. A quick blow to the side of her head from Koby effectively knocked all the steam out of her.

Koby took Flossie to a pre-dug hole on the other side of the field. The rest of the slaves quietly followed behind them. He ripped the back of her shirt open to expose her smooth slender back, then he made her lie face down over the hole with her protruding pregnant belly snugly fitted within the depression. Once he had her positioned just right, he checked to see that all the field slaves were assembled and turned to Mr. Mike for further instructions.

Flossie heard the whip whistle through the air just before it struck. A trail of fire landed on her back from shoulder to hip. She screamed, choking herself on a mouth full of dirt. The sound of the whip could be heard all the way to the Big House. Old Man Etienne came out on the porch to watch.

The overseer swung that whip back and forth until sweat dripped down his face. He put all his strength behind every swing, grunting in satisfaction each time a piece of her flesh came away from her body. He cursed Flossie as he beat her, calling her every name but the child of God with each swing of his wicked whip.

Jessy couldn't take it anymore. Her face was bright red with tears. She screamed, "Lord Jesus, help that chile!" as Masta Mike tried his best to beat poor Flossie and her unborn child into the sun-baked Louisiana earth.

Flossie was beyond feeling. She'd passed out after the third lash. Mr. Mike kept on swinging, watching Flossie's unconscious body jerk involuntarily with every swing of the lash. There was blood speckle on his clothing when he finally tossed the whip to Koby, his face flushed and his chest heaving from his exertion.

"One of you nigras get this piece of shit back to her cabin and get her patched up for work tomorrow!" he barked.

Then he turned his mean eyes on the assemblage. "Let this be a lesson to any one of you lazy bastards that think you are going to get away with not giving me a full day's work." He looked down at Flossie's shredded back. "The only thing that's keeping me from stripping all the skin off her back and leaving her to the buzzards is the sucker she's carrying."

He looked toward the Big House porch where Clidamont Etienne was lounging like a mediaeval king. "The Etiennes might not take kindly to me damaging their merchandise without their leave."

He tipped his hat to Clidamont Etienne, hopped on his horse, and rode away.

CHAPTER 23

Maison Plaisir, Storyville District, New Orleans

~

ONIQUE'S DELICATE WRIST beat like the wings of a butterfly as she busily fanned herself, more from aggravation than from the heat. Julien Etienne's voice was an unpleasant distraction as he droned on and on, drowning out the beautiful piano music the talented Reynard was playing in the parlour. It was Monique's job to listen intently and smile sweetly in response to all the empty inanities she heard night after night from her high-class patrons, but tonight she was distracted.

Her keen gaze repeatedly shifted in the direction of the hallway leading downstairs. By law her establishment catered to only white gentlemen, but tonight there were six magnificent specimens of black male pulchritude conducting a clandestine meeting in one of the private rooms in the lower level of her house. Monique was as nervous as a cat walking a tightrope over the churning waters of the Mississippi River.

When a handsome free man of colour offered her an exorbitant amount of money to allow him and what he cryptically described as several of his "personal associates" to utilise her secret back room, she had given her consent with reservations. Monique was an astute business woman, always careful not to do anything that would jeopardise everything she'd managed to build over the years.

God knew she didn't need the money. Monique was a wealthy woman. She ran *Maison Plaisir*, "House of Pleasure," the most exclusive brothel in New Orleans. She used a great deal of her wealth to buy the freedom of the women who worked for her.

Monique's all-white clientele was serviced by some of the most beautiful women in the state, ranging from light, bright and damn near white to complexions as deep as the smooth rich black of the Africans from Uganda, and everything in between. The popular brothel catered to a well-heeled clientele. It was an architectural jewel in the centre of a row of elegant mansions on Basin Street between Iberville and North Robertson Streets in the Storyville district.

Norman, her black doorman who once served as her butler, was twice the size of a royal naval ship and lethal with fists and pistol. She trusted him implicitly. He'd proven over the years to be more than competent when it came to barring entry to all but the wealthy planters, their sons, politicians and other scions of New Orleans society having membership in the exclusive house of ill repute. Not even Norman would be able to save her if any of her white patrons determined there were freemen of colour in one of her little-known rooms downstairs. If her secret was discovered there would be hell to pay. Yet, other than the fact that Monique was wringing the delicate lace of her hanky in obvious nervousness, her face showed none of her disquiet.

There had been something about the big, tall man who said his name was Rephidim that compelled her to say yes to the meeting, albeit against her better judgment. Now she was having second thoughts.

What kind of name is Rephidim anyway? she thought. She'd never heard of such. She had to admit that the man's appearance was just as exotic as his name. She just hoped Rephidim and his associates handled their business and put as much space between themselves and *Maison Plaisir* as possible. She didn't want or need any trouble.

"I declare, you are not paying attention to a word I am saying."

Monique had the grace to blush as she returned her full attention to Julien Etienne, the son of a prosperous River Road planter. She plastered an artificial smile on her face as he continued to wax poetic about his family plantation, a plantation she would never have the opportunity to visit unless it was by way of the kitchen or as his future wife's maid.

They were standing near the libation table in a tastefully decorated sitting room of a whorehouse, conversing with one another as if they were at a planter's ball. Julien's mouth was saying all the right things, but Monique knew his spirit. She knew what Julien was thinking as his hungry eyes took in her appearance, finding no fault. He both desired and despised her.

Monique had the manner and dress of a well-bred plantation lady. She was the only woman wearing unrelieved white, her signature colour. She looked lovely with her thick auburn hair piled high atop her head in a soft riot of curls. Diamond earbobs sparkled at her delicate ears, and a matching necklace and bracelets graced her slender neck and wrists. A silk umpire gown designed by the most popular *modiste* in the city hugged her full breasts and clung to her rounded hips. She was a vision.

Julien and his contemporaries would beat the skin off her flawless back and hang her from the highest tree if she ever tried to grace their front door. Monique knew her place. She would forfeit her life if she forgot it.

She had honed her skills at masking her true feelings during the years she had lain beneath the heaving body of her protector. Now she belonged to no man, and she liked it like that. She was a cool customer, showing none of her inner disquiet on her outer countenance.

"On the contrary, I am captivated by the beauty of your home, Mr. Etienne. I am sorry if I appear to be preoccupied, but, alas, I feel the beginnings of a migraine coming on. I hope you will forgive me."

She simpered and batted her long eyelashes to add effect to her practised lie. He was standing far too close for comfort. She could smell the whiskey on his sour breath.

Monique knew all about young master Julien and his sadistic family. It was only through a benevolent twist of fate and a white sire and grandfather that Monique didn't find herself subjected to the same brand of cruelty as that meted out to the slaves on Magnolia Hill.

She had met Julien's grandfather Clidamont Etienne twice. The first time, old man Clidamont had taken a knife to the face of one of her girls, permanently disfiguring her, and there was nothing she could do about it. The second time was when he brought his two grandsons to her establishment to be "initiated" into manhood.

The two brothers were as different as night is to day. Julien was pretentious, foolish, and cruel. A bad combination if she ever saw one. While his older brother, Henri, was quiet and more subdued in personality, Henri visited her establishment less frequently than Julien did, and only for appearance's sake. Henri's proclivities tended to lean in "another" direction, but what takes place in Monique's establishment stays behind the walls of Monique's establishment.

Henri had been unable to perform with the young beauty his grandfather had chosen for him. Nevertheless, Monique had it on good authority that he performed like a stallion when offered a young nubile male. Henri's secret and that of the other well-heeled members of New Orleans society were safe with her. Her life and her continued financial prosperity depended upon discretion.

Julien was a frequent, if unwelcome, visitor. Like his grandfather, he too had a penchant for violent sex. Monique had trouble with the weak-chinned whelp in the past beating up on one of her girls. Norman warned him that he would be permanently banned from the house and his membership revoked if there was any other incidence of violence on his part. Norman said Julien merely looked him in the face with his flat cold grey eyes and responded, "I'll have to relay your warning to my father, nigger," with a smile on his lips that would have frightened a lesser man.

Monique had more than enough protection on the premises with Nathan and four other men who worked for her, but she'd be lying to herself if she said Julien's less than subtle threat to Norman didn't unnerve her. The insinuation that his father would intervene if he was not allowed to have his way troubled her.

Monique's aim was to make money—a lot of it. The only way to accomplish that was to please even the most discriminating member. You have to spend money to make money. The parlour at *Maison Plaisir* was a virtual garden of black beauty, ranging from ivory to the deepest ebony.

Attention to detail was paid to every aspect of Monique's girls' appearance, from the perfumes and lotions they smoothed on the soft skin of their bared shoulders and *décolletage*, to the delicate French lingerie hidden beneath elabourately appointed frocks in every colour of the rainbow.

Monique's girls were not just exotic and beautiful. They were also intelligent, well-spoken, and accomplished in pianoforte, needlepoint, or singing. The lively conversation, tinkling laugher, and enticing perfume of Monique's girls stimulated the male patrons. The things these girls could do behind closed doors could not be repeated in mixed company.

The white man's hunger for black flesh was voracious. Monique was merely providing a service. The investment she put into each of her girls was well worth the return. Their appearance and comportment easily equaled their white counterparts, and their talents in the art of pleasure rivalled even the most notorious *demi-mondes* in Paris. *Maison Plaisir* was known to have the best of everything—women, wine, and atmosphere.

Monique was no longer interested in entertaining Julien Etienne nor did she want to listen to any more of his drivel. He had been monopolising far too much of her time. There were many important personages in attendance tonight, and now it was time for her to attend to some of her other guests.

"Who would you like to entertain you this evening, Mr. Etienne?" she asked by way of dismissal. "I have two lovely new girls from Barbados who might interest you. I assure you that both are pliable and eager to please."

Julien caressed his chin, appearing to ponder her question. "What if"—he paused to look Monique directly in the eye—"what if I told you that I don't want either of the new girls? In fact, truthfully, I am not overly interested in any of your lovely girls tonight."

With that, his eyes swept the parlour, dispassionately taking in the bevvy of beauties. He lowered his voice so only Monique could hear what he would say next. "What if I want *you*, pretty lady?"

Monique was floored. She'd sooner lay with a poisonous snake than allow Julien Etienne to touch her. He repulsed her. His appearance and manner made her sick to the stomach.

Other than a slight hitch in her breath, her face didn't betray her thoughts. She quickly plastered her routine tight smile on her face.

"I am flattered that you find me desirable, Mr. Etienne, but, unfortunately, I am not for sale. Not now. Not ever. Since you are not interested in any of the girls, there is a high stakes poker game going on in one of the back rooms. Maybe you'd like to try your luck at a game of chance? I will send my majordomo to you, and he will assist you with your needs for the evening."

With her head held high, Monique breezed regally past Julien with her silk skirts gently swaying against her slender legs, leaving a soft waft of expensive perfume in her wake and Julien glaring at her back.

CHAPTER 24

⌒‿

"FOLD," NICO said, throwing his cards down in disgust.

"Shit. Me too," Antioch stated, following suit.

Ajuma turned to Gilead with one dark brow raised and a question in his bright green eyes.

"Hell, I fold too," Gil said, before throwing his cards down on the table in a fit of pique. Ajuma had won every hand that night. It seemed lady luck was on his side.

They were downstairs in one of the private rooms at *Maison Plaisir*. An upscale house of ill repute run by a beautiful Octoroon named Monique Dubonnet. Rephidim, who had made the arrangements with the Madame, was stretched out in a corner chair with his booted feet crossed at the ankle, his hands clasped across his taut belly, and a cowboy hat covering his face. A glimpse of his five o'clock shadow could be seen on the part of his chin not covered by the hat.

Antioch had finally managed to catch up with the warlock who would set up the meeting with the demon, Devius, in the back room of a seedy bar in the French Quarter. Everything was arranged. They would meet Devius tonight on *Beer Shahat*. The warlock assured him that, for the right price, Devius would disclose specific information relating to Ephraim's disappearance.

Simeon was chain-smoking, pacing back and forth like a caged tiger, anxious to get going. The hairs at the nape of his neck were standing on end. Something didn't seem quite right to him. He wanted out of the whorehouse—like yesterday—but they couldn't go anywhere until two A.M. when Boaz and his special crew were scheduled to get back from their current mission in Algiers. They had several hours to kill. The brothers were enjoying a few drinks and a quick game of poker before they set out on their mission.

Ajuma had a look of satisfaction on his face. He'd won every hand and gotten a tidy sum in the process. It was now time to rub it in.

"Well, brothers, I hate to empty your pockets and run, but I've got a yearning to spend some time with my woman before we pull out later tonight. So, if you gentlemen will please excuse me, I will take my leave."

Clamping his cheroot between blinding white teeth, Ajuma unceremoniously scooped up his winnings and rose to take his leave. Their proposed meeting spot was not far from Magnolia Hill Plantation. He would have more than enough time to see Flossie and meet his men at the rendezvous location. He tipped the rim of the wide-brimmed hat he habitually wore to conceal his features in a jaunty fashion and stood.

Nico stood to pat Ajuma on the back. "You know you are one lucky bastard. I expect an opportunity to recoup my winnings as soon as possible." Nicodemus was probably the most outgoing and affable of the Brothers of the Dark Veil. He was also one of the most powerful. He could slice the throat of a demon and still maintain an angelic smile on his handsome face.

Ajuma laughed. "Your request is duly noted, Nico. I welcome the opportunity to challenge each of you—any time, any place. Is anybody else leaving?" he asked.

Gilead threw back a stiff shot of whiskey and slammed the glass on the table before responding. "Not me. I plan to take a minute to wet my whistle before I meet up with you guys later."

Nico couldn't resist putting in a dig. "A minute is probably about all it will take for you to wet that little whistle of yours, Gil."

Antioch couldn't restrain himself from getting in on the ribbing. "Here, here. I am all for getting the old whistle wet or, even better, getting it blown."

"And I will second that!" chortled Rephidim.

Contrary to what they would have their king believe, each of them had sampled the charms of humans on more than one occasion. The women at *Maison Plaisir* were renowned for their beauty and comportment. No way were they going to pass up an opportunity to enjoy their charms tonight.

Now turning serious, Ajuma addressed his brothers. "Alright then, I will meet you all at the point of rendezvous at two hours past midnight. My men will meet with each of your troops at the gateway in the swamps.

Rephidim tipped his hat up to reveal one eye. "Just make sure you don't attract any undue attention when you leave, Ajuma. I wouldn't want to cause the lovely Monique the kind of trouble she would face if one of her white patrons sees you leaving here. She took a big risk allowing us the use of her facility tonight. I would hate to have her kindness blow up in her face."

"Ah, so it's the lovely Monique now, is it? Are you thinking about crossing over like Ajuma here?" Gilead asked with a mischief smile on his face.

Rephidim was quick to disabuse Gilead of the notion. "I will have to take a pass on that, Gil. Monique Dubonnet is lovely, but I personally prefer the strength of a preternatural female. Give me a strong long-legged Nephilim woman who can take a pounding without breaking and a deep vein bite without passing the fuck out any day."

Antioch joined in. "Here, here."

Rephidim licked his lips when he recalled his earlier conversation with Monique Dubonnet. "But you have to admit that is one fine-looking woman. If I was going to stick what I got inside something human tonight, I couldn't think of a nicer piece to do it with. I'd dig deep in my pocket for some time with her, but I don't think she is for sale. What a pity," he whispered.

When Gilead threw back yet another shot of whiskey, Simeon's droll voice sounded more than a little bored. "Why bother with a glass, Gil. Just tip the motherfucking bottle up."

Gil rolled his eyes and said, "Fuck you, Sim!" before pouring himself another glass of the premium liquor in a deliberate manner to provoke him. He took a deep swallow, never once taking his eyes off Simeon's impassive face.

"As I was getting ready to say before I was so rudely interrupted by Brother Sim the governess, I am not quite as discriminating as you brothers. I fully intend to stick what I got as far up in one of the human lovelies in this establishment as it will go. I further intend to enjoy every single minute of it. What say you, Sim?"

Simeon ignored Gil's question, instead turning to Rephidim with a question of his own.

"What do you know about the woman who owns this establishment, Reph? Can she be trusted?" He needed some kind of assurance to quiet the sense of unease flooding his spirit.

"I thoroughly checked her out before I made my approach, Sim. Monique Dubonnet is an Octoroon with skin so white her African blood is virtually undetectable. In spite of her white blood, she is a legendary beauty.

"Like her mother, Monique is the descendant of a white plantation owner from Santo Domingo. Only one sixty-fourth African blood runs through her body, but because of social conditions, she is barred from the upper echelons of white society."

The brothers listened in silence, fascinated.

"Monique followed in the footsteps of her mother and became a *placée*, the adored mistress of a wealthy white man. He comfortably installed her in a well-appointed house on Rampart Street. She had servants to wait upon her and her every desire met.

"Her protector was married, but he spent more time with Monique in the little house on Rampart than he did with his wife and children. For appearance's sake, he kept a separate residence right next door to the home he'd bought for Monique. Theirs was a long-standing relationship of convenience resulting in two children, both boys.

BEHIND THE DARK VEIL

"It is illegal to educate mixed race children in New Orleans, so her protector arranged for the education of the two children Monique bore him. Both of her sons are studying in France, following in the footsteps of their uncle Bernaud who was educated abroad and is now a prominent New Orleans physician. One is studying to become a doctor and the other a barrister. Having even less black blood than their mother, her sons will be able to easily blend into society as white men."

Rephidim's demeanour was introspective. "I must admit that I admire Monique Dubonnet's tenacity and resourcefulness. When her protector fell victim to an outburst of yellow fever and suddenly died, she could have had the choice of any one of the wealthy planters lining River Road and beyond. She had no desire to become the *placée* to yet another white man nor did she desire to marry a Creole man of colour. So, she sold the house on Rampart as well as several pieces of expensive jewellery her lover had given her over the years, and bought a much larger home in the Storyville District. The rest is historey. She will not betray us. She has too much to lose."

CHAPTER 25

⁓

*A*JUMA GHOSTED UNDETECTED out the back entrance of *Maison Plaisir*. He was halfway around the block before he materialised. Seconds later, he felt gold dust kiss the surface of his skin. Nicodemus had caught up with him.

"I will walk a part of the way with you," Nico said.

They didn't have far to go. Ajuma's horse was tethered at a stall just around the corner. They proceeded in the direction of the stables. The cool night air was a pleasant contrast to the stuffy smoke-filled room in the bordello. They walked in silence for a time.

"Well, Nico, what mischief will you be getting into on this fine night, pray tell?" Ajuma inquired.

Nico turned to Ajuma with a feigned look of indignation on his handsome face. "I beg your pardon, Ajuma. Me? Involved in mischief? Never!"

The sound of Ajuma's laughter rumbled from the pit of his stomach, disrupting the quiet night. There were few pedestrians about and even fewer carriages.

"Well, pardon me, brother, for misjudging you," Ajuma said sarcastically. "But aren't you the brother who was forced to climb out of the bedroom window of the wife of Michael of the House of Yomyael butt naked?" Ajuma didn't leave time for Nico to rebut. "If I recall the circumstances correctly, didn't you land on a prickly rose bush during your last-minute escape?"

Nicodemus' expression turned sheepish. He was guilty as charged of everything Ajuma said and so much more. His manservant had been left with the task of pulling thorns out of his black ass for days, but that didn't mean he would acknowledge his brother's assessment of his escapades.

"Now that's not fair, Ajuma, and you know it! I've got a weakness for the fair sex. I'm my father's son. What can I say? Shit, before you found your Flossie, you were just as bad, if not worse than I am. So, shut the fuck up."

Ajuma chose to ignore the latter part of Nico's statement. "You are damned right. You have a weakness for the fair sex, Nico. The only problem is that you don't discriminate between those who are available and those who are already spoken for."

Ajuma was fearful that one day Nico was going to get caught fucking someone else's woman and end up getting his head cut off. He had much love for the brother. He didn't want anything to happen to him. Ajuma's expression changed to one that was more serious. "Just promise me that you will be careful, Nico. That is all I ask."

"I will, Ajuma. I will," Nico said, his face unusually serious.

The two brothers clasped hands and bumped shoulders, promising to meet a few hours hence before they separated at the next dark corner.

<hr/>

Dog may be man's best friend, but besides Zion and the Brothers of the Dark Veil, Ajuma's horse Kehilan was his. He was a high-spirited, bold Al Khamsa Arabian stallion with a dark bay coat accented with white markings on his feet and his chiselled face.

Kehilan was an equine thing of beauty. Sheer perfection with a long slender neck, high withers, a deep barrel chest, short back, excellent depth of hindquarters, a lean body, and long legs. As in all things of beauty, he was extremely temperamental.

BEHIND THE DARK VEIL

Kehilan was one of five horses gifted to Ajuma, King Zion, Nicodemus, Simeon, and Antioch from the Prophet Muhammad. The others were named Seglawi, Abeyan, Hamdani, and Hadban. The king and the brothers gave their horses the names of their sire. Each horse was a first generation *Al Khamsa*, an Arabic term which roughly translates to mean "the five" original Bedouin stallions whose loyalty was tested by the prophet and proven to be steadfast and true.

Kehilan had proven his bravery and loyalty to Ajuma many times over, but under the best of circumstances he didn't take kindly to being shut away behind the doors of anyone's stable. Ajuma could hear his horse's restless motion and his distinctive whinnying before he even rounded the corner toward the stable. Kehilan rose up on his hind legs as soon as he saw his master.

"Calm down, boy. Did you think I forgot you?" Ajuma asked, gently running his hands down the horse's flank to calm him. "How 'bout we take a nice leisurely ride to the country. Would that put me back in your good graces?"

Kehilan threw back his graceful head. His intelligent eyes indicated he understood everything Ajuma said to him. Ajuma pulled a juicy red apple out of his pocket by way of apology, then waited patiently for Kehilan to finish his treat. Horse and rider became one as they took off at a leisurely canter, leaving the dark streets of the city behind them.

Ajuma's thoughts were on Flossie as the clip clop of Kehilan's hooves pounded the dirt road leading to Magnolia Hill. His pants grew tight in the crotch at the thought of her. The gentle jolt from Kehilan's canter served only to aggravate his anxiety. Ajuma picked up the pace.

They were rounding a sharp curve in the road when Ajuma and Kehilan froze like statues in the centre of town square. Three of the most despicable human beings, and Ajuma was being extremely generous with that assessment, were blocking the road leading to Magnolia Hill. The grimy fellows appeared as if out of nowhere, like lazy fat possums coming out of the woods to feast on fresh road kill. They were slave patrollers.

The fact that Ajuma hadn't picked up on the stench of their collective unwashed bodies was a testament to how absorbed he had been with thoughts of Flossie and the mission he and his brothers would soon embark upon. Patrollers were the scum of the earth. They would lie in wait on the dark roads at night, making a living by plundering, stealing, and fetching rewards for the return of helpless runaways.

"Well, lookit what we got us here, Jonas. Hew wee! I declare. This must be our lucky night."

The one named Jonas dismounted his horse, scratching his crotch as he drew closer to Ajuma to get a better look.

"Why, I believes you might be right, Clem. We got ourselves a big bright-skinned buck in his prime, sittin' astride a piece of horse flesh like he's the king of one of them thar heathen countries from across the waters. And look at them thar eyes on him. Ain't never seen eyes that green on a buck before. Betcha he's one of them thar halfbreeds, ya think?

Ajuma sighed in frustration. *I don't have time for this shit on any given night, and I especially don't have time for it tonight.* All he wanted to do was get to his woman and his son. *Was that asking too much?* Apparently, it was, because now he would be forced to deal with the human trash before him.

The man named Jonas drew his pistol, aiming it dead in the centre of Ajuma's chest. "Now I wonder how he came to be in possession of such a fine horse, don't you, Clem?"

Jonas must have been infected with lice. Now he was scratching his grimy neck and his dirty armpits.

"Well, Jonas, truth be told, I was thinking the exact same thing myself," the lowlife replied.

Clem was tired of playing their little cat and mouse game. He wanted answers. "Whar'd you get that thar hos, bwoy?"

Ajuma didn't like his manner and he cared even less for the man's tone. Having already sized up the patrollers and assessed the situation, he didn't deign to reply. He merely looked down at the three men from the lofty height of his horse with a look of disdain upon his keen features. Kehilan was getting a bit antsy. *It will be best for all concerned to terminate this untimely exchange as quickly as possible,* he thought.

Clem turned to Jonas and the third man when Ajuma didn't answer. "Looks like the cat got his tongue, huh? He musta stole that hos, Jonas. That thar hos is way too good for the likes of him. Bet ya some rich planter is missing a horse and a buck, if ya ask me."

Nobody asked you, asshole. Ajuma could have kicked himself for being so careless. He should have taken the route through the swamp. He could have tethered Kehilan in the wooded area that led into the swamp and doubled back to the slave quarters without detection. That way he would have avoided this encounter. In his haste to get to Flossie, he'd forgotten all about the poor white trash that patrolled the parish roads on constant lookout for slaves who were out after curfew.

Many of the slaves weren't trying to run away, but were merely trying to sneak in a nocturnal visit with family or friends who lived on other plantations or travel to the homes of the few free persons of colour who lived in the area. It was not unusual for lovers to be sold to separate plantations. One or the other would either brave the patrol-ridden dark roads which connected the plantations on River Road, or never see one another again.

Up until this point, the third man had remained a dark, silent spectre in the background. Ajuma felt waves of menace flowing from him. He guessed the third patroller, whom they called Jim Bob, was a man of action and few words. Jim Bob dismounted the sway-backed nag he had been sitting astride and moved to stand not two feet from Ajuma with eyes so evil he would have frightened a lesser man. But Ajuma wasn't a man.

Jim Bob's voice snapped Ajuma back to attention. "He asked you a question, bwoy, and I intend to get an answer. I'm gon' ask you one more time, and I ain't fittin' to ask ya agin." The patroller followed up his verbal threat by letting loose a noxious glob of thick brown tobacco juice while uncoiling a thick long whip he'd pulled from the side of his saddle.

He handled the whip in a threatening manner. "Now, where in tarnation did you steal that horse from, bwoy?" Jim Bob's nostrils flared when his threat was again met with silence.

Singularly, Ajuma doubted any one of these bottom-of-the-barrel bullies would have approached a male slave at night or during daylight hours, for that matter—that is, not unless they had a weapon to back them up. They were cowards, all, deriving courage while in a crowd by preying upon those weaker than themselves.

Jim Bob stared Ajuma in the eye in an unsuccessful attempt at intimidation. One side of his jaw bulged like he was a human bullfrog or had a large tumour inside his cheek. He spat another long stream of tobacco which just barely missed Ajuma's pant leg, splashing instead against Kehilan's side.

Now that shit just ain't right. Disrespect me if you want, but not my damn horse.

Jim Bob addressed his cohorts without taking his eyes off Ajuma for a second. "Well, he's way past curfew, and I would bet my hairy left nut he ain't got no papers on him either. I say we forgo the bounty they probably got on him, string him up, and take that fine-looking horse he stole."

Another wad of thick tobacco juice shot out of his mouth, this time landing on the tip of Ajuma's boot. Ajuma dismounted. The one named Jonas was right. This was their lucky day. Ajuma was about to put all three of these motherfuckers out of their misery. Ajuma may be black, but as a Nephilim, unlike his human counterpart, he had options.

He moved with superhuman lightning speed from his horse to within an inch of where Jim Bob stood. His eyes were unnaturally bright, appearing to have fiery lanterns in their depths. The deadly smile on his face revealed the tips of bright white fangs—fangs which were growing longer by the second.

Jim Bob raised his hand to strike Ajuma with the handle of his whip. Before he could lower his hand to deliver the blow, Ajuma reached in and through the startled man's chest cavity, puncturing ribs and shattering bone to wrench out the man's beating heart. Ajuma latched on to his neck with his lethal fangs before the body hit the ground, taking deep gulps of the dead man's blood.

The sharp report of a pistol and the resulting sting in Ajuma's right shoulder brought his attention back to the other two men. He dropped Jim Bob like a handful of hot coals and stalked Jonas.

Clem ran off into the woods. Ajuma was unconcerned with Clem's futile attempt at escape. He knew he wouldn't get far. He shook the shoulder wound off as if it was merely a bee sting and advanced upon Jonas with single-minded intent.

Ajuma's preternatural senses picked up the ripe earthy smell of human waste. The man had soiled himself. Jonas tripped in his haste to get away and was now crawling backward, cutting his wrists and hands on the sharp rocks in the road. Jonas was unable to string two coherent words together to beg for his miserable life. He saw his own death in Ajuma's eyes and started to blubber.

Ajuma took his time before striking. He wanted to savour the moment. The offal lying on the ground before him had intended to "string him up" and steal his horse. Ajuma was curious as to how many innocent people of colour had been accosted by the man he was about to kill. Well, he wouldn't be around to terrify any more innocent slaves.

Ajuma knelt beside the terrified man and whispered in his ear, "Like you said earlier, today is your lucky day." He drank his fill before snapping the man's grimy neck.

By the time Ajuma caught up with and dispatched Clem, his cock was hard and he was on blood overload. Fighting and feeding always made Nephilim warriors want to fuck. He jumped back in the saddle and continued on his journey. He really needed to get to his woman quickly.

CHAPTER 26

Magnolia Hill Plantation

⌒

*A*JUMA GHOSTED INTO the small cabin occupied by Flossie and his son with the taste of death in his throat and human blood spatter saturating his clothing. A frown lit his handsome face. His sense of hot need was now replaced with a thick, thorny ball of fear. *Something is wrong.*

He found Flossie huddled on a cot in the far corner of her cabin, directly in line with the ambient light of the hunter's moon shining through the cabin's solitary window—a window which had no glass and no shutters.

Ajuma's small son slept peacefully at the foot of his mother's cot with soft snores falling from his sweet little mouth. Ajuma sent a subliminal message to the child.

Sleep well, little warrior. Sleep well. Your papa will visit with you next time. This visit is for your mama.

Because of Ajuma's powers of suggestion, his son would not wake up, even if the walls of the flimsily constructed cabin were to fall down around him. He knelt to lovingly kiss the toddler on his open mouth and stroke his baby-soft cheek.

Ajuma moved as silently as a phantom, quickly divesting himself of his soiled clothing, dropping each item on the hard dirt-packed floor before he returned to the cot where Flossie slept.

169

She must have sensed his presence. Her luminous dark brown eyes suddenly opened, luring Ajuma deep into her magnetic gaze. He had been unable to think of anything but his need to touch her, to kiss her—to show her in a manner far more powerful than words how much he loved her—since the last time they were together. He could not have kept himself from her, even if his life depended on it.

Ajuma would be the first to admit he was a cold-blooded killer, but there was something about the tiny woman who bore him one child and was about to bear another that soothed his spirit and gentled his heart. Flossie represented life and everything that should be, even if it wasn't. No shackles of human slavery could bind the blinding white light generated by her spirit.

Ajuma knew they were star-crossed lovers—that he was destined for heartbreak as she aged and eventually died while he remained young—but he was thankful for every second he was allowed to bask in her light. The Ancient of Days' blessings were always enough. He would take what was offered, and be glad.

Something came over Flossie the moment her man entered the cabin. Suddenly, the pain in her back diminished from teeth-clenching agony to a dull monotonous drone which, though it still competed with the discomfort she felt from her advanced pregnancy, was almost bearable.

A short while ago she couldn't even lie comfortably on her side, and she certainly could not lie on her back. So, she had been forced to lie in an awkward position somewhere in between, trying not to aggravate her injuries. Now, all she wanted to do was hold Ajuma and feel his big strong body pressed against hers.

Up until the time Ajuma placed his gentle hands upon her, she had been unable to find surcease from the mental or the physical pain the overseer had inflicted. Ajuma made everything more bearable—the fields, the animosity of the other slaves, and the constant fear that one of the Etiennes would come out to the field one day to finish off what Mr. Mike had started. Somehow she knew Ajuma would come to her tonight. Her spirit had cried out to him and he had come to her. *Thank God he is here.*

Flossie's hungry eyes travelled the length of the magnificent man that was all hers. His thick, long arousal was proudly displayed, causing a white-hot blast of desire to slam into her like a bolt of lightning. The feeling was so intense, she was forced to close her eyes for a minute. Ajuma always affected her like that. She opened her eyes again, her gaze filled with both love and longing.

Eyes that bore the secrets of antiquity stared back at Ajuma with joy and something else in their mysterious depths. Was that pain Ajuma detected? Ajuma knelt on the dirt floor beside the cot, reaching for Flossie's hand as he tenderly placed his other hand upon the belly that was swollen with his child. He could feel the life they'd created together moving restlessly inside her petite body. A son or daughter he and Flossie had made from their love. His eyes never left her face as he kissed her belly. He drew her small hand to his lips, kissing the work-hardened calluses on each finger one by one before he placed a tender kiss in the centre of her palm. He sat so close to her that they shared one breath.

"How fare you, my love?" he asked.

Flossie could feel a rumble in her chest from the deep base of his voice. Everything about him made her melt inside. She traced his handsome face with the tips of her fingers as if she was trying to memorise every stark angle on his beloved face by touch alone. Never had she beheld a man more splendidly made. Truly, he was beautiful to behold.

"I fare much better, now that you are here, Ajuma," she whispered.

Ajuma loved the way Flossie said his name. She enunciated every syllable like they were notes to her favourite song. He reached for her. Flossie visibly flinched when Ajuma sought to gather her in his arms.

"What's wrong, baby? Did I hurt you?" he asked anxiously.

Flossie lowered her eyes. The air in the cabin changed as she retreated physically and emotionally. Ajuma noted a marked stiffness in her movements as she attempted to place some distance between herself and him.

Ajuma lifted her into a sitting position so as not to cause her additional pain. He gently lowered one shoulder of her cotton shift and then the other, allowing the shift to pool around her waist. Her perfect breasts were ripe and swollen with breast milk. Her nipples were dark and succulent and as hard as South American cocoa beans. She was womanly perfection.

A five foot, 100-pound slave girl had captured the heart of the fierce Ajuma. She had the power to lay him low where the most powerful demon could not. He intended to look at every inch of her little body before he buried himself deep inside of her, taking her slow and hard. Gently, he turned her around and the air in the cabin froze.

"Who did this to you?!"

The skin on Flossie's back that had once been so beautiful and smooth to the touch was now covered with a crisscross pattern of painful welts from just below her neck to the juncture where the small of her back met her buttocks. Some of the welts were still oozing blood.

An invisible hand reached inside Ajuma's chest, painfully squeezing his heart to the point of bursting. He was finding it difficult to breathe. Blood-red tears streamed down his cheeks.

Flossie immediately started to cry—not from her injuries, but from the anger they generated in Ajuma. She'd never seen this side of her gentle giant before, and it frightened her.

His large hands shook as he gently folded Flossie's tear-stained face within the protection of the same hands he'd used just a short while ago to snuff out the life of three sub humans. Ajuma could barely contain his rage. He was ready to kill again. He had the evidence before him that his woman—the mother of his child—had been beaten worse than a beast of burden.

"Flossie. I swear by all that is holy, upon the light of The Ancient of Days and all his angels, upon my very soul, that I will kill the animal that did this to you," he vowed with his teeth bared and a murderous look on his countenance. "Every white on this godforsaken plantation will die tonight!" His voice shook with conviction.

Flossie was frightened. Ajuma's green eyes, which were so warm and tender but a moment ago, were now murderous and as cold as ice. A hint of lethal fang was showing between his full lips. A tic pulsed in his chiselled jaw as he ground his teeth in seething rage. She was afraid he would lose control and endanger them all. Flossie tenderly kissed his lips, trying to soothe him, not unlike she would soothe little Jacob after a fall.

"I know you are angry, love. I know. Please calm yourself. I do not want anyone to overhear us. Please." She took his face in her hands and stared directly into his eyes. She needed to cut through the thick haze of rage and get him to face reality.

"If you kill every white on this plantation, more will come to take their place. They will rain down upon us like locusts with their weapons of death and destruction until they stomp every black man, woman, and child into the dirt beneath their feet. They will not only come during the night but during the day as well, when you and your army of angel men will be powerless to help us."

Something in the tone of Flossie's voice managed to penetrate the red-hot curtain of rage in front of Ajuma's eyes. He didn't mean to frighten her with his anger. He did not fear for himself. He feared for Flossie's safety and that of their children.

Flossie's concerns were valid. The slaves lived in flimsily constructed cabins which were built close together, enabling voices to drift upon the wings of the wind. If the wrong person overheard his raised voice, they could well report his comments to the overseer and bring down the wrath of the whites upon his family. If something happened to his loved ones because of hastily spoken words in the heat of anger, he would never forgive himself.

CHAPTER 27

⁓

*A*JUMA PLACED HIS forehead against Flossie's, taking several deep breaths to compose himself. She was right. It would be foolhardy in the extreme for him to lose control now, but he had to do something. It takes a lot out of a male when he can't protect his family, especially when he can't protect his pregnant wife and child.

It didn't matter that he and Flossie had not been joined before a Nephilim cleric. She was his wife in spirit, if not in name. At that moment Ajuma felt the full weight of the impotence the black slaves felt every minute of their miserable existence, and it humbled him.

Flossie was right. If he was to lose control he would surely sound the death knell for his entire family and other innocent slaves. Or even worse, he would compromise the existence of others like him. Be that as it may, before he left this night, he fully intended to know the name of the one who had beaten his woman. He would make him pay. He was also resolved that no one would ever abuse his woman again.

"Listen to me, love. I have to lead a squadron on a fact-finding mission tonight. It should not take me long. I expect we'll be in and out in a few hours. I will come to you tomorrow when all are asleep. I intend to take you and little Jacob away from this evil place. No one will ever hurt you again."

Flossie couldn't hide her puzzled expression. "But you said there was no place for me and little Jake in your world. You said there was constant battle. That you would not be able to keep us safe from the supernatural predators that hide behind every shadow and abound at nearly every turn. I recall you also said there were entities out there that would seek to harm those you love to bring you down. What of your people, Ajuma? Will they accept us?" she asked.

Over the past two years, Flossie had come to understand that this gift from the gods she called husband was a temporary one and that she should savour every minute they had together. Although she was afraid to have a life without him, she knew the price she had to pay to keep him was to accept that one day she would lose him.

"I would not have you jeopardise your position with your brothers and your king, whom I know you love and respect. Your king will not be pleased to find humans in the midst of his people. I cannot allow you to betray the trust of your people for me, Jake or our unborn babe. I love you too much for that."

The curse of immortality Ajuma wore like a heavy winter cloak was both his shield and his burden. He was determined to make Flossie understand that, in light of her recent beating, everything had changed.

"Flossie, honey, listen to me. Everything I said was and is true. I cannot deny it. Yet, you and the children will be much safer with me than you are here. I would gladly give my life for my king as well as my brothers, and have proven my loyalty more times than can be counted, but if I can't keep you in my life, I will be no good to anyone, including myself. Now that I have found you I realise how empty my life was.

I will talk to Zion. He is a hard male, but he is also a fair male. Most importantly, he is my brother and my dear friend. Somehow, I will convince him to allow you and my children to live among the Nephilim."

He looked into the eyes of the proud slave woman who had captured his heart. Every day Ajuma spent amongst the human slaves filled him with more respect for Flossie and for them. In his estimation, they fared relatively well, considering what they were forced to endure. They had been taken away from their homes with no means to return; stripped of their language, culture, and religious practises; and beaten and forced to labour for people whose ancestors were still crawling around on all fours and dwelling in caves long after the African continent became civilised.

176

Yet even though they were surrounded with injustice at every turn, they exhibited a strength and resilience he'd never seen before. Having been to hell and back, Ajuma could state without equivocation that Magnolia Hill was a big chunk of hell on earth.

Little Jacob and the unborn babe Flossie carried have the blood of angels running through their veins. They share his blood. He had to make Zion understand Flossie and his children will be no threat to the Nephilim Nation.

Flossie couldn't help but be excited about the prospect of sharing the remainder of her life in Ajuma's world. Nor could she help but notice the worry line which appeared between his handsome brows. She smoothed it away with her thumb, pulling him closer until they shared one breath.

"Just kiss away the pain, baby," she whispered. "Make me forget this afternoon. Make me forget this evil place. Just love me. Love me baby."

Ajuma did as his woman asked until two hours before sunrise.

❧ ☙

Without his big horse, his whip, and his brace of pistols, Mike Tolliver was nothing more than a cowardly, illiterate, vicious bully with rotten teeth and body odour. His betters referred to him and his ilk as poor white trash, and that is exactly what he was.

There were a lot of Tollivers—eleven to be exact—and not a one of them was a twin. His drunken father kept putting babies in his mother's belly and beating on her until she was plumb worn out. The line between the beating and the fucking started to blur and Mike and his siblings eventually found it difficult to differentiate one from the other. After the youngest Tolliver, Clem, was born, his momma just closed her eyes and died.

Things went from bad to worse after his mother died. His poppa couldn't stay sober for long enough to care for the passel of kids he'd made. He stayed gone for long periods of time, drinking up most of the little money he made doing odd jobs and gambling away the rest, leaving the Tolliver youngens pretty much to their own devices.

When their father's bloated body was found washed up on the banks of the Mississippi River, not one tear was shed. The Tolliver children stoically buried their father's rotten corpse behind the barn and kept it moving. They later erected a still on the site of his grave, and started to sell moonshine and engage in other illegal activities to put food on the table. Now all they had was each other. The older kids looked after the younger ones as best they could.

They lived in a rundown, ramshackle farm on the outskirts of town. Every last one of them was a liar and a thief. They lied to survive and to keep one step in front of the law. They stole to keep food in their stomachs and clothes on their backs.

There were only two Tolliver girls. Both made their money on their backs. Beanie, the eldest girl, died at a young age from that nasty woman's disease. To this day, the other Tolliver girl, named Franny, was considered to be the community whore, with a bunch of snotty-nosed, pissy-pants bastards to prove it. Each of Mike's nieces and nephews were ugly as sin, taking after their slow-witted, cross-eyed mama. Not a one of them could claim the same father.

Without a doubt the Tollivers were accustomed to a degraded standard of living. Jim Bob, Clem, and Jonas were patrollers, and for the past four years Mike was employed as the overseer at Magnolia Hill. The other brothers ran the still and engaged in other illegal endeavours when they weren't behind bars. They were outcasts from respectable society and forced to exist on the fringes of the social order they envied. They were looked down upon by their white betters and slaves alike.

Mike Tolliver slammed the half-empty bottle of Kentucky bourbon on the rough-hewn hard wood table in his cabin, wiping his mouth with the back of his grimy hand.

There was a bristling sound as his sweaty arm made contact with his unshaven face. He took in his surroundings with disdain. His humble beginnings didn't keep him from envying those who had more, nor from resenting the good fortune of others. His employer forced him to live in a cabin not much better than the slaves. There was a narrow cot in one corner, the chair he was sitting on, and the wooden table upon which sat his bottle of bourbon.

Mike was rip-roaring drunk, despite the fact he would have to rise early to see the cane harvested and sent to the mill. He narrowed his pale blue eyes, staring at the amber liquor swirling in the bottle. To the Etiennes he was no more than a paid slave, hired to do their dirty work, and he hated each and every one of them, from the youngest to the oldest, extended and close. If he could gather every Etienne in a locked room, he would surround the room with dry straw and light a flint. Yes. He would burn them to cinders, and that would be too good for the lot of them!

He hated the fact that he, a white man, was forced to enter through the back of the house whenever he had occasion to speak with Etienne Senior or Junior. Even the two Etienne children looked down on him as if he was dirt. Never once was he invited to sup with the family. They treated him like he was not good enough to sit at their table.

It wasn't right that one family had so much and he had so little. The Tollivers could live for a month off of the food Clidamont Etienne fed his pigs. *The black savages eat better than I did when I was growing up*, Mike thought.

Mike was filled with hubris, and his excessive pride had no outlet. He could see no means of bettering his circumstances. He had no education, and he didn't have a good family name. He felt blocked from advancement, thus creating a level of frustration he satisfied in the only manner a Tolliver knows: with violence. He took his anger and frustration out on the backs of the slaves under his charge, knowing they could do nothing to defend themselves.

His wrist still hurt from the beating he gave that Flossie gal earlier. Watching her tight little butt cheeks clinch together through the thin cotton shift she wore made his dick jerk each time his whip struck home. Even now he was aroused by the memory of the beating.

Tomorrow I will seek her out again. I will drag her little black ass in the barn and have at her.

As far as Mike was concerned, there was nothing better than pregnant black pussy. It felt like sticking his dick in sweet hot butter. He took another big swallow from the bottle of bourbon thinking maybe he'd make that big black buck Koby, who's been eyeing her, watch while he fucked her.

What the fuck was that?

Mike thought he heard the sound of rushing wind outside his cabin. Before he could stagger to the door to investigate, a gold-flecked fog filtered through the cracks and around all four sides of his cabin door. Mike's eyes grew large with amazement which quickly turned to fear as the mist coalesced into the form of a man.

A hot steam of urine ran down his pant leg. Standing in front of him was a big black green-eyed nigra with huge fangs. He was nearly twice the size of the biggest slave on Magnolia Hill. No matter how many times Mike blinked his eyes to discount the obvious, he could not deny the fact that he was looking at a black angel—with wings.

CHAPTER 28

Maison Plaisir, New Orleans

~

A FAMILIAR FEELING of breathlessness had been creeping up in increments all day, threatening to take hold of Simeon of the House of Ramuel. By the time he'd met up with his brothers later that evening his initial discomfort had escalated to heart palpitations and an uncomfortable tightness in his chest. The uncomfortable feelings escalated after Ajuma and Nicodemus departed *Maison Plaisir*. Simeon was sweating like a pig and having difficulty breathing. It felt like the walls were closing in on him, and the ceiling was dropping to meet the floor.

Sometimes sounds on the wrong side of the Dark Veil were just a little bit too loud, and the sights and smells a little too rich for his ultra-sensitive preternatural senses. Simeon needed to step away to find some sense of balance, lest he become unglued.

It wouldn't be the first time he checked out without notice. Rephidim, Gilead, and Antioch probably thought he was being rude when he ghosted out of the smoke-filled room to find a serene retreat away from the raucous banter of his brothers in the manicured courtyard of *Maison Plaisir*. Still, he knew he had to get out of there, or suffocate. *I have to get myself together. I can't afford to lose control.*

Tonight he would need all of his faculties about him. His soldiers and his brothers were depending upon him. *If only I could shake the feeling that something fucked up is going to happen.*

Simeon was a loner. He kept his suspicions to himself. In an effort to calm his racing heart, he took deep, slow breaths of the cool night air, clutching the back of an iron bistro chair with all his might.

The courtyard wherein he stood was elabourately designed and heavily scented with the creator's own perfumery of a densely planted variety of flora and fauna. Thankful that he was alone, he stilled his mind to allow the beauty surrounding him to seep in. These episodes of anxiety were becoming more and more frequent of late. It was a battle to get control. He managed to do so—again—but each time it grew more and more difficult.

When Simeon was sufficiently calm, he struck a flint, illuminating the sharp plains of his chiselled features, and placing the upper portion of his black clad figure in sharp relief. Moments later the sweet fragrance of his cheroot perfumed the night air.

He inhaled deeply, filling his lungs, and releasing the smoke through his sensuous mouth and noble nose. He looked back toward the well-lit house. His eyes mere slits against the smoke. Though the hour was late, the sound of revelry could still be heard.

He was a handsome male, tall and lean, with rock-hard rippling muscles, smooth dark skin, and piercing eyes that were so dark they appeared almost black. A potent air of sensuality surrounded him. Yet he hadn't been with a female in over 100 years, and he didn't anticipate his situation would change in an equal amount of time.

Simeon knew that he needed to get his head straight so that he could go back into a place where he had once been held prisoner—a place where he had been profoundly scarred both emotionally and physically and had nearly lost his life. He tossed the half-finished cheroot away, thinking he'd step through the portals of hell a million times if there was even a slim chance he could find out what happened to young Ephraim. Unlike his brothers who saw it as a challenge each time they entered the hells and lived to see another night, it was never easy for him.

Simeon still couldn't get the image of Ephraim's sister out of his mind. The sight of that beautiful young girl's tear-stained face continued to haunt him. She held herself responsible for what happened to her brother.

Simeon was no stranger to how it felt to lose a loved one, to betray your own blood and suffer the guilt from that betrayal every day of your life. Young Sara lost her brother, and Simeon lost his sister. In that respect they were kindred spirits.

When Watcher Angel Shemyaza turned down Zuet's offer to join forces against Attiq Yomin's warrior angels, Zuet swore to capture and destroy every single Nephilim that walked the earth. Shemyaza's sons, Zion and Shiloh, secreted the Nephilim away just before they were captured along with Nicodemus, Antioch, Rephidim, Boaz, Gilead, and Simeon. Zuet was determined to ascertain the location of the members of the Nephilim Nation. For 200 years each of them was subjected to the worse form of torture, but nobody broke.

Then one day Zuet's son, Travail, came to the cell in the lowest level of the seven hells where Simeon was being kept. He had captured Simeon's sister. When Simeon saw the fear in her eyes he broke, begging and pleading for Travail not to hurt her. He remembered debasing himself, crawling on the filthy dirt floor covered with vermin and faeces, promising anything—everything—if Travail would just let her go.

He told Travail where he thought the Nephilim were hidden, and they tortured and killed his sister anyway—right in front of him. Fortunately, Zion had the foresight to realise that any one of them could break under the right combination of torture. He had not shared the *real* location of the Nephilim with anyone but his younger brother Shiloh. So, nothing was lost but Simeon's dignity, his self-respect, and his precious sister's life.

Simeon acknowledged his motives for wanting to bring Ephraim's killer or killers to justice were less than noble. Maybe he saw this quest as a means of redemption. Or, maybe it represented something more. *What I wouldn't do to be able to erase the pain in Ephraim's sister's beautiful eyes when I tell her that I personally destroyed her brother's killers.* Maybe, just maybe, he could make her see him as something other than the soulless savage demon killer he had become. Maybe…

Who was he fooling? Thousands of years of repressed shame and rage threatened to explode inside of him with every breath he took. Even if he rubbed his skin off to the bone, he'd still have the taste of death and torture on his tongue and the smell of the seven hells polluting his soul. He'd never be clean enough for any female.

Simeon was just about to light another cheroot when a branch snapped nearby. His body went on instant alert. A familiar and decidedly unpleasant odour wafted into the courtyard on a grey cloud. Seconds later a shadow darted past the back door, then another. He stepped behind a large topiary to conceal his presence. The demons were coming in droves. They came up from the earth and misted one by one into the stately mansion where his brothers were screwing their brains out, unaware of the pending danger.

He knew something fucked up was going to happen. They'd been set up by that goddamn warlock! Had Simeon not been outside, it would have been a full-scale ambush. He sent a mental message to Antioch, Gilead, and Rephidim.

"Put your cocks in your pants, boys. We've got uninvited company," he said before ghosting back inside the house.

It was killing time.

A Portal in the Atchafalaya
Swamp Outside of Magnolia Hill

When Ajuma finally arrived, Nicodemus was pacing in the clearing with an angry look on his face. Timing was everything. They were going into the hells where Zuet, the sworn enemy to the Nephilim, ruled. Anything could happen. Yet Ajuma arrived thirty minutes late, leaving him and

Boaz with their respective squads, cooling their heels in the mosquito-infested swamp. Nico lit into Ajuma as soon as he saw him.

"Where in the fuck have you been, Ajuma? We were getting ready to leave without you!"

It was rare that the ever affable Nicodemus became angry and rarer still when he unleashed that anger on one of his beloved brothers. This time he was royally pissed off, and with good cause. Nicodemus' anger was mixed with a healthy dose of fear. He had no way of knowing whether or not Ajuma had encountered demons or met with some other disastrous fate on his way to or from Magnolia Hill. He'd been beside himself with worry. That worry served to stoke the fires of his anger.

Ajuma's night had been fucked up since he left the city. He didn't need this. He felt his temper rise, although the only evidence of his mounting irritation were the muscle that was pulsing like a runaway heartbeat in his jaw and his frightening green eyes which were now narrowed to the size of slits. Ajuma's palms were itching. He wanted to shut Nico up with a fist to the mouth—knock out a few of those pretty white teeth he was so damn proud of. Instead, he clamped his fists at his side. He was still reeling with bloodlust from killing that piece of shit overseer. He forced himself to calm down. He would not strike out at Nico for speaking the truth.

Nico was standing in Ajuma's personal space with a look of disappointment on his face. "Bo and I have been trying to mind-meld with you for the past half hour, and all we've gotten is a blank wall of silence. That is all kinds of fucked up, man, and you know it," he added, accusatorily.

Boaz was leaning in a negligent fashion with one foot against a tree and a twig clamped between his teeth. He had yet to say a word in censure to Ajuma, but his expression spoke volumes. There was no doubt in Ajuma's mind that Bo was just as upset as Nico. If Ajuma didn't hear what Bo thought about his tardiness tonight, he would no doubt hear it later.

In the past, Ajuma's mind had been an open book to his brothers, as were theirs to him. They shared one another's thoughts through a special form of telepathy they called mind-melding, which enabled them to communicate with one another and work in concert as an indestructible fighting unit.

Ajuma had blocked his mind to Nico and the rest of his brothers while he was with Flossie. He knew he'd fucked up. He just wished Nico would let it go so that they could get on with the mission. Nico wasn't done yet. It seemed he intended to get everything off his chest.

"How could you leave us waiting here with a bunch of green-behind-the-ears recruits while you greased your knob inside your human, Ajuma?" Nico asked, shaking his head in frustration. He could not fathom what his otherwise reliable brother saw in that human—what he saw in any human, for that matter. Other than a quick fuck and occasional source of life-sustaining elixir, Nico had no use for them.

The kettle that was containing Ajuma's anger had come to a boil, and the lid was about to blow off. "That human you speak of with so little respect is my wife, Nicodemus, in every sense of the word." His sharp tone silenced Nicodemus as effectively as a muzzle over his mouth.

"Her name is Flossie." Ajuma's eyes raked Nicodemus from head to toe with disdain. "I know someone like *you* will never be able to understand what I feel for her. You have never felt that way about any female. You are far too busy sticking your cock inside every available hole without regard to the pain you leave behind to know what love is."

Nicodemus flinched at the cruelty and accuracy of Ajuma's words.

Ajuma's next words were spoken with soft precision. "Hear me and hear me clearly, Nic-o-fucking-demus. I will not stand by while you or anyone else maligns my woman!"

This time Ajuma didn't even try to hide his anger. His chest heaved and his nostrils flared. His bright green eyes were ablaze with emotion. He had yet to experience a leave-taking as heart-wrenching and difficult as his departure from Flossie and his son had been. He fully intended to provide Flossie and his children with the protection afforded behind the Dark Veil. Like it or not, his brothers were just going to have to get used to the idea.

He took comfort in knowing that soon they would be with him permanently. Now was as good a time as ever to let his brothers know that he would demand they afford his woman and his children the same respect they gave him. He would start with Nico and Boaz.

He'd said his piece, then stood quietly and defiantly before Nicodemus, Boaz, and the curious eyes of the Gibborim soldiers who had been taking in the heated exchange. It was then that Ajuma realised that the only squads present were his, Nico's, and Boaz's.

"Nico, you are so full of shit that it's coming out your goddamned mouth," Ajuma said with rancour. "I see the rest of the squads aren't here. Yet, you jump down my throat like I have committed a cardinal crime for getting here late. Tell me. Do you hate the fact that I am in love with a human that much, brother?"

Nico couldn't believe this shit was happening. He'd fought side by side with Ajuma since the days the Prophet Enoch walked amongst men. Shit. *We've been to the hells and back.* Never would he believe this brother would fall victim to the same weakness of their fathers to love a human—a human slave, at that.

The Brothers of the Dark Veil had a cardinal rule. Take your pleasure when and where you can, but never allow yourself to become involved emotionally. It was obvious that Ajuma's association with the human was having a dilatory effect on his work and wreaking havoc with his mind.

Nico wanted to strike out at Ajuma, but he caught himself. Obviously, love makes you speak and act foolishly. He realised he was not serving the greater good by verbally lambasting him. Just as quickly as it rose, Nico's anger faded away.

"Please don't be cross with me, Ajuma," Nico said in a more repentant tone. "All I am trying to say is that you've been shutting us out ever since you met *her*. You've lost your focus, man. We were trying to mindmeld with you earlier to let you know that we had been set up. Antioch, Gil, Sim, and Reph are currently stuck at *Maison Plaisir*, battling a horde of demons. They were ambushed. There was no way they could hide the fight from the humans. They will have to erase the memories of every single human at *Maison Plaisir*. There is no way they will be able to get here in time. So, Ajuma, it looks like it's going to be just us.

CHAPTER 29

⁓

AJUMA LOWERED HIS head in shame. Nico's revelation made him feel like shit. Nico was right. He had lost his focus, but that didn't take away from the fact that he loved Flossie and his son. He would be better able to dispatch his duties once he knew his family was safe on the other side of the Dark Veil.

Nico placed his hand on Ajuma's shoulder. "Listen. When we have more time, we will sit down and speak of this. I admit it will be difficult for me, but I will try to have an open mind about you and your human—excuse me, your Flossie."

Ajuma nodded in agreement.

Now that Nico's tirade was finally spent, Ajuma looked over with a question in his eyes to where Boaz stood quietly. "You got anything you want to add, Brother Bo?"

Boaz spit out the twig he was chewing and pushed away from the tree to approach them. He'd predicted from the start that Ajuma's association with the human would create problems for all around. It looked like his prediction had been right on point. Since Nico had already said everything he was thinking, Boaz looked Ajuma in the eye and replied, "Nope." He and Ajuma would have a sit down, "come to Jesus" talk when they returned from their mission, but now was not the time nor the place for such a discussion. If they didn't pull out soon, the small window they had left to meet Devius would be lost.

Ajuma used the moment of uncomfortable silence to relay his encounter with the slave patrollers on River Road and his murder of the overseer who had beaten Flossie. He refused to apologise to Nicodemus or Boaz for his tardiness or his actions. Given the circumstances, they didn't expect him to.

"Listen, we'll have to work out our differences later. Right now we have a mission to complete," Boaz said with quiet determination.

Ajuma, Nico, and Boaz veiled their horses in preparation to leave. All business now, Ajuma turned to Nico and Boaz. "Who else knew we were going to meet at *Maison Plaisir*?"

"Monique Dubonnet, of course, and the warlock," Boaz replied.

"We can rule Monique out," Nico said with assurance. "She has no way of knowing who and what the Nephilim are. Rephidim made sure of that before he approached her."

"Well, brothers, that only leaves the warlock." Ajuma took a quick visual inventory of his squad. "He knew exactly what he was dealing with when Antioch approached him to set up the meeting."

"Alright, let's just say the warlock double-crossed us," Boaz said. "Who's to say the whole mission isn't compromised? Dare we proceed? This may be a major ass-fuck."

Nico was quick to agree. "I don't know, man. The little hairs on the back of my neck aren't just standing on end. Those motherfuckers are dancing."

Ajuma looked in the direction of the Gibborim squads that were anxiously awaiting their orders. "Truth be told, I'd feel a hell of a lot better if we had seasoned soldiers on this one." More than two-thirds of the squads would be going to the hells for the first time. Ajuma pinned Nico and Boaz with a piercing green-eyed gaze. "But we're not going to accomplish anything if we stand here with our thumbs up our asses. I say we roll."

In silent agreement, they collectively ghosted to the nearby portal and made their descent into the hells.

BEHIND THE DARK VEIL

꩜ ꩜

The Valley of the Shadow of Death
Third Level of the Hells

A frown marred Emanuel's handsome face, and fear filled his eyes. They were in the Valley of the Shadow of Death. In spite of what the biblical text revealed about this desolate place, Emanuel was more afraid than he'd ever been before. He had more than a rod and staff for protection, yet he was not comforted. He'd had no clue what he was getting into when he signed on for his first foray in the hells, and now there was no turning back.

Emanuel, Jihad, and their friend Kai all served under General Akibeel. They had been in training camp together, and during that time became fast friends. When an opportunity arose for them to go on a mission with the Brothers of the Dark Veil, each of them jumped at the chance to serve.

All three had volunteered for this mission for personal reasons, but only Emanuel and Jihad had been chosen. They were extremely disappointed their friend Kai would not be able to embark on this experience with them. Maybe he would be chosen for the next mission.

Emanuel volunteered because he had a lovely wife to support and a baby on the way. Jihad volunteered because he wanted to marry Dreama of the House of Shemyaza. Kai volunteered because he wanted to move up in rank and enjoy the higher pay grade that would accompany the promotion that would ultimately result from the successful completion of the mission.

Right about now Emanuel was wondering who had gotten the better end of the deal, he and Jihad or Kai, because nothing could have prepared him for the sights, sounds, and smells he was experiencing. *Nothing.*

The combined squads were progressing single file, with General Akibeel leading the front, General Urakabarameel holding the centre, and General Danel taking up the rear. Emanuel was the last soldier in the line-up, right in front of General Danel and behind his friend Jihad. Emanuel had a hard brick of fear in his belly that was literally making him sick to his stomach.

Emanuel picked up his pace to catch up to Jihad. His legs were shaking so badly, he feared he would trip and fall and maybe get snatched up by some demonic monstrosity with razor-sharp claws and vicious teeth. He didn't want to get separated from the rest of his regiment. In a whisper he prayed none of the other soldiers would hear, he made what he considered to be a shameful admission. *Maybe I made a grave mistake coming on this mission. Nothing is as I thought it would be.*

Growls, yelps, and screams rent the air, battling with other malevolent sounds as the weak were run down, viciously torn apart and devoured by stronger beings only to somehow rematerialize so that they could suffer all over again. It was maddening. Sweat ran down Emanuel's face to pool under his collar as they silently marched on.

The valley pulsated with bestial sounds of a salacious nature. Wet, slavering sounds that made Emanuel's face grow hot with embarrassment. These sounds were the very heartbeat—the pulse—of the third level of hell known as *Beer Shahat.*

The leaves on the few trees they passed, and the blades of grass upon which they trod, were an unnatural greyish-black hue. The grass crunched like brittle straw beneath their booted feet. Small creatures of the night decided they would make an appearance, their beady little eyes following the Nephilim with curiosity. Each wore unnatural cloaks of darkness and had nightmarishly distorted appearances.

Suddenly the landscape changed. They were no longer traversing the terrain by foot. Following the lead of their superiors, they now floated an inch above the ground. The low-lying area over which the troops floated contained a sediment-filled basin, dotted with what appeared to be small patches of land. On every patch of land, there was some form of monstrous apparition with hideously deformed features and out-stretched arms. Fork-tongued sentinels with male and female genitalia entreated them in seductive tones, requesting that they come just a little closer. Each one fervently assured them they would do no harm and would make the soldiers feel real good.

"My, my, my, what a pretty boy you are," said one of the monsters to Emanuel. "Come to me, my little half-breed angel. I will give you pleasure beyond your wildest dreams. Let me debauch your body and your soul."

"Come, my children," shouted yet another whilst holding his heavy genitals. It had huge ponderous breasts with bloody nipples. It licked its lips in a lascivious fashion as the soldiers hurriedly passed by. Repulsed, Emanuel turned to spit in their direction.

Ajuma stopped him just in time. "Do not acknowledge them, Manny. These creatures are damned until the end of time. They are cursed to exist on their small patch of land, without food, water, or human contact."

Emanuel looked puzzled. "But can they not merely swim to the nearest shore?"

"No, they cannot," Ajuma replied, breaking off a branch from one of the nearby trees. When he threw the branch in the water, it sizzled and completely disintegrated within seconds. What Emanuel had presumed was water was actually some type of hellish acid. He marked his movements more carefully from then on.

Emanuel's eyes were as huge as a frightened child. He watched in amazement as a vulture-like being with extremely hairy human legs swooped down the side of the valley wall. The long arm of one of the island monsters stretched out to capture the airborne creature and, with superhuman strength, drew the beast toward it.

Emanuel looked on in fascination as the half vulture/half human was ripped to pieces and devoured. Pieces of its flesh landed in the acid water, sizzling upon impact. The flesh disintegrated, obliterating every trace of the winged beast.

Emanuel shuddered. That could very well have been him suffering the same fate. He decided right then and there not to allow Generals

Urakabarameel, Danel, or Akibeel out of his sight. He intended to stick to his superiors like glue.

Emanuel relaxed a bit when they left the Valley of the Shadow of Death behind them. It felt like the whole squad expended a collective sigh of relief. He hoped the danger was behind them as well. Emanuel waited until General Danel went up front to speak with General Akibeel.

"Jihad," he whispered, "I don't know about you, but this place gives me the fucking creeps. I cannot explain it, but I feel like something with big ice-covered feet just walked over my grave."

Jihad nodded his agreement without turning his head. Even though they hadn't seen a single soul for the past few miles, he too felt like he was being watched.

"Good, I'm not crazy," Emanuel thought, just before another chill went down his spine.

Ajuma's attention was drawn to the rear when he heard the whispering. "You soldiers okay back there?"

At first Ajuma was hesitant to bring rookies with them on this mission, but they had to get their feet wet sometime, and there was no time like the present. He fell back to check on the soldiers bringing up the rear.

"To be honest with you, General Akibeel, Private Jihad and I were just commenting on the fact that although we haven't seen a soul other than those demonic monstrosities back in the Valley of the Shadow of Death, we feel there are eyes boring into the back of our heads. With all due respect, sir, they don't feel friendly." Emanuel couldn't keep his voice from shaking. "Are there no others in this vast wasteland but us and the monsters, General Akibeel?"

As if on cue, Emanuel heard the plaintive cry of a lone vulture and the response of other predators of the night. A wintry chill raced down his spine. They were surrounded by darkness so profound that even with their acute preternatural vision it was difficult to penetrate.

Ajuma was impressed with Emanuel's sense of perception. "You are right, Private. We are not alone. There is a hierarchy in the land of the damned. Even now we are being watched and our powers measured.

You must be ever vigilant. Trust no one and never let your guard down. Those who watch may know we are here, but we will not let them know our purpose."

The tortured moans and cries of the wicked ricocheted off massive boulders surrounding the blackened earth. The boulders formed walls that went higher than the eye could see, totally blocking out the sky, and rendering this place utterly devoid of light, hope, and any vestige of goodness.

"Gentlemales, welcome to hell," Ajuma stated dramatically, before he returned to the front of the line.

When Jihad told Dreama he'd volunteered to go on a mission in the hells, Dreama told him about her conversation with that crazy old bat who ran around King Zion's Baton Rouge plantation, prophesying gloom and doom. She begged him not to go.

Jihad had scoffed at her concerns, telling her that the old female was off her gourd and that she shouldn't lend any credence to anything that came out of the mentally defective female's mouth. He remembered puffing up his chest and boasting, "I'll walk through the fiery gates of hell for you, baby." *What a joke*, he thought.

Now was the time to seriously rethink his previous proclamations of bravery. At the moment, he was worse than a frightened child hiding from the bogeyman under his bed covers. *If I am so damn brave, then why in the hell are my knees about to buckle and my teeth chattering loud enough to wake the dead?*

When Jihad signed on for this mission, it was with the assumption that each of the seven generals would lead a contingency of twelve to fifteen men into the hells. Instead, the other generals were stuck in New Orleans battling demons, leaving only three squads, thirty-six Gibborim soldiers in total, to complete the mission at hand.

There is relative safety in numbers. Jihad was feeling none too safe at the moment. The only thing that kept him from crying like a baby and turning tail to run was the picture in his mind of his sweet Dreama. If he wanted to distinguish himself and rise in the ranks so that he and Dreama could afford to get married, he would have to "man up" and make it through this mission and every mission that followed.

CHAPTER 30

⁓

GENERAL URAKABARAMEEL GAVE the neophytes a sorely needed pep talk before they stepped through one of the gateways leading into the hells. His exact words were, "Only a goddamn fool would walk through the hells without fear. Being fearful doesn't make you a coward. It makes you aware of your surroundings, and it makes you smart. So, don't try to be no damn hero. The true definition of courage is when you can proceed in the face of your fear." He ended his gruff pep talk by adding, "Keep your eyes and ears sharp and you might just get out of here alive."

Well, that was the understatement of the fucking year, if ever there was one, Jihad thought. He was so scared he couldn't think straight.

They had made it through the Valley of the Shadow of Death and were now walking single file down a dark funky labyrinth leading to *Beer Shahat,* the third level of hell. The tunnel would lead them directly into the entrance of a popular bar called The Nasty Secret, which was frequented by low-level demons. Jihad took some small comfort in the knowledge that his friend Manny had his back, and behind Manny was that bad-ass Brother of the Dark Veil, General Boaz Danel.

Each soldier was strapped head to toe with weaponry. They also wore masks covering the lower portions of their faces to keep the thick murky air in the tunnel from getting inside their mouths. The smell in the tunnel was worse than an overflowing outhouse in hundred-degree weather. The masks also served the purpose of filtering out some of the nauseating stench.

The tunnel seemed to go on for miles, winding, curving, and veering off in myriad directions like an underground maze. Its interior was so dark Jihad could barely see the back of the soldier right in front of him. He nearly collided into the poor bastard, running up on his heels, so anxious was he to not become separated from his squad.

The mind plays funny tricks on you when you can't see what's up ahead. Your imagination can run wild, and sometimes you think you see or hear things that aren't really there. Other than the sound of their collective heavy breathing, there was complete silence—at first. Then Jihad thought he heard something. It was a wet crunching sound that could only have been made by a set of monstrous jaws and sharp lethal teeth. It sounded like something was greedily tearing into flesh, muscle, and bone with its mouth open. The sound made Jihad sick to his stomach. All he wanted was to get this bit of nasty business over with so that he could get back to his baby Dreama.

Jihad was no man's coward, but at the moment he was scared shitless and didn't care who knew it. Fear had a hold on him so tight that he worried he would lose the contents of his bowels.

Now wouldn't that be something to bandy about in the barracks? he thought. *I'll feel much better once we put this tunnel behind us. Just a little ways to go,* he kept telling himself. *Once General Akibeel is able to rendezvous with the spy he was charged to meet, we can get the hell out of here. No pun intended.*

Jihad strained his superhuman eyes to see up ahead. His heart started to race. *Was that a bit of light ahead, and did I hear music? All praises to The Ancient of Days!*

The soldiers ahead of him picked up their pace, following General Akibeel through what appeared to be a set of batwing doors. Ready for any and everything, Jihad took a deep breath when it was his turn to enter through the swinging doors. It took him a moment to adjust his vision to the dim lighting. When he finally did enter the bar, he surveyed his surroundings in a glance, his previous trepidation slipping away like a lost memory.

Why, Jihad thought, *it's just any ordinary run-of-the-mill bar—larger and more raucous than most, but a bar all the same.* Were it not located in hell, it could easily be taken for any number of drinking establishments in New Orleans or Baton Rouge.

⁂

For a moment all conversation stopped as the bar patrons sized up the new arrivals. The squad of Nephilim scanned the bar like western desperados with a challenge in their eyes and their lethal-looking weapons visible for all to see. This was showdown time. If something was going to happen, they would be ready for it.

There was a collective sigh of relief once the generals gave the go-ahead for the men to fan out through the bar. Music, conversation, and laughter amongst the patrons resumed.

Ajuma did a thorough scan of the bar to ensure there was no threat. Finding none, he approached one of the bartenders. "Barkeep, I'll have drinks for all my males. Now!" he demanded in perfect Dimoori Sheol. In a much lower voice he said, "I am here to meet with someone. I was instructed to inquire as to his whereabouts at the bar upon my arrival."

The demon, Devius, was Antioch's informant, but Ajuma saw no reason to disclose that information to the bartender.

The bartender nodded toward a closed door off to the right of the bar. "Go through the door on my left and proceed down the hall. The one you seek is behind the third door on your right."

Ajuma gave Nico and Boaz a prearranged signal, thanked the bartender, and hastily headed through the door.

After Ajuma left to meet with Devius, Nico told the men to have a good time, but to remain vigilant. They spread out through the bar, each finding their own form of diversion.

Emanuel made his way over to Jihad. "I don't know about you, Jihad, but after that trek through that shitty smelling tunnel, what I need about now is a good stiff drink and a hot bath. I think I'll take the general up on his offer."

Jihad could not have agreed more. When he got a chance he fully intended to find out whether or not Manny heard some of the weird things he'd heard while in the tunnel. The two friends headed toward the bar.

The long-panelled bar took up most of the space, its rich mahogany polished to a splendid shine. In fact, it was so clean Jihad could see his face on its surface. Around the base of the bar was a gleaming brass foot rail. A row of evenly spaced spittoons were positioned on the floor right next to the bar, and several pristine white towels hung from the bar ledge for patrons to wipe beer suds from their moustaches or the sweat from their brows.

A massive stone fireplace took up an entire wall. Inside the fireplace was a huge boar, slow roasting on a spit. The grease from the beast's succulent skin sizzled and popped, dripping into the fire beneath it. Jihad's mouth watered at the delicious smell.

The bar was crowded. Three handsome bartenders were serving several patrons, mostly men, lining the bar. Jihad placed his and Manny's order. "Two whiskies, neat," he said before turning around to survey the occupants of the bar.

Jihad counted about ten tables with chairs in the common area, all of which were occupied by either females or couples. Pretty barmaids in skin-tight, low-necked dresses and frilly white lace-edged aprons balanced trays laden with steaming hot food and drink for the patrons at the tables and in the gaming area.

Hanging directly behind the bar in a place of prominence was a nude painting of a beautiful redheaded woman. The portrait was flanked on each side by taxidermy heads of a bear and a moose with large flat palmate antlers intact. The woman who'd modelled for the painting was at that very moment entertaining the patrons with a sassy little ditty about a husband finding another man's shoes under his wife's bed. She was accompanied by a little man with thick black-rimmed spectacles wearing a long-sleeved white shirt with a black wrist band, black trousers, and a little black coachman's cap. The little man exhibited skillful artistry as his deft fingers fairly flew across the keys of the tinny sounding piano.

Drinks in hand, Jihad and Manny wandered over to the gaming area to observe one high stake game of chance after another. There was faro, poker, three-card monte, brag, and dice. Jihad noticed a lot of money exchanging hands. In another section of the bar, several men and a few women were playing billiards. In yet another section, a lively game of darts was taking place. Everyone appeared to be having a good time. Jihad and Emanuel relaxed.

It wasn't long before the Gibborim soldiers were approached and propositioned by several of the single females and a few of the men. Already, some of the soldiers were in dark corners whispering seductive promises in the ears of the women or entwined in the arms of other women on the dance floor. Jihad couldn't help but notice General Urakabarameel, a renowned womaniser, seated on a bar stool with a long-legged beauty precariously perched on his lap. Except for Jihad and Emanuel, most of the members of the squads were similarly engaged. Both handsome young soldiers were spoken for and content to watch.

Emanuel married his lady Angela over six months ago. Their first child was due sometime in the spring. He had no desire to betray his lady's trust. The only problem was that Manny was an exceptionally handsome Neph, which made him a veritable magnet to the ladies. Tonight was no different.

It was when Manny was trying to discourage the amorous intentions of yet another female patron in the bar that Jihad noticed the same foul smell they'd encountered in the tunnel. This time the smell was worse— closer and far more concentrated.

CHAPTER 31

⌒

*J*IHAD HEARD A tearing sound. The sound emanated from the ceiling and was slowly travelling toward floor level, like dry rotted wallpaper being peeled from a wall. The veil of existence within the confines of The Nasty Secret was slowly being lowered, revealing the true nature of each and every occupant within the bar. The Nephilim were now exposed to things as they truly were and not as they had appeared.

Jihad spun around in confusion. Everywhere he looked was an abomination. The surface of the pristine bar was now covered with cuts, nicks and filth. The bar was manned by three monstrous looking bartenders. A cryptid, a hairy beast, and a foul-mouthed shapeshifter replaced the handsome humans who previously tended the bar. They were frantically filling orders for drinks that put the fire in "firewater." The drinks were actually blazing. Jihad immediately dropped the glass of whiskey he held as it took flame, threatening to burn his hand off.

A coterie of devils, demons, imps, and rebellious angels now stood at the crowded bar, drinking the fiery beverages proffered and pissing where they stood. The barroom floor was a stinking mess of puddles of piss and excrement, which the evil beings cavorted upon without a care.

The pretty redheaded songstress was a wrinkled slack-jawed witch who was now performing aberrant sex acts on a raised dais while an orchestra of naked priests (save for their clerical collars) played a discordant cacophony of chamber music in sync with the wicked witch's salacious grunts and moans. Standing behind the performers were two twelve foot tall angels of punishment garbed in tattered loin cloths. They were flaying the skin from the backs of a group of young nubile succubae with fiery barb-studded whips.

The wages placed on the heated games of faro, poker, three-card monte, brag, and dice were not for money as Jihad had previously thought, but for body parts. There was a raucous game of billiards underway between the demon Cagrino, better known as Chagrin, and the demon called Malphas. Cagrino had the appearance of a yellow hedgehog and Malphas, a president in hell and commander of forty legions of demons, had the face of a crow and the body of a man.

Instead of billiard balls, the evil demons' cues struck the bloody eyeballs purloined from demons unfortunate enough to have lost their wagers against them. Everywhere Jihad looked there was complete and utter madness.

Quite a few of the big guys were slumming that night. Abaddon, commander of the Sixth House of Hell and ruler of the Abyss, was in the far corner of the bar playing a game of darts. Instead of using the customary circular dart target, the hideous demon, whose body was that of a warhorse and whose face was that of a human, aimed the steel-tipped darts at an angry demon he'd shackled to the wall.

The demon's face was covered in bloody puncture wounds and riddled with steel-tipped darts. Each time Abaddon's dart hit its mark, his poisonous scorpion's tail spun like a wagon wheel and he chortled with glee.

Jihad caught the scream in his throat before it exited. What he had previously been led to believe was a wild boar was actually a man, impaled anus to mouth upon a ten foot pole, slow roasting in the heart of the hearth. The smell of burnt human flesh was pervasive. He had no time to become ill. A second later the Nephilim were under attack.

⁕ ⁕

The barkeep directed Ajuma to a room that led down a dim hallway. It was partially lit with wall sconces made of human skulls. Ajuma knocked on the third door on the right. When he received no answer, he turned the knob and entered. The slow, steady plop of something dripping and the metallic smell of blood drew his eyes upward. Hanging from a wooden beam in the ceiling by a thin wire that had nearly sliced through his neck was none other than his informant, Devius. Ajuma turned abruptly to exit the room and slammed into the chest of the biggest demon he'd seen in at least 500 years.

Well, what do you know. They'd been set up again.

Jihad and the other soldiers were already fighting for their lives when Ajuma sent out a mental alert.

"Get the hell out of there. We've been set up. The lifeless body of my informant is hanging from the rafters in a room behind the bar, and I am engaged in a battle with the biggest motherfucker I've seen in centuries. Leave at once!"

The bar became the scene of a vicious melee, with sharp-clawed, fire-breathing demons bearing down on well-trained Nephilim armed with swords, axes, daggers, clubs, and pole arms with spikes and hammers. Under Nicodemus' command, every member of the Nephilim team drew their weapons, prepared to battle their way out of the nest of demons.

Nicodemus resembled an avenging angel as he separated heads from the bodies of one demon after the other with his mighty sword. Black demon blood ran from the tip of his flame-bladed great sword as he advanced to his next victim, slicing the demon from shoulder to groyne before he could even raise his clawed hand to defend himself. Everything went to shit real fast when Gaap, a mighty prince, high president in the hells and commander of sixty-six legions of demons, walked in with his entourage, blocking the Nephilim exit and stripping away the remainder of the Dark Veil behind which the roomful of demons had previously hidden.

Jihad thought he would lose his mind as one horror after another materialised before his eyes. He snapped out of his shock soon enough. One of the demons twisted Manny's head clean off as he stood right next to him. Hot blood spattered on Jihad's face and chest. Emanuel's headless body did a macabre little jig before it finally dropped to the floor. Jihad stepped over his dead friend's body without a backward glance. He would have to mourn him later. It was time to fight or die.

The piano player gracefully pushed away from his instrument to take the arm of the old crone as the battle between the demons and Nephilim raged around them in a well-orchestrated dance. Together, the unlikely pair stepped from the dais with their eyes focused squarely upon the thick gold chain Jihad wore about his neck, a long-ago gift from his angelic father and a source of protection.

The crone was nude from the waist up. Her flat wrinkled breasts hung to her waist like empty cow udders, swinging with every step she took. Around her scrawny neck was a grimy chamois sack. Within the sack were pieces of bones, graveyard dirt, shells, and other items so foul their damp, decaying odour seeped through the sack, polluting the air around her. Her consort and erstwhile piano player was none other than Mammon, the wolf-faced demon of riches and avarice. The demons made their way through the fighting to Jihad.

"Give me that bauble around your neck, boy, and I might just let you live," Mammon whispered in a gravelly voice. His mouth was full of huge sharp teeth. He made a nasty wet sound as he licked his hairy lips in a rapacious manner.

Not to be undone, the crone grasped one of her flat wrinkled breasts in her hands—hands with razor-sharp curled fingernails. Keeping her eyes upon Jihad in a seductive manner, she lifted the deflated sack to her mouth and flicked her long, black forked tongue across the grey hairy nipple.

"Give him that bauble around your neck, my young green lad, and I just might let you die—*easy*," she commanded.

Jihad shivered with revulsion. He fought the urge to scratch himself when he saw cockroaches crawling out of the crone's nostrils, ears, and beneath the hem of her tattered filthy skirt. Instead, he raised his sword and issued a challenge of his own.

BEHIND THE DARK VEIL

"How 'bout I keep the bauble around my neck and give you two abominations a taste of this cold hard steel instead?" came Jihad's fearless reply.

The old crone was clapping her hands like an excited child when, out of nowhere, a huge sword materialised in Mammon's hand. The demon advanced on Jihad with lethal intent. Jihad's only warning that he was about to strike was the hissing sound that came mere seconds before Mammon dealt his first blow.

Jihad felt the air on the side of his face stir as Mammon's blade cut through the air, barely missing his shoulder. Mammon put driving force behind the strike. The near miss put him slightly off balance.

Jihad took advantage of the misstep to parry and thrust, drawing first blood. He opened up a thin cut across the demon's chest. Black tar-like blood oozed through the rent shirt. For the next ten minutes the sound of metal upon metal, the crone's gleeful laughter, and heavy breathing filled Jihad's head.

Jihad was well trained. He and the demon were evenly matched, both moving back and forth jockeying for position and looking for an opening in which to strike. The now enraged demon viciously swung his sword, forcing Jihad back into a table. Jihad nearly slipped and fell in a puddle of filth on the floor. He righted himself just in time to avoid yet another thrust to his face. This time the demon's sword came down so hard that it shattered the table behind him, breaking it in two.

Mammon was wearing Jihad down with the ferocity of his attack. In the background the crone yelled, "Shank him. Shove that sword up his ass. I want to see it come out of his mouth! Kill him. Kill him. Kill him," she chanted.

The demon seemed to grow stronger by her words while Jihad's strength was starting to wane. His hands were sopping wet with sweat. With each blow of the demon's sword against his, he found it more and more difficult to hold on to the handle. He blinked repeatedly as sweat ran down his face, burning his eyes. It took everything he had to defend himself against the demonic blows Mammon was virtually raining down upon him.

Mammon had the advantage, but instead of delivering the killing blow, his wolf face took on a parody of a smile as he methodically delivered slices across Jihad's chest and arms, severely weakening him from loss of blood. The crone's comments seemed to drift to Jihad from a great distance.

"Slice him up. Shove a pole up his ass and roast him on the spit. Nothing tastes better than roasted Neph on a spit," she chortled.

Jihad was just about finished. His sweat-stained clothing clung to his body. His legs were quivering and his muscles so weak he could barely lift his sword. Just then, he saw an opening. He mustered the strength from somewhere to plunge his sword to the hilt into Mammon's belly. The look of surprise on the demon's face was worth every wound Jihad received.

Jihad staggered, barely able to remain on his feet, as the demon vanished in a puff of greyish-black smoke. Before Jihad could right himself, a huge demonic eagle swooped down from the rafters to snatch the weak warrior up with its talons, bursting through the ceiling with its prize.

CHAPTER 32

Grato Quies, Baton Rouge

~

REAMA HUNG HALF on and half off her bed, her eyes filled with tears, as bitter bile splashed in the bucket she kept at the side of her bed. She was perilously close to falling out of the bed, as weak as a kitten, by the time she was done throwing up.

She had emptied her stomach numerous times during the day, and was far too weak to make it to the chamber pot to toss her accounts. Her parents may have tried to keep her innocent about many things concerning males and females, but there was no doubt about it: she was pregnant with Jihad's child.

It was high noon. Every member of the Shemyaza household was locked behind the shuttered windows and demon-warded doors of their respective resting places. They would remain so until nightfall when the world of the Nephilim would again come to life. Dreama was far too sick and too worried to sleep.

She dreaded what her mama would say when she told her she was with child. When she thought about the look of disappointment she would surely see in her beloved pater's eyes, all she could do was turn her tear swollen face into her damp pillow and cry herself a river. This was not the way she and Jihad wanted to do things.

Jihad was going to go to her pater and offer for her properly. With her pater's blessing, they would then approach King Zion for permission to wed. They would have a big wedding. All their family and friends would be in attendance.

This is not the way it is supposed to be!

The Nephilim ascribed to many of the same moral codes as their human counterparts. Pregnancy outside of wedlock is a shameful thing. Other than cases of rape, the onus and subsequent punishment is placed squarely on the shoulders of the female. Males will be males. Many will say she should have known better to keep her skirts down and her legs closed. If a pregnant female's lover chooses not to make an honest woman of her, she will be subjected to ostracism. In many cases she and her child may well be forced to live among humans outside of the protection of the Dark Veil, a frightening thought in and of itself.

Thank The Ancient of Days that Jihad is not that type of male. He will be home soon, and he will make everything right again, Dreama thought, finally drifting off to sleep just before nightfall with a prayer of thanksgiving on her lips.

⁓ ⁓

The tapers had long burned out, and normal sounds of the estate quieted for the night. Animalistic growls and grunts joined the wet sounds of sexual intimacy and of King Zion's massive headboard pounding against the wall.

Delilah's thighs were spread as wide as they could go. She was wide open in every way. Zion was taking advantage of her vulnerability like a bandit robbing a loaded stagecoach in the darkest hour of the night.

Zion was never gentle with her, but tenderness and a gentle touch were the last things Delilah needed or wanted. She wanted the wild beast in full divine rut that could stroke the farthest reaches of her body and make the surface of her skin tingle from his touch.

He pinned her down, as his muscular ass clenched, plundering her body with deep bold strokes that touched the bottom of her womb and beyond. Delilah opened her mouth to scream from the intense pleasure.

Zion raised his hand to cover her mouth and part of her nose, silencing the mantra of, "Fuck me, Zion—want me, baby—need me—love me." She screamed instead inside her head as his mind melded with hers. She was having trouble breathing. Her heart went tight inside her chest because she knew he didn't care.

Delilah was a married woman with a husband who adored the very ground she walked on. She could picture him now, pacing the floor in the beautiful home he had built for her, while their king fucked her senseless.

Zion was magnificent, a beautiful black god with coal black skin as smooth as velvet, a wild mane of thick hair the colour of midnight, and the golden predatory eyes of a Bengal tiger. Delilah realised she could never have Zion's heart. He was wild and untamable. His body would have to suffice for now.

Zion Shemyaza had his fangs buried at her jugular. His cheeks hollowed as he sucked down deep gulps of her life-sustaining blood. She gave her blood and her body willingly. He could have all she had to offer and more. Delilah was a selfish, self-centreed bitch without a care for anyone but herself, but Zion Shemyaza she loved to distraction. She'd do anything to have him.

Zion was inside Delilah's mind and her body as far as he cared to go, as far as he would allow himself to go with any female. He heard her plaintive passion-filled plea loud and clear while blocking his mind and his heart to her probing touch. She scratched his scalp with her sharp nails, tugging his face in position to take his mouth in a kiss. Zion turned his head away, keeping what she craved from her. He'd never allow a bedmate to taste his lips. The act of kissing was far too intimate.

He felt it keenly when Delilah finally gave up and gave in, surrendering to his superior will and the small portion of himself that he was willing to give. She was no different than the millions of women he'd bedded in his long lifetime. He was a king. She was only giving him his due.

He rose up on his muscular haunches, never losing contact with her grasping snatch. He grabbed her by the waist, bringing her up with him. They were breast to chest, belly to belly, cock to cunt.

Delilah was tall for a female and sturdily built. She loved Zion's special brand of rough handling. He lifted her body as if she weighed nothing. The tip of his prodigious cock was all that remained inside her opening. Then he slammed her down to take every inch of him to the hilt again and again, moving faster and faster, until her insides burned from his possession.

Zion threw his head back and roared like a jungle lion at the time of release. Delilah could feel his cock swelling inside of her, rippling from tip to balls. She whimpered when Zion pulled out, splashing his hot seed on her chest and belly.

Delilah was grinding a phantom and her chest was heaving as she tried to catch her breath. Something in her mind was pounding from the devastating absence of Zion's splendid body. What Delilah originally thought was her heartbeat pounding in her head was actually someone pounding on the door of Zion's bedchamber.

Zion ghosted to the door with his fangs distended, his cock still glistening with Delilah's cum. His forehead furrowed. A disturbance of this nature at this time in the morning did not bode well.

"What?!" Zion barked in a voice that would frighten Nephilim and demons alike. His manservant, Jon, stood on the other side of the door, nonplussed. He was totally oblivious to his master's state of nudity and the heavy smell of intense sexual congress that was billowing out of the room behind him.

"I apologise for the interruption, Sarrum," Jon said in his customary cultured tone of voice. "There has been a recent development of which you need to be made aware."

Zion nodded solemnly. He stepped back and bade Jon to follow him to his sitting room while he donned a dressing gown. The door to Zion's chamber was wide open. Delilah lay spread-eagle upon the bed with her legs brazenly splayed open and her cunt gaping from hard use. Jon had seen her kind over the centuries. He didn't spare a glance in Delilah's direction, and he didn't waste any time once they were seated in Zion's sitting room.

BEHIND THE DARK VEIL

"It's about the mission, Sarrum. There were casualties and many wounded. All of our dead have been recovered save for one of the privates under General Akibeel's command. All the other generals await you downstairs in your study. General Akibeel is in the barracks now. He intends to choose two more Gibborim to accompany him back into *Beer Shahat*. He is bound and determined to retrieve the soldier's body before the demons get an opportunity to desecrate it.

⁓◦⧼ ⧽◦⁓

In the space of a few short hours Kai had oiled every leather saddle in King Zion's stable until they shone like new money. It was nervous energy, but he had to do something to keep himself busy until the soldiers returned—or lose his mind. He was willing to perform just about any mundane, mindless task he could think of to keep his mind off the mission his friends were on and the fact that he was not with them.

When one of the king's stable boys led General Akibeel's Arabian stallion into the stable, Kai knew his friends were back from the mission. Anxious to hear every aspect of their adventure, he dropped the rag he'd been using on the saddles and ran to the barracks to meet up with Jihad and Manny.

He suspected Jihad's return would bring a smile to Dreama's pretty face. He hadn't seen much of her of late, but on those occasions when their paths did cross she appeared to be unaccustomedly morose.

Kai's excitement soon turned to despair when a ragtag bunch of Gibborim serving under Generals Boaz, Akibeel, and Urakabarameel walked past him with solemn faces. They carried the shrouded bodies of their comrades. He ran up to a soldier he was acquainted with.

"Hey, Michael, where are Jihad and Manny?" he asked.

Michael pointedly ignored Kai's question and kept walking.

"Surely Michael heard me," Kai said to himself with a perplexed look upon his face.

213

Each of the soldiers made a point of turning their head away from Kai when they saw him approaching. Kai knew without being told that both his friends were dead.

When he learned of the mission to retrieve Jihad's body, he volunteered to go.

Dreama's screams rent the air, raising the hackles of all who heard her. She was in the kitchen when she heard the news of Jihad's death. She dropped like a rock where she stood. She'd been inconsolable ever since, refusing to eat, drink, or bathe. Mavis was at her wit's end as to what to do.

On the other side of the plantation, the Widow Solonge stirred from a troubled sleep. She was not alone. A hybrid demon named Afriti sat at the foot of her bed. Centuries ago, Solonge and Afriti formed an unholy alliance. Solonge wanted to see the sons of Satan suffer for torturing and murdering her children while Afriti wanted revenge against one of them in particular, the demon who sired him. Solonge's voice was as rough as sandpaper when she addressed her uninvited guest.

"So, it has begun," she stated with resignation.

"Yes. It has begun exactly as I told you it would," Afriti stated. "In two days' time an unwed Anakin girl will leave the protection of the Dark Veil under a cloud of shame. She will bring grief to her family and cast a pall over all who live here. Her suffering will be nothing in comparison to what is coming to one of the king's honour guard. After much suffering and grief, the door will be opened for Zuet's enemies to pierce the veil that will thwart him. You will help me to achieve my revenge, and I will help you to achieve yours."

The demon offered his wrist to Solonge, and she drank from it.

Two days later Dreama was gone.

CHAPTER 33

Magnolia Hill, Slave Row

~

EPHILIM BLOOD AND saliva have miraculous healing properties. The blood Ajuma shared with Flossie the previous night went a long way toward accelerating the healing process. If only she had been given a few days' reprieve from hard labour, at least the physical portion of her ordeal would have been a distant memory, if not the mental. But slaves are considered to be less than the beasts of burden that cart the cane from the fields. They were seldom, if ever, given the luxury of healing from their abuse. When Flossie limped to the cane field the next morning, her body was stiff and her flesh still burned where the lash had kissed it.

The slaves were working under the blazing hot sun without supervision. While the cat is away, the mice will play. What the field hands were doing couldn't exactly be characterised as playing, but they were certainly taking advantage of the fact that there was no Mr. Mike, no Josiah, and, most importantly, no mean-as-hell Koby breathing down their necks as they chopped the cane at a more leisurely pace than usual. Even at the slower pace, every swing of the machete birthed a new form of agony for Flossie. She paused to rub her lower back and swipe the sweat from her brow.

It was high noon, and they were still working when word of Mike Tolliver's murder was passed from slave to slave in heated whispers

215

down row upon row of sugar cane. They collectively ceased working altogether when Josiah, one of the more popular gang leaders, rode up signalling everyone to break for lunch. The field hands barely afforded Josiah an opportunity to get off his horse before they converged.

"Is it true, Josiah? Is Mr. Mike really dead?" asked Cleofus, one of the field hands.

"I swear afore Gawd," Josiah said, his eyes gleaming with vengeful excitement, "Mr. Mike be dead as a door knob." He looked in the direction of the Big House to ensure he was unobserved, then chortled.

Unlike Koby, Josiah never did take pleasure in hurting his own people. He did what he had to do when asked, but he didn't like it. Without Mr. Mike to crack the whip, the slaves were standing idle on the fringe of the fields while Josiah weaved an astounding tale.

Ever the outcast, Flossie stood on the periphery of the circle of slaves forming around him. She just knew she hadn't heard Josiah correctly. When he repeated himself, Flossie literally froze where she stood, allowing Josiah's words to wash over her like acid rain.

"Mr. Mike dead? That can't be possible. Ajuma promised he wouldn't touch him. Oh, my God. Ajuma, no!" She clamped her palm over her mouth to keep from crying out.

Flossie thought no one was paying any attention to her strange behaviour because Josiah had centre stage, but she was wrong. Minnie, the same slave who smirked in her face when Koby dragged her for the vicious beating of the day before, was now staring her down with a look of speculation in her dark eyes. One of the slaves exhorted Josiah to start at the beginning, so he did.

"When Mr. Mike didn't show up in the field this morning, me and Koby went up to the Big House to find out what Massa Claude wanted us to do. Well, Massa Claude was mighty riled up. He followed us back to Mr. Mike's cabin straight away, fussin' and cussin' and callin' Mr. Mike white trash and such. He said he wasn't paying that no-count bastard to lay abed while they's work to be done."

"I swear before almighty Gawd, we smelled him before we put our feets on the front porch. Massa Claude was all gussied up with them fancy boots of his that go jingle-jangle with every step. He pulled out one of dem thar fancy hankies he keeps in his pocket, and he covers up his long nose like this."

Josiah mimicked Claude Etienne's mannerisms with the hem of his sweat-stained cotton shirt. He even went so far as to stick his pinky out like he was having a spot of tea from a dainty tea cup. He presented a ludicrous picture of his betters in his disrespectful affectation.

The slaves twittered at his tomfoolery. It was obvious that Josiah was deriving a great deal of pleasure in drawing his storey out, but when the laughter finally died down, the expression on Josiah's face changed from that of a jokester to one of a haunted man.

"Then Massa Claude say, 'Nigga, go on in and find out what be keep-ing Mr. Mike.' Now I tell you true. I wasn't finna go nowhere near the inside of that cabin. Nosiree, stepping through Mr. Mike's door was the last thing old Josiah wanted to do. Cause all of us knowed he was dead. Couldn't nothing livin' smell that powerful bad."

"I looks at Koby. Koby looks back at me. Then Massa Claude say: 'Both of you niggas best to get to steppin' if yah know what's good for yah.' I swanny," Josiah continued in a much lower voice, looking around to make sure no one was coming. "I ain't never seen nothing like it in all my born days."

Josiah took a deep breath to collect himself while each of the slaves waited with bated breath for his next words. It wasn't every day they got to gloat over the death of someone who'd made their existence a living hell. They would probably host a celebration on Slave Row later on that night, but right now they wanted every single detail.

"Mr. Mike was mean as a snake and that's a fact, but even he shouldn't have died like that. I tells you, he died hard. I wouldn't have believed it myself if I didn't see it with my own two eyes. Looked like the devil himself ripped Mr. Mike's head clean off his neck and shoved it all the way up his ass."

The slaves didn't get a chance to react with more than a collective gasp because at that moment, Koby rode up on the big brown carriage horse Massa Claude allowed only him to ride around the plantation. The expression on his face was ten times meaner than Mr. Mike's had ever been. Without a word, Flossie and the rest of the hands hustled back to the field. Flossie's back screamed in protest and her baby kicked as she bent to retrieve her machete to commence work under Koby's watchful eye. For the first time since Flossie had been sent out to the field, the slaves sang as they worked.

At day's end, aching and beat down with fatigue and fear, Flossie rushed to hide several items near the river bordering Magnolia Hill. These were items she cherished and intended to take with her when Ajuma came for her and Jacob later that night.

Her stash was piteously meagre, consisting of handmade ceremonial artefacts her mother had given to her as a child and clippings from select medicinal herbs from her garden. All were carefully wrapped in white linen and hidden from sight behind a big rock. She hoped to earn her keep among Ajuma's people with her gift of healing.

Upon her return from the river she went through the motions of picking greens from the little garden outside her cabin to prepare Jacob's dinner. She kneaded dough for biscuits as the funky smell of collards and fatback boiling in a big metal pot over the fireplace filled the cabin. She kept telling herself, "This will be the last meal I cook in this hell-hole." But even as the words passed her lips, she really didn't believe it.

Her mama's name was Sorrow. Flossie's name should have been Misery, because all her life she'd been beaten down with it. Now she couldn't conceive of anything else. Even if a pot of joy was placed in the palm of her hand, she feared it would be snatched away. Instead of feeling excited that she would soon be putting Magnolia Hill behind her, she found her heart and spirit to be as heavy as her swollen belly.

Something bad is gonna happen. I smell it in the air.

BEHIND THE DARK VEIL

Flossie was afraid. Her fear was rooted in the knowledge that there had to be some ramifications for Mr. Mike's murder. Low-class or not, white folks don't sit quiet when one of them turns up dead.

The air around her felt like a powder keg about to blow, and she didn't want to be anywhere near when it did.

Flossie wasn't hungry, but she and Jacob ate. The food lay like a rock on the bottom of her stomach. After they had eaten, there was nothing to do but wait, worry, and watch for the secrecy that one could only grab hold of late at night. It seemed time stood still as she awaited nightfall.

Jacob could sense his mother's disquiet. The usually rambunctious little boy was unaccountably subdued. Even when Flossie sat him on her lap to recount stories of Africa and the proud kings and queens Ajuma had told her about—kings he had actually met—she found no comfort.

Hurry to me, Ajuma, love. I need you.

She couldn't wait for Ajuma's return—couldn't wait to put Magnolia Hill and all its dark memories behind her once and for all so that they could make new memories as a family. Little Jacob didn't even know Ajuma was his father. They could not risk the baby telling anyone about the big green-eyed angel man who visited their cabin at night and disappeared before the light of day. Jacob thought Ajuma was a wonderful dream that lingered on the tip of his childish mind in the first breaths of a new day. Flossie found comfort rocking her sweet little boy in her arms.

Finally, Jacob fell asleep. Flossie held the beautiful son created from Ajuma and her love, closed her eyes, and allowed the possibilities to wash over her like a gentle breeze as she too drifted off. Hers, however, was a troubled sleep.

CHAPTER 34

⁓

*N*EARLY ALL OF the planters on River Road wore fashionable low-heeled, square-toed shoes with buckles. Not Claude. He wore custom-made Hessian boots with silver-tipped tassels, and riding spurs that sliced like razors into the flesh of any horse he rode. The tassels made a tinkling sound, similar to wind chimes, with every step he took. There wasn't a slave on Magnolia Hill who did not fear Claude Etienne's familiar footfall.

Flossie was abruptly wrenched from a sound sleep by the tinkle of those dreaded boots one second before her cabin door was kicked in, spraying splintered wood everywhere. There stood Claude Etienne, larger than life, and flanked by three other planters, representing a small contingency of what they called the River Road Militia.

God have mercy on Flossie's soul.

Claude stood in the opening where the flimsy cabin door had once hung, breathing hard with unholy fire in his slate grey eyes. Flossie quickly cast her eyes down. She'd seen enough in that first glimpse to recognise his intent. Claude's eyes were as cold and unyielding as the metal on his pointed toed boots where Flossie now focused her attention. His eyes told Flossie this showdown was a long time coming.

Claude was almost as big as Ajuma—six foot, two inches in height and at least 250 pounds—but his body was soft and pudgy around the middle from a dissolute lifestyle while Ajuma's entire frame was rock hard and covered with thick muscles. Claude's massive presence blocked

221

out the light of the setting sun and sucked the air out of the small cabin. Flossie stood in the middle of the cabin with her arms wrapped around Jacob, frozen with fear. She immediately transferred that fear to her two-year-old son, who clutched her skirts and began to whimper.

No one on Magnolia Hill wanted to draw the attention of Claude Etienne. The hate and fear the slaves felt for Mr. Mike was nothing compared to what this man generated. He was evil, wicked, and depraved, a veritable plantation "Boogey Man" to whom enslaved mothers threatened to send their children whenever they misbehaved. He was a slave's worst nightmare.

Claude's companions fanned out in the small cabin, blocking all means of escape. It was an exercise in futility if ever there was one since there was only one way in and one way out of the cabin, and Claude's big body was blocking it.

"I want to know who made that little niggah you are holding and who put that other suckah in your belly," Claude demanded, without preamble.

He reasoned that since no one on the plantation claimed the deed, it had to be a slave from another plantation. That same slave was probably the one who was guilty of murdering his overseer for tanning her hide on the previous day. He'd done a thorough investigation since Tolliver's body was found. One of the slaves reported hearing a man's raised voice coming from Flossie's cabin the night before. Flossie gulped so loud it sounded like a gunshot in the cabin.

"Where is he, wench?"

Flossie was smart enough not to ask who the "he" was. Even if she wanted to, she couldn't. She could only open and shut her mouth like a fish out of water. Each time she attempted to answer, she was unable to force out any sound. Fear had a stranglehold on her throat and had snatched her ability to speak.

What am I supposed to say? The father of my son and unborn babe is an angel, and he's in hell right now killing some damned demons? Don't think so. That would get me killed on the spot.

BEHIND THE DARK VEIL

Claude knew the effect he had on the slaves. He gloried in it, but it wasn't just Claude who relished the fear he generated. The demon within, Tyranny, was experiencing near orgasmic pleasure in what he knew was about to come. His brothers Travail, Hindrance, and Salacious had taken up temporary residence inside the bodies of Claude's companions, and they liked the fit just fine. All three demons whispered in the men's ears, egging them on. In a voice as smooth as silk, Claude asked Flossie again.

"I'm gon' ask you one more time where that buck of yourn is, wench, and I want the right answer." Then he focused his gaze on her crying son. "And you better shut that squallin' piccaninny up before I have old Nestor here do it for yah!"

Nestor French stood by like a hungry wolf, his wicked, yellow-toothed grin striking an even deeper cord of fear in Flossie and her son. Nestor had a reputation for performing unnatural acts with little boys.

"I got something to stuff his mouth with right here!" he promised, fisting his groyne and licking his thin wet lips. He looked like he was itching to harm little Jacob, who was at that point crying his little heart out.

Flossie clamped her hand over her son's mouth so hard, all you could hear was the muffled sound of aborted whimpers trapped deep in his little throat. Claude was waiting for a response. The look in his eyes let Flossie know he didn't plan to wait too much longer.

Flossie's mind was racing. She had to think fast. Obviously someone had either seen or heard Ajuma on the last night he came to her cabin. Her tongue felt like sand paper. She cleared her throat and tried to swallow, but there was no spit left in her mouth to moisten her dry throat. She could see no way out of the dire situation.

Ajuma, please help us. I don't know what to do. I don't know what to say!

"Massa Etienne." She cleared her throat yet again. This time her voice was a little stronger. "Massa Etienne. I'm real sorry, Massa, but I don't know what you talkin' 'bout. There was a man in my cabin last night, but I don't know his name. He must be a Maroon, Massa. He sometime come into my cabin at night and have his way wit' me. I swear 'fore Almighty God I ain't seen him since we laid down to sleep last night. When I woke dis mawnin' he was gone, Massa, and that be the truth."

Claude moved closer to Flossie in an attempt to magnify the degree of intimidation. His strategic move wasn't necessary. He could have been a mile away and Flossie would have been just as terrified. She was afraid to move so much as a muscle. He drew closer and closer, sopping up her personal space like a sponge in shallow water.

"Well, Nestor, George, Parker, this here niggah wench said she telling me the whole truth, so I guess that's what it is just 'cause she say so, right?" he said, deferring to each man in turn with a questioning look on his face.

George Raveneau addressed Claude without taking his rapacious eyes off Flossie. He reminded Flossie of a rabid dog who had its prey cornered and completely at its mercy. He too had a bad reputation of cutting and burning his slaves' genitals and being especially cruel to his young wife.

"Personally, Claude, I don't believe her," Raveneau said, flicking out a pocket knife to casually clean beneath his fingernails. Raveneau then turned to the other two men. "How 'bout you, Parker? Nestor?"

Both Parker Villareale and Nestor French responded in the negative as Flossie knew they would. It was inevitable that each would deny the veracity of Flossie's statement. After all, this was a game of cat and mouse. Flossie knew which role she played.

Ajuma had escaped their evil clutches. Someone would have to pay, and it looked like that someone would be Flossie. She silently prayed they would not hurt Jacob or her unborn baby. She had never been so afraid in her entire life.

Claude stepped within an inch of Flossie. She could smell the liquor on his breath and that special brand of stench that oozes out of white men's pores just before they do something really evil.

"Well, it looks to me like we got us a consensus. Do you know what the word consensus means, gal?" Claude asked.

Flossie was not expected to answer his question, so she remained silent.

"It means that nobody believes your lying black ass."

With that, Claude took off his thick leather belt with the big silver buckle and struck Flossie a vicious blow across her face. The first blow connected with her mouth, busting her lips open and knocking out all of her front teeth. Flossie hunched her body in a vain attempt to shield Jacob and her belly from harm.

The second blow hit Flossie in her right eye. Everything moved in slow motion after that. Claude swung his belt with vicious intent, destroying her beautiful face, while Nestor, George, and Parker moved in from all sides. The last thing Flossie remembered was Parker's blow to her stomach that sent her and little Jacob reeling across the cabin. Then, darkness.

Flossie came to, surprised she was still alive. The pain was so bad she wished that she wasn't. She was still on the floor where they'd left her. Her face was battered. One eye was swollen completely shut and her lips were split and bloodied. She nearly choked on the thick metallic taste of blood filling her mouth. She spit the blood out, experimentally running her tongue over her teeth. There were pieces of jagged teeth and empty spaces where her front teeth and two of her side teeth used to be.

The pain in Flossie's right eye was indescribable, like someone had shoved a piece of metal in the socket. But it was nothing compared to the pain she felt in her lower extremities. She whimpered like a wounded animal when her brain sent out the signal for her body to move.

Agony pulsated from every part of her body. Her cotton skirt was splattered with blood and rucked around her waist. Her blouse was pulled up, exposing her swollen breasts and her pregnant belly. She gagged, nearly choking, when she saw pieces of bone protruding from the side of her calf. What she couldn't see were the human bite marks on her breasts, her neck, and her thighs.

There was blood and crusty, dried semen around that place between her thighs and buttocks that screamed with pain from the inside out. She barely had enough strength to cover herself. It took every bit of power she possessed to move her head to take in the rest of the cabin.

When Flossie looked over and saw little Jacob's lifeless body, his head twisted in an unnatural position, and his little pants pooled down around his ankles, a moan rose up from the soles of her feet, gaining power as it travelled through her body and up to her mouth, exiting in what was later described in the slave quarters as a scream from the graves of all their murdered ancestors.

CHAPTER 35

Grato Quies, Baton Rouge

~

NICODEMUS EXHALED THE sweet and slightly pungent hemp through his nose and mouth. It was a particularly potent blend given to Zion in 2859 B.C. by Shen Nung, the Red Emperor of China. Zion and Nicodemus sat before a campfire, walled within a cloud of whitish grey smoke in the wooded area bordering the northern lands of *Grato Quies*. Nicodemus passed the clay pipe to Zion, then leaned his head back and closed his eyes to feel the full effect of the aromatic cannabis.

To an uninterested observer, Zion and Nicodemus were just two friends passing time in the woods. Both were dressed casually. Although they carried weapons, none were readily visible. Neither of them expected any trouble of the demon variety. *Grato Quies,* and every rock, tree and blade of grass on the thousands of acres of land surrounding it, belonged to Zion. It was impenetrable.

Neither had been able to rest, so anxious were they to lay eyes upon Ajuma who had been gone a full sennight. Rather than pace the floor, they ghosted from the manse and set up camp directly in front of the supernatural doorway in and out of the hells, as well as the lower levels of the heavens, to await Ajuma's return.

Only those with hyper-acute senses or mystical knowledge of the universe can discern the locations of The Ancient of Days' gateways, and even fewer can access them.

The hemp had a hold on Nicodemus.

"Zion?" he asked, breaking the comfortable silence.

Zion's eyes narrowed against the acrid smoke as he touched his taper to the fire and lit the bowl of the clay pipe. Red, yellow, and gold embers blazed as he took deep, measured pulls to make sure the cannabis burned evenly on his inhale. Zion waited for the smoke to flood his lungs and seduce his senses before he answered in a desultory voice.

"What?"

"I've got an idea," Nico replied.

Nicodemus was legendary for the outrageous nature of his numerous ideas. Most of them involved engaging in outlandish escapades of some sort with females who either belonged to someone else or were otherwise off-limits.

"Oh, Ancient of Days, please spare me." Zion chuckled, rolling his bright gold eyes in dramatic exaggerated fashion. He looked up toward the sky as if his words would reach the seat of heaven. "I am almost afraid to ask you what your idea is. The last time you had an idea, I ended up being the subject of much speculation at an Octoroon ball that you neglected to tell me we were crashing until *after* we arrived. That night, more than a dozen human mothers sized me up as husband material for their unwed daughters. Thanks, but no thanks, Nico. I am not interested in any of your ideas," he stated emphatically.

Instead of being put off by Zion's playful censure, Nicodemus proceeded to outline his plan as if Zion hadn't spoken. "Why don't you discard that air of kingliness you wear like a second skin and let's go out and have some fun,?"

Nicodemus noticed Zion had allowed the pipe to burn out. He snatched the pipe out of Zion's hand and proceeded to fill it with fresh hemp and lit the bulb of the pipe with a taper.

BEHIND THE DARK VEIL

All Brothers of the Dark Veil held a bond of love for one another, but none were closer than Zion, Nicodemus, and Ajuma. It had been a long time since the three friends had been able to enjoy one another's company. Zion was busy in his role as king of the Nephilim, and Ajuma had been wrapped up in Flossie. Nicodemus missed spending time with his two favourite Nephs a great deal. The sound of Zion's voice cut into Nico's thought.

"Where in tarnation do you propose we go?"

Nico was like a child with a new toy, ever hopeful that Zion might reconsider his proposal. "Well, how 'bout we go into town for a spell and make nice with the humans?"

Zion immediately shook his head in the negative. One experience at a human party with Nico was more than enough for him. "That's your thing, not mine. I have no interest in humans other than their role as an occasional food source." Zion held out his hand. "Give me the pipe."

When Nico sought to argue, Zion repeated himself.

"Give me the pipe, Nico."

Nico reluctantly passed him the pipe, fully intending to revisit the subject later.

"Well, then come along with me while *I* play with the humans, Nico said, pressing his case. He was still convinced he could bring Zion around. "I don't know why," he said with a smirk on his full lips, "but women swoon at the mere sight of you. All you need do is get them weak and wanting from your devastating good looks, and I'll take care of the rest. Then we can erase their memories, and ghost out of town like phantoms in the night. Come on, Zion. It will be fun!"

Before Zion could respond, a cloud of gold dust shimmered around the gateway. First, Kai, then Dawud, and then Mikel ghosted through the gateway with their sheet-covered burden carefully anchored between them. When Ajuma ghosted out of the gateway, road weary and covered in demon spatter, Zion and Nicodemus were right there waiting for him.

❦ ❧

Magnolia Hill

Ajuma's single-minded pursuit to get his woman and child away from the clutches of Magnolia Hill overshadowed all other concerns. He'd worry later about what to say to Zion when he showed up on the other side of the Dark Veil with a pregnant human and child. Zion was his friend. He would just have to find the words to make him understand.

At the moment Ajuma was more concerned about how Flossie would react to his being a few days late. *She must be frantic with worry*, he thought. He vowed to dedicate himself to making it up to her for the rest of her life. First, he had to get her and his son out of that hell-hole.

The lands that made up Magnolia Hill abutted a river on one side and wooded area on the other. The river provided irrigation for the growth and juicing of the sugar cane, Magnolia Hill's life blood. It served as an essential source of hydration for the livestock and for washing.

The woodland provided lumber for building and fuel for the boilers and for cooking. Flossie's cabin was located in a coveted area on Slave Row. It was the last cabin at the end of the row, right next to the woodland and the communal water pump shared by all the slaves.

Ajuma swore to himself that if any additional harm came to Flossie or his son, he would drain every drop of water in that river and burn down every tree in the woodlands *after* he finished with the guilty parties. He would not sit by quietly if Flossie was forced to endure another beating.

Ajuma ghosted to the end of Slave Row to find someone else living in his beloved's cabin. It was clear to him that something untoward had occurred because there was a blanket where the rickety door had once been, and there were broken pieces of wood lying about in front of the cabin. Nothing was as Ajuma had left it a sennight ago.

BEHIND THE DARK VEIL

His incorporeal nostrils flared as he hovered above the roof. He felt like howling at the moon when he smelled the familiar scent of Flossie's sweet blood coming from the flimsy walls and the packed dirt floor. His heart seized inside of his chest.

Ajuma remained a golden mist, ghosting the length and breadth of what he and Flossie frequently referred to as that little piece of hell on earth. He hovered and inhaled deeply, seeking Flossie's and Jacob's scents as he ghosted over every single cabin in Slave Row. He searched the smoke house, the mill, the boiling house, the curing house, and the distillery. He even searched the trash house, the workshops for the blacksmiths and carpenters, and the cabin of the overseer he'd killed. Flossie and little Jacob were nowhere to be found.

Ajuma felt and smelled a pervasive demonic presence when he finally paused to hover over the house Flossie called the Big House, where the whites lived, but for the first time in Ajuma's life he wasn't concerned with the demons. Let the demons have the wretched place and everyone in it, for all he cared. He hadn't returned to the Magnolia Hill shit hole for anything but Flossie and his son.

Finally, Ajuma ghosted to the one place he'd deliberately avoided. For this search, he took on corporeal form, fully visible and more vulnerable than he'd ever been. He didn't walk. Muttering a prayer in Enochian under his breath, he staggered through the wretched patch of land on the outskirts of the plantation that held the remains of Magnolia Hill's slaves like a man whose senses were dulled with hard drink.

The sadness Ajuma felt the moment he took physical form in that graveyard made him weep. He felt all the pain, and hopelessness, and despair, and a million other emotions rise up from the graves and seep into his soul like chords of an angry choir. Those emotions joined the knowledge that he was responsible for whatever happened to Flossie and his son. She had begged him not to seek retribution for her beating. The guilt took his breath away.

With every step he took, something inside of Ajuma fractured and died. Something picked away at his spirit like a vulture, leaving it as bare as the bones of the oldest corpse in that burial ground. The temperature there was at least fifteen degrees cooler than anywhere else on the plantation. It matched the coldness that was creeping up Ajuma's legs, threatening to encase him. It was mid-summer in Louisiana, yet Ajuma's teeth chattered like he was standing barefoot on an iceberg.

And then Ajuma found it—two freshly dug graves under the leafy bow of a huge magnolia tree, the only tree in the cemetery. One grave bore the name of his son Jacob on a crudely cut piece of wood. The other had no headstone at all. For an infinitesimal moment, that nameless *something* that protects you when a devastating hurt threatens to tear you apart would not allow Ajuma's mind to face what was obvious. When reality did finally hit, Ajuma dropped to his knees and howled like a wounded wolf.

Consumed with the belief that there was neither rhyme nor reason for The Ancient of Days taking his woman and his son, Ajuma went more than a little mad. He clawed through the dirt covering the unmarked grave with his bare hands, muttering Flossie's name in Enochian, the language of the angels, while blood-red tears covered his face.

I have to see her one more time. Attiq Yomin, I beg you. Just let me hold her in my arms one more time.

He wanted to take the bodies of his wife and son with him to the other side of the Dark Veil, to honour them in life as he would never be able to in death. By the time Ajuma's crazed eyes reached the surface of the plain pine wooden box, several of his claws were ripped off, his fingers bloody and shredded.

CHAPTER 36

Grato Quies, Baton Rouge

~

ZION'S GOLD EYES narrowed with determination. Nico and Hamdani were gaining on them. Soon they would be neck and neck with Zion and his stallion, Seglawi. The sleek coats of the stallions were slick with sweat and their ears plastered flat against their noble heads. Both were hot-headed alpha animals, with preternatural equestrian speed and a will to claim victory in all things.

Zion and Nicodemus held the reins like Bedouin masters as Hamdani and Seglawi's powerful hooves pounded beneath their bodies. Each was bent forward, urging the stallions on to even greater speeds as they raced through the thick humidity of the Baton Rouge night with the hot wind beating against their faces. Both were determined to win the race.

Zion and Nico rode bareback, controlling the direction and pace of the fiery Arabians with the strength of their strong muscular thighs and sheer dent of will. Both stallions and riders were as one as their powerful bodies moved gracefully with every roll and dip. It was a thing of utter beauty to behold.

They were approaching one of three streams running through Zion's property when Ajuma's agonising cries cut through the pounding of their heartbeats and the horses' hooves. Both Nico and Zion immediately slowed the horses before skidding to a halt. Without a word, they ghosted to Magnolia Hill. Ajuma needed them.

ᆨᇰ ᇰᆨ

The Old Slave Cemetery, Magnolia Hill

Nicodemus took in the scene in an instant. Ajuma was hunched over an open grave not far from a fresh plot with a wooden marker bearing the name Jacob. Nico could only assume that the open grave belonged to Flossie. A shaft of pain ran through him for Ajuma's loss. Nicodemus looked toward the horizon. He wished Ajuma had time to mourn his loved ones, but the sun would block out the moon in short order. They dared not tarry.

Nico was prepared to share his thoughts when Ajuma reached inside the grave. Ajuma's intent was clear. He planned to rip off the top of the plain pine coffin that separated Flossie's body from his awaiting arms, to do only The Ancient of Days knows what with it.

Zion immediately sprang into action, grabbing Ajuma shoulders from behind. He unceremoniously tossed Ajuma backward and away so that he landed several feet from the grave. Ajuma jumped up like he was on a spring board.

He turned on Zion and Nicodemus in full battle mode, with a deep foreboding growl in his throat and his fangs and remaining claws distended. Zion cautiously backed away with both hands raised in an effort to calm Ajuma.

"Take it easy, brother. We are here to help, not harm."

But Ajuma's eyes were too shrouded in grief to see his closest friends. In his fractured and wounded mind, all he could see were two huge beings that were trying to keep him from his beloved.

He attacked.

It was all Nico and Zion could do to control him. They didn't want to hurt him, but if they didn't subdue him soon, more likely than not, he

234

would kill every single human on Magnolia Hill. And *that* they could not allow. The secret to their continued way of life was to keep the humans ignorant of their existence.

Nicodemus barely ducked out of the path of one of Ajuma's lethal swings. "Aw shit," he muttered.

Ajuma's eyes were wary as Zion and Nicodemus circled him, looking for an opening. They had to get out of there immediately. Zion moved a rock telepathically to distract Ajuma. He then caught him in a bear hug from behind while Nicodemus punched him senseless.

"I'm sorry, my brother." Nico delivered a paralysing blow to Ajuma's jaw.

They could not allow Ajuma's uncontrollable grief to be the catalyst that would jeopardise the safety of the Nephilim Nation. Zion didn't bother to apologise for his next action when he realised Ajuma was starting to stir. He pulled up one of the crude wooden headstones and slammed it against the side of Ajuma's head. Ajuma dropped like a bag of rocks.

When Ajuma came to they were back at *Grato Quies*. Nicodemus was sitting astride his chest. Pain ripped into him so deeply and so profoundly that it literally took his breath away. His son was dead. Flossie was dead. Even though he was still breathing, he was as good as dead too. There was no longer any need for Nico to restrain him. He was empty inside, and he didn't care whether he lived or died. There was no more fight left in him.

Nico had never betrayed Ajuma's confidence about little Jacob, not even to Zion. Ajuma was making him nervous. Nico didn't know what was more disturbing, the crazed maniac he and Zion had to physically restrain back at Magnolia Hill or the empty shell lying motionless before him. Ajuma didn't resist as Nico and Zion half-walked, half-carried him to the main house.

⁂

Jessy muttered to herself as she ran barefoot through the slave graveyard. "I ain't nowhere nears used to trucking with no haints, but I declare

I'd walk a mile through a cane field full of spooks if it means I can get me some more of that simple-minded man's good loving. Ooh wee. That boy can go." She needed to slip back into her cabin before sunrise, and the only way she was going to accomplish that would be if she cut through the graveyard.

Jessy had slipped away earlier that night to visit a slave named Tom she was sweet on at the Raveneau Plantation. He was big and a little slow, but he loved every inch of her big-boned, red-haired, yella body— funny-looking grey eyes and all. He'd shown her just how much he liked her, over and over again on top of a pile of fresh tossed hay in the Raveneau barn. *Lord have mercy that be one big, sweet man!*

Jessy had also stopped by the slave infirmary at Raveneau to check in on Flossie. The only other midwife within twenty miles was an old slave woman named Reba who lived on the Raveneau Plantation. She was half blind and not nearly as skilled as Flossie, but she was better than nothing.

That is where Ole Massa Clidamont had the coachman take Flossie for her delivery. He said he didn't give a shit if she died pushing it out, but he was determined to get that sucker out of her before she went.

Jessy shook her head as she picked her way around the random headstones. *It's bad luck to step on somebody's grave. Lord, seeing what they done to poor little Flossie liketa broke my heart. Now Flossie be scarred up just like her mama, Sorrow, had been.*

Jessy was halfway through the graveyard when a chill raced down her back like someone had just stepped on her grave. She quickly concealed herself, and then she saw him.

Jessy didn't know what he was—a demon, angel, or something in between. The only thing she knew for sure was that he wasn't human. Jessy was frozen in fear, huddled in a puddle of her own piss, hiding behind an old wooden headstone. She prayed to the dear Lord he would not sense her presence.

She'd decided to call him a haint for lack of another name for him. He was kneeling near Flossie's little boy Jake's grave. He had goldenbrown skin and bright green eyes. It looked like he was crying, but the tears coming from his eyes were as red as blood. *Oh, god...his teeth.* Jessy clamped her hands over her mouth to keep from crying out. His teeth were long and sharp as an animal's with the claws to match.

Curiosity temporarily overrode Jessy's fear when the haint started to dig up ole man Rodney's body. *Now why in tarnation was the green-eyed haint trying to dig up ole Rodney?* she wondered. Even though the haint was muttering in a strange language, Jessy could feel his pain as clearly as if he'd touched her.

Before she could puzzle out an answer to her questions, two more haints popped into the graveyard out of thin air. She knew they weren't human either. *I ain't never seen nuthin' human appear out of nowhere like that.* One was as handsome as the green-eyed haint, but the other looked more like an angel than a spirit.

Then they started to fight. They growled and snarled like the pigs in Massa's trough when they get to fightin' over a juicy choice bit of meat. The beautiful one who looked like a black angel pulled a headstone out of one of the graves like it was little more than a piece of hay from the barn, and he brained the green-eyed haint, knocking him clean out. Right before Jessy's startled grey eyes, all three of them haints disappeared like big clouds of star dust.

Jessy waited a long time before she gathered up the courage to move. When she did, she ran for all she was worth and didn't stop running until she was leaning against the inside of her cabin door. Even if she lived to be as old as ole man Rodney, she would never ever forget what she had seen this night.

CHAPTER 37

Slave Row, Magnolia Hill

~

LOSSIE HELD HER body as still as a post, so afraid was she to waken the sleeping giant of pain inside of her. She could smell new rain leaking through the holes in the cabin's roof. The smell danced with that of salt pork and fresh garden vegetables simmering in a stew pot. Someone was moving around in the cabin. Flossie turned her head and squeezed her good eye shut, feigning sleep.

This must be what it feels like to be dead, she thought. *Each breath is just a waste of time until I can give up the ghost. All they will need to do is bury me.*

The River Road Militia had beaten more than one baby out of Flossie on the day they found Mike Tolliver's desecrated body. She'd been carrying twin baby girls. Two days after she delivered, Reba patched Flossie up as best she could, and the coachman loaded her and the babies in the back of a buck wagon and transported them back to Magnolia Hill.

Now the babies were one month old, and Flossie had yet to look at them, hold them, or name them. She didn't want to love them. She reasoned that if she allowed herself to love them, she'd surely lose them, just like she'd lost Ajuma and Jacob and everybody else she loved. Flossie couldn't abide any more pain. It would incinerate her and carry her off with the next wind.

Flossie's mind wondered back to that last night she and Ajuma were together. He said he was going to take her and little Jake away from

Magnolia Hill and that no one would ever hurt them again, but her son Jacob was dead and buried. Ajuma didn't come back as he promised, so he must be dead too.

Hattie Mae's familiar voice tunnelled its way through the surface of Flossie's grief like an earthworm through moist soil. Hattie Mae was a short nut-brown woman well past her middle years with big hips, bow-legs, and a thick head of silver-grey hair she wrapped around her head in a crown. She was a handsome woman who always spoke her mind—that is, whenever there were no white folk around.

"Ain't no need for ya to try and play possum, gal. I know you wake. They's gon' be some changes today. I'm sick and tired of you laying 'round feelin' sorry for yaself. Ain't like you the only one whose neck the white man done stepped on. Just about everybody on this here planta-tion been touched by the evil inside those Etiennes."

Flossie listened to every word Hattie Mae said, but she wasn't ready to *hear* her. The pain was too raw. She kept her eyes closed and her breath-ing even. *Maybe if I don't turn around she'll go away.* Flossie just wanted to be left alone so that she could wither away and die, but the woman would have none of it.

"You gon' eat this here broth I made for you, or you gon' choke when I shoves it down your throat. You choose."

Flossie felt the metal taste of a spoon prying her parched lips open and the taste of broth on her tongue a second before the broth raced down her throat to block her airway. She started to choke. Her brain automatically turned on its coughing mechanism.

It appeared even though she wanted to die, her body was not in agreement. Flossie was forced to swallow first one then another spoon-ful of the warm broth.

"That's right, gal. You ain't ready to die yet," Hattie Mae stated in a sing-song voice as she coaxed yet another spoonful of soup between Flossie's busted lips. "You got two youngens to take care of."

"And just in case ya wonderin'," she said, "we done named one of your babies Perline after my own mother and the other Minette after that white woman come visit Massa Clidamont for the governess job last year. Ain't right to let innocent babies go without a name," she mumbled. "It's right sinful if yah ask me." Flossie knew Hattie Mae didn't expect her to respond to her chatter, so she didn't.

"Nothing you can do 'bout that dead baby boy of yourn, but there's a whole lot you can do about the two girls. Don't want to leave them to the devil's mercy, now do ya?"

It eventually turned into a test of wills with Hattie Mae staring unflinchingly into Flossie's ravaged face and Flossie staring right back with her one good eye. It felt odd for Flossie to open both eyes and see a dark curtain over the other.

All Flossie could do was look at Hattie Mae through her one good eye, wishing they'd beaten her hearing out of her so that she would never again hear someone utter Jacob's name. The pain was starting to stir again, but this time it was in her heart. Flossie didn't want to think about Jacob, and she certainly didn't want to talk about him. When Flossie thought about what they did to her baby, she wanted to die all over again.

A couple of months ago, Hattie Mae wouldn't have spit on the best part of Flossie, and now she was spooning soup into her mouth. The fates were wagging their fickle fingers in Flossie's face and laughing at her expense. Somebody should have told her that all she had to do for acceptance was to have her son taken like a woman and murdered and get herself beaten within an inch of her life. She was now officially one of them.

"That's right," Hattie Mae said. "Eat, live, and maybe you might just be able to pay young Massa back for what he did to you and your boy. Eat, gal. You know it was that nasty Minnie what sicced Massa on you. And now she struttin' her skinny ass around with a new calico skirt, a brand new pair of shoes, and a steady supply of rock candy."

Hattie Mae finally had Flossie's attention. She would eat. She would gain her strength. She would make Claude Etienne pay for what he did to her if it took the rest of her life. She'd make his old man pay for bringing him into the world. She'd make Claude's sons pay just because they were his, but first she was going to make Minnie pay. Flossie continued to swallow until she was too tired to open her mouth, then she slept.

⊷ ⊶

Flossie never recovered from the beating administered by Claude and the River Road Militia. She suffered a stroke right after she delivered the twins. Besides being horribly disfigured, she was now partially paralysed on the right side of her body. Since she could no longer work in the fields, she was reassigned to work in the kitchen.

Cook watched Flossie struggle from her pallet on the kitchen floor. Cook knew better than to offer aid of any kind. She'd nearly had her head bitten off the last time she tried to help her. She'd be damned if she'd give that heifer the chance to do it again.

"That's a proud one," she thought. "Always was, but man falleth before pride," she mumbled under her breath. No sooner did the words cross Cook's lips when Flossie stumbled and nearly fell over the lazy hound that slept on the kitchen floor.

By the time Flossie righted herself on the crude piece of wood she used as a walking stick, her face was drenched in sweat. She was so sick to her stomach she thought she would lose last night's supper. Flossie gritted what teeth she had left with the same sense of determination that had her walking, albeit only with the help of a walking stick, when everyone thought she would never walk again.

Flossie's hands shook as she laboured to the scarred wooden chopping table where the ingredients for the noon-day meal were already laid out. She focused on the table and the stool in front of it like it was the promise land. To spare Flossie her dignity, Cook turned her back to stir something simmering in the big cast iron stew pot. She was humming a familiar spiritual in a rich soothing alto that reminded Flossie of trees heavy with sweet fruit in the summertime. For the life of her, Flossie couldn't recall the name of the song or the words. She was glad Cook chose not to witness her struggles. Finally, Flossie landed heavily onto the wooden stool. Cook addressed Flossie with her back to her.

"You can start choppin' up those carrots and pullin' the greens off the stalk for cleanin'. After that I got some onions for you to chop. When you are done, you can pull the feathers off those birds over there."

Cook nodded in the direction of four fat headless hens lying in a metal pan on the floor with flies buzzing around them. The chickens reminded Flossie of herself, bloody and wounded. Only difference between them and her was they were already dead and she was just half-way there.

Six months had elapsed since the beating, and Flossie still didn't want to touch or look at her babies. A young slave girl named Callie had lost her baby to the lung sickness. She acted as wet nurse to Flossie's babies. Either Jessy, Hattie Mae, or one of the other women on Slave Row would take the babies home with them at night. The babies were getting love from everybody but their mama.

The day was progressing normally with Flossie assisting Cook in various tasks and Cook humming as she worked when Callie marched into the kitchen straight from the fields with one plump baby under each arm. Flossie's mouth dropped open in incredulity when Callie plopped one baby right in Flossie's lap and the other right in front of her on the rough wooden table where she had been chopping vegetables.

"Here," Callie said with a look that dared Flossie to defy her. "These your babies. I didn't feel the pain from you pushin' 'em out, and I damn sure didn't feel the pleasure from making 'em!" She slammed her palm down on the table to make sure she had Flossie's attention.

"These your damn babies, not mine, and I swear 'fore God you gon' take care of 'em."

With that, Callie turned her wide calico-covered hips around and marched right back out of that kitchen.

Flossie reacted like someone had put poisonous snakes in her lap and on the table. She stared at the edge of that scarred wooden table like it was the old wooden cross that white folk put so much stock in. She refused to look at the infant wriggling around on its rough surface nor the one in her lap.

She couldn't move. She couldn't allow herself to look at them. If she never saw or touched those babies it would have been just fine with her. To acknowledge them would mean she would have to acknowledge Ajuma, and she wasn't ready for that. She'd only just accepted that Jacob was lost to her forever. It was too soon to take on any more grief.

Yet Flossie couldn't stop herself from smelling their innocent sweetness. She couldn't stop herself from hearing the sweet cooing sounds they made as they communicated with each other in baby angel-speak.

Cook stood off to the side, waiting to see what would happen. She slowly put down the rag she'd been holding to move closer to where Flossie sat with the baby on her lap. Flossie's hands hung limp at her sides. She hadn't moved to steady the wobbling infant. The only things holding the baby steady were the barrier of Flossie's body and the edge of the table. Cook didn't intend to stand by and watch that crazy fool gal let the baby fall on the dirt floor and bust her little head open. She was ready to spring forward and catch that baby before she came to any harm.

The baby sitting in Flossie's lap started to wobble, almost falling backward. The baby fisted the front of Flossie's thin cotton shirt in her delicate little hand. Against her will, Flossie's gaze caressed the baby's face to look into a pair of moss green eyes just like Ajuma's. From that moment on, she was lost.

CHAPTER 38

⁓

$\mathcal{I}$T SOON BECAME a familiar sight to see the little ones fast asleep or playing on a blanket on the kitchen floor, while their mother toiled in the hot kitchen. In time Flossie grew stronger. She would always have a limp, but soon she was able to get around without exhaustion and without the assistance of her walking stick.

In addition to her work in the kitchen, Flossie resumed her healing and midwife duties. The inhabitants of Magnolia Hill grew accustomed to seeing Flossie's wizened figure limping around the plantation with her scarred face, her one milky eye, and her little green-eyed, dark skinned babies.

The girls were identical in every way, but where Minette was perfect, little Perline was born with a twisted little foot and the beginnings of a small hump between her little shoulder blades. Perline had been a breach baby. Instead of turning her in the proper position for birth, the midwife pulled Perline out by her foot. Perline's deformity was a result of her leg being broken at the hip when she was pulled out of Flossie's body. The foot the midwife used to pull Perline out of the birthing canal was broken and was never properly set. Little Perline would be fortunate if she was able to walk at all. That did not matter to Flossie. She adored both of her daughters. They represented an enduring gift of love that would sustain her the remainder of her life.

Her daughters became her life. She knew she would never see Ajuma again. Were it not for her twin daughters and her son's grave, which she

245

visited frequently, she would have thought Ajuma had been a figment of her imagination.

When the pain of her loss became almost unbearable, she had but to look over at her two precious little girls to know that Ajuma had not been a dream. Both of her daughters had inherited their father's moss green eyes. Her angel man had not been a dream. He was real.

Naberius, a demon with three bird heads and the body of a bent over cock, had been dogging Claude Etienne's booted heels all day. More than anything, he wanted in, but there were already more high-level demons taking up residence in Claude's body than he cared to count. There was no room for a low-level peon like him. Any mischief he wished to stir up would have to be of the external variety.

Earlier that day, Claude's favourite dog, June Bug, bore a litter of eight puppies. One of the puppies was born with only three legs. Naberius whispered an evil suggestion in Claude's ear. Claude grabbed that ill-formed puppy by the scruff of its neck and bashed its defenceless little body against the privy wall. Naberius actually came on himself when the dead puppy was then thrown in the nearby hog trough.

The sound of the hogs fighting to get at the tasty little morsel was music to Naberius' ears. Demon seed dripped down his thigh when he pranced around, doing a little demonic dance, cackling with glee. Naberius was the demon of evil intent. It didn't matter if the victim was animal or human. As long as there was pain and suffering that would eventually result in death, he was well and content. Word of Claude's cruelty had already reached Flossie when later that day he paid an unexpected visit to the kitchen, along with his trusty lap dog Koby, who was as full of the devil as he was.

That was the day the twins first came to Claude Etienne's attention. It was winter. The toddlers were about three years old. They were lying within sight of their mother on a raggedy old blanket on the warm kitchen floor. The old hound dog they fed scraps to was lying nearby.

Naberius' eyes lit up when he saw little Perline's twisted foot. Right then and there he decided little Perline was not worth the money it would cost to feed her. He made it a point to share his assessment with Claude while at the same time compelling Claude to take Flossie's lame child, kill her, and throw her in the hog trough like he had done with the puppy. Sensing some mayhem afoot, several other low-level demons wanted to take control of the situation, but Naberius held centre stage and did not intend to give it up. It was his time to shine.

Flossie tensed when she heard the familiar jingle-jangle of the silver tassels on Claude's dusty boots. She didn't have to worry about Claude, Clidamont, or any man, for that matter, forcing his attention upon her. No man would ever look upon Flossie with desire again. Her beauty had been destroyed when the whip ripped open her back and the belt ruined her face. It was just as well, since she would never again suffer a man's touch after what was done to her. Yet, there were other ways someone like Claude Etienne could hurt her. She had good cause for concern.

Claude didn't just enter the kitchen; he commanded it and he didn't come alone. Magnolia Hill harboured a nest of demons. These demons could be sensed but not seen by most humans. Each demon battled for supremacy and for control of the human residents on the plantation, white and slave alike. There were more than enough unwitting hosts to go around on Magnolia Hill.

Claude was big, sweaty and smelly. He sat the evil he carried around him all the time smack dab in the middle of the kitchen floor, like a heavy set of luggage.

Flossie schooled the expression on her scarred face to hide the hatred that always crept to the surface when any Etienne was around.

"Whose suckers are these?" he asked, knowing full well who the children belonged to. Flossie had no choice but to answer.

"They mine, Masta Claude."

Flossie tensed as he walked closer to the children so that he could get a better look at them, squinting his grey eyes into the shape of bullets. His eyesight was starting to fail him.

"What the hell is wrong with this one?" he asked, pointing to little Perline.

"She fine, Masta Claude, 'cept she can't walk," was Flossie's reply.

Claude spit a thick glob of stinking tobacco on the floor just inches from the children. "She don't look fine to me. In fact, I think it's a crime to waste good hard-earned money on a worthless crippled slave who won't be able to earn her keep."

Claude took a moment to let his words sink in. He liked to toy with the slaves, to treat them like flies whose wings he could pull off at a whim. He could feel the misery start to rise in Flossie. It made him feel powerful, like he was the king of the world and not just the acting master of his father's plantation.

Flossie started to shake all over. Something bad was about to happen. She could feel it. Claude confirmed her worst fear with his next words.

"Why, I'm of half a mind to feed that good-for-nothing sucker to the hogs," he stated, prompting Flossie to start praying.

Olodumare, have mercy. It's 'bout to happen all over again. The devil's bout to take another chunk of my heart. Soon there won't be none left. Have mercy Lord!

"No, please, Masta Claude, no," Flossie said in a whisper.

Flossie begged for her daughter's life, swearing that Perline would be made useful, that she would earn her keep. When her pleas fell on deaf ears, she fell to the dirt floor and started to pray even louder.

The ugly slave woman's prayers were angering Naberius. He wanted to see her suffer if only to shut her up. Cloaked in the veil of invisibility, Naberius sidled over to Claude. As the demon drew closer, Claude experienced an unexplainable sexual rush. Claude's penis sprang to life when Naberius ran his long black tongue along the outer ridge of his ear.

Naberius stared at the children. If he didn't know any better, he would swear both the children could see him. Their large green eyes followed his every move. He found this to be very interesting indeed—something he would have to investigate more thoroughly later. Right now, all he wanted was to see what the inside of that crippled human's head looked like. He needed to shut that black bitch up. Not to be swayed from his original intent, Naberius returned his focus to Claude, whispering softly in his ear.

"If killing the dog made you feel good," he said, "just imagine how good it will feel to kill that little deformed niggah! Bash her head up against the wall, and watch her blood flow! Do it now!" he commanded.

A host of minor demons and imps popped in, prancing, dancing, and cheering like spectators at a bloody event in a Roman arena.

Suddenly Claude's hands itched to grab hold of Perline, to tear her apart, to rend the little girl from limb to limb. He didn't just want to kill Flossie's child. He had an uncontrollable compulsion to beat her brains out.

No sooner did Naberius make his obscene suggestion when a member of the *Harab Serapel*, a hideous demon-headed raven of greed, covetousness, and unbridled lust named Emesis, dropped into the room like a huge albatross. It took advantage of Naberius' momentary shock and outrage to drape a preternatural cloak of protection over both of Flossie's children. Now the inner nature of both children was inviolable to the demons. They could see the children, but they could not see *inside* them.

Undeterred by the presence of the other demons, Emesis quickly whispered in Claude's ear, planting his own special form of compulsion to supersede Naberius' previous command. Seconds later Emesis exited the room as quickly as he had entered, disappearing in a puff of smoke along with the remaining imps previously vying for a place on Magnolia Hill.

Claude scratched his head in confusion. His previous thought had evaporated from his mind like mist on a foggy morning. He reluctantly consented to let little Perline live. Before Flossie could express relief or gratitude, he said, "Since you put so much stock in the little runt gal, you gon' give me the healthy one instead."

Claude turned to Koby. "Snatch that little niggah up and follow me!" he demanded.

"Nooooooo!" Flossie screamed, sobbing at his feet. She was losing her mind. *God, I can't take no more.* She thought even God could not be so cruel, but he was just that cruel.

That day Claude and Koby took little three-year-old Minette away from Flossie. Cook grabbed hold of Flossie to keep her from flinging herself at Koby, who laughed as he carried the squirming little toddler in the direction of the trough where they kept Claude's killer hogs.

Flossie's mouth opened in a silent scream when she heard her baby cry out and the rooting squeal of the hungry hogs. After that there was silence. Flossie's good eye rolled to the back of her head as she slumped in Cook's arms.

CHAPTER 39

⌒‿

$\mathcal{F}$ LOSSIE LOOKED OVER at Cook's ample chest rising and falling in sleep, then she checked to make sure Perline was in a deep restful sleep on the pallet next to her before getting up to leave the kitchen.

Minutes later Flossie was standing outside the hog pin in search of a trace of Minette. The night was dark as most nights go and her vision was faulty, but there wasn't a hand, or foot, or even a scrap of cloth left of her baby. It was like Minette had never existed anywhere but in Flossie heart and mind and on the face of her twin sister.

Flossie's expression was one of resolution as she walked back to the wooded area behind her old cabin. Her gait was uneven, but she made good time. The last slave to claim the cabin moved out two days later. She claimed there were haints visiting from the nearby graveyard, and now the cabin remained empty.

Most of the slaves were too afraid to venture anywhere near the cabin, especially late at night. Flossie wasn't afraid. She'd already been dealt the worst from the hand of the living. No need to fear the dead.

Flossie pulled back the rock that she'd hidden her ceremonial artefacts under years ago, sighing with relief to find the little white bungle was still there. Taking painstaking steps to combat the throbbing in her calf, she made her way even deeper into the woods to the altar where she had first met Ajuma.

This would be the first time Flossie had come to the altar since her son's murder and the very first time she would beseech the Orisha

251

pantheon of gods to empower her to do baneful majick and do harm. That night Flossie vowed never to speak Ajuma's name again, not even in her mind. For a brief time, he had represented hope. Now she knew she had none.

Minnie had her eye on Clyde for a long time, but it wasn't till his woman Velma got sold off for stealing that Minnie saw her opportunity to get him. Clyde was a fine-looking buck with smooth light-brown skin, a big muscular build, and a randy look in his eyes that made Minnie feel like someone grabbed her in the crotch and squeezed real tight. He was well worth the effort it had taken Minnie to set his woman up for a crime she didn't commit.

Clyde worked in the boiling house where they processed the cane. Like the carpenter, blacksmith, and other trained slaves on Magnolia Hill, he lived in a larger cabin than the rest of the field hands and enjoyed extra rations. Minnie could do a lot worse than Clyde, and that was a fact.

Velma wasn't the only slave on the hill Minnie had brought low. She had betrayed Flossie for the price of a calico skirt, a second-hand pair of shoes, and a bag of rock candy.

When Minnie ran into Clyde coming from the barn that afternoon, she made it a point to rub up against him real sexy like. She promised him a piece of rock candy. To let Clyde know she was more than willing to give him a lot more than the candy, Minnie grabbed the thick package between Clyde's thighs before he went about his way. She whispered in his ear, "All you need to do is show up at my cabin come dark, and you'll be in for a real treat."

When Clyde showed up at Minnie's cabin that night he was more interested in the candy than he was in the woman. Since Minnie was willing, he'd be a damned fool to turn down what she was offering. Clyde may be guilty of many things. Being a damned fool wasn't one of them.

BEHIND THE DARK VEIL

He wasn't in the mood for foreplay. He was still missing his Velma something fierce. Any other woman he laid down with was just another hole to temporarily ease the ache in his chest that seemed like it was never going away.

His jaw puffed out, Clyde sucked on a big piece of rock candy while Minnie lay beneath him, grinding her fully clothed body against his and panting like a bitch in heat. There wouldn't be any hugging and kissing or sweet words between those two—just some hard fucking, and a nod goodnight when he was done. She'd be lucky if he spoke to her if he ran into her the next day.

Anxious to get the deed over with, Clyde rose up to pull out his cock. Minnie could see it clearly from the candle burning on the floor beside her pallet. She licked her lips like she'd just finished some of that rock candy Clyde was sucking on. It was thick and hard and leaking at the head, and she was hungry for it. She hiked up her skirt and spread her legs wide.

Clyde pressed the head of his cock to her opening. He frowned as he met a barrier when he tried to stick it in. He knew for a fact Minnie was no innocent. She'd already been with most of the bucks on Magnolia Hill and half in the parish. She was a doorknob. Just about everybody had already had a turn.

Minnie was as puzzled as Clyde. She was hot and bothered and itching to feel Clyde's hardness buried deep as it would go inside of her. Clyde reached for the nearby candle, then pushed Minnie's legs up so that her knees were near her chest. He shone the light of the candle between her thighs and leapt back when thousands of fat white cockroaches came streaming out of her opening. Clyde dropped the candle and ran like her cabin was on fire.

Clyde didn't waste any time telling the blacksmith about his experience with Minnie. The blacksmith shared the storey with the carpenter, and so on. Soon, the storey spread to the slaves working in the Big House and the entire length of Slave Row.

Meanwhile, Minnie was in the slave infirmary, trying to scratch her insides out and screaming her fool head off. Albino roaches were now streaming out of every opening on her body—her eyes, her mouth, even out of her ass. Nothing they did could help her.

～❦ ❦～

Meanwhile, Koby was riding up and down the rows of sugar cane, his hand itching to unleash the sting of his whip on the back of the next field hand foolish enough to whisper about Minnie or anything else. They'd yet to replace the overseer.

Maybe if I do a good job and work these niggahs real hard, Massa will let me keep the job.

He soon had his opening. A piecing scream sounded from the direction of the slave infirmary. Jessy's head involuntarily shot up, and Koby was on her in a second, pulling his whip out as he approached. Koby didn't bother to drag Jessy to the whipping post. The rage was on him too strong. He beat her right then and there, wielding his cruel whip until she could no longer hold her hands up to protect herself. Jessy curled in a ball while he went to town on her. Koby didn't stop whippin' on Jessy until his arm got tired. Only then did he pause to look around for someone else to hurt.

His message was clear. If they didn't keep working, he would be more than happy to give any one of them some of what Jessy just got. The rest of the field hands chopped cane as if their lives depended on it. They kept their heads down and held their breaths until Koby coiled his whip, jumped astride his horse, and headed to the sugar mill.

Koby arrived to find up to a dozen boys and men hard at work in the intense heat inside the mill. The heat and the stench of rotting cane always made Koby feel like he was going to throw up. Finding no fault there, he moved on to the building where the slaves boiled the cane juice. His chest swelled in anticipation of a confrontation when he caught Clyde joking around with a slave named Josh while ladling scrum from the surface of the scalding liquid. They carefully transferred it to a kettle where the syrup from the scrum would be reduced to crystals. Koby never did like Clyde, and now he had an opportunity to do something about it.

Koby reached for his whip, planning to catch Clyde unawares and beat the tar out of him. He charged toward Clyde and Josh with his teeth bared and the whip raised above his head, but the heat in the sugar house was so intense and the humidity so thick that Koby slid on the wooden floor, lost his footing, and toppled head first into the scalding liquid bubbling in the cistern. Koby could feel the skin falling away from his face, neck, and arms when Clyde and Josh pulled him out of the boiling hot sugar.

He lingered in agony for three days before he finally died from his injuries. Minnie died the next day. Flossie's was the last voice they heard before they met their maker.

"Save a place for Claude and Clidamont when you gets to hell."

Made in the USA
Middletown, DE
18 September 2024

60582332R00161